Billionaire Undercover

THE BILLIONAIRE'S OBESSION
Hudson

J. S. SCOTT

Contents

Prologue

Taylor

Seven Years Ago...

E very person on Earth was going to experience profound grief at some point in their life.

It was just a fact, unless that person was a sociopath, or so removed from reality that they weren't capable of feeling any type of emotion.

For some, that event happened early, with the loss of a parent or even both parents, or maybe a very beloved grandparent.

For others, it happened in their *adult life*, when they completely understood death and dying, and the very real fact that their relationship with that person who was leaving this world would never be there for them again.

Not in this life, anyway.

I just wasn't sure I was ready for *that* to happen to *me* right now.

Not when the elderly man I was looking at in a hospital bed was my entire world.

I didn't have siblings to lean on, another parent, or any other family who was going to understand how I felt.

It was just me, and Mac Tanaka, the only parent figure or family I'd ever known.

And once he was gone, I'd be completely and utterly alone in the world at the age of twenty-one.

I started to panic as I sat beside Mac's hospital bed, holding his hand, wondering what in the hell I was going to do *without* him.

He'd been my father figure, my teacher, my friend, and the only person wise enough, in my opinion, to run to with *any* problem I had. Mac gave levelheaded advice. I'd always been able to count on that.

Not that the elderly man hadn't always encouraged me to be free-thinking and independent.

He'd always warned me that I was only going to share a small part of my life with him because he'd been in his seventies when he had taken on the challenging task of raising an eleven-year-old girl.

Now, ten years later, I was feeling robbed because our time together had been way too short.

But dammit! I needed to be strong for *him* right now since he'd always been there for me.

"I can see that brilliant brain of yours working, and you're thinking much too hard, Tay," Mac said in a weak voice, sounding out of breath every time he talked. "You're ready to tackle the world on your own. You just don't know it right now. It's way past time for you to start living your own life, instead of taking care of me."

There wasn't a single hint of an accent in Mac's voice. Even though his parents had been born in Japan, the guy was as American as apple pie.

He drew on his Japanese heritage for wisdom and philosophy, but embraced his position as a first generation American, and *this* culture, too.

I think that's something that had always fascinated me about Mac.

"I've never minded taking care of you," I protested.

He smiled weakly, his face pale and wan. His skin was almost the same color as the starkly white sheets and pillowcase. "Maybe not," he agreed. "But you've put off your education for too long."

I didn't mind that, either. Yeah, I'd always wanted to go to Stanford to pursue a career in geology, but there had been no question in my mind, when Mac had been diagnosed with cancer three years ago, that I was going to wait.

I'd put my acceptance with the prestigious university on hold, because honestly, I was all Mac had, too.

I'd never once regretted that decision. In the beginning, he'd been able to take care of himself, but over the last year or so, he'd really needed me.

"I'll get to Stanford someday," I assured him. "Now just rest, Mac."

As I watched his eyes flutter shut, I instinctively reached for my necklace Mac had given me, and closed my eyes.

He'd presented the pendant to me on my sixteenth birthday, and I'd rarely taken it off since that day.

It was a fierce dragon with a long cage tail that protected the pearl inside.

Mac had told me to touch it every time I felt nervous, so I'd remember that I was gentle, but also incredibly strong and powerful.

Generally, wrapping my hand around the symbol helped, but I was starting to think I wasn't as courageous as Mac thought.

Breathe, Tay. Just breathe.

I could hear Mac's encouraging voice in my head, his younger, stronger tone as he'd taught me to find serenity inside myself, even when my entire world felt like it was in chaos.

I took one deep breath and let it out.

Followed by another.

And then one more.

I can do this. I can keep my shit together for Mac. I owe him that, and so much more.

As I opened my eyes, and squeezed his cool hand lightly, I told myself that I didn't need to grieve yet. Mac was still with me, and I was going to appreciate every second I had.

He'd been my rock in the past, so it was time for me to be his damn boulder.

That was exactly what I did for the next several days, until the night that Mac had quietly left me, comfortably passing away in the middle of the night while I slept, curled up in a recliner beside his bed.

I crumbled because I didn't need to be his boulder or his rock anymore.

For a long time, I was simply a mass of tiny pebbles, scattered a million different directions, before I found the strength to move on.

Chapter 1

Hudson

The Present...

"Something needs to happen right fucking now. Three of our geologists were captured *nine days ago* while they were on a short exploration mission that should have been completely safe," I said in a low growl to the other three people sitting around the large conference table at Montgomery Mining headquarters. "Why the hell we *didn't* hear about any of this until *today* is irrelevant at the moment. Our focus is to get our other two Montgomery Mining team members out of Lania alive, and the clock is ticking right now."

Generally, I didn't lose my cool because I knew it was counterproductive as the head of this company, but at the moment, I was sitting at the very edge of my patience.

Probably the *only* reason I wasn't going off right now was because one of those three team members who had been captured by guerilla forces was sitting at the other side of the large conference table, and she was fragile at the moment.

In fact, Harlow Lewis looked like she was barely capable of sitting upright for much longer.

I'd already fired the people responsible for not contacting my brothers and me the second they'd gotten word about the fate of one of our exploration teams.

I'd been gone to Seattle for *nine damn days* to attend my cousin Mason's wedding festivities with my two brothers. It was the *only time* all three of us had been away from our San Diego headquarters for that long since we'd saved the corporation from the brink of going under. Still, it was nine damn days, right?

What could possibly happen without one of the three of us here in such a short amount of time?

Those optimistic, comfortable thoughts had been completely obliterated when my brother Jax and I had come back to the office this morning.

I'd learned that some really bad shit could happen in a hurry, even in a monster company like mine that usually worked like a well-oiled machine on a day-to-day basis.

I'd returned to a goddamn nightmare situation.

"We did tell our upper management that we would be unavailable for nine days," my brother Jax mused aloud from his seat beside me.

"For fuck's sake, I *didn't* tell our executives *not* to call me if three of our employees were taken hostage and in a dire situation. I would definitely classify *that* as an emergency, in which case, I *did* tell them to call us. This isn't a small issue; it's a damn crisis, and we should have been involved in the hostage negotiation from the very beginning. We own the company."

I took a deep breath, knowing I had to contain my edginess. I'd spent the last fifteen minutes listening to Harlow Lewis spill out her story between anguished sobs, knowing that if we'd been involved from day one, we wouldn't be in the situation we were facing right now.

The FBI negotiation process had been too damn slow.

Nine days was an eternity to waste when you had a hostage in the hands of Lanian guerillas. They weren't exactly known for their humane treatment of captives.

Apparently, upper management had negotiated Harlow's release with FBI assistance in our absence, but we still had one man missing, and an intern in captivity who had been doing a summer internship under Harlow's supervision.

Son of a bitch! How had three of our geologists ended up being captives of Lanian rebels in the first place? It didn't make any sense.

Number one…now that the previously war-torn country had been at peace for several years, and a new generation of leadership had taken control, Lania had been on its way to becoming a highly desirable tourist destination in the Mediterranean.

Number two…all of the rebels were *supposed* to be gone. There hadn't been an incident in Lania for the last two years, and before that, there had only been a few minor protests.

Number three…why was I so damn furious right now that numbers one and two were apparently bullshit?

If there was *any* rebel activity, we damn well should have known about it.

I looked at my younger brother Jax, and I could tell he was feeling the same way I was at the moment, even though you'd never know it by looking at his face. However, I knew my brother, and there were always a few small tells he couldn't hide from me that clued me into exactly how he was reacting.

My youngest brother, Cooper, had decided to stay in Seattle for a few weeks to connect with some old college buddies. But if he were here, I knew he'd feel the same outrage Jax and I were experiencing right now.

Goddammit! This shouldn't be happening.

But it was, which is exactly why I'd called in the *third* person in the room.

I turned my gaze to Marshall, the leader of the volunteer rescue task force that was simply known as Last Hope, and tried to gauge his position.

Jax and I had put in an urgent call to Marshall the moment we'd heard about the kidnapping. As usual, he'd showed up within a few hours with all the relevant information needed to try to perform a rescue attempt.

Unlike Jax, the former Commander Marshall *was* really hard to read. His calm demeanor under pressure, and kick-ass skill as a previous leader of one of the Navy SEAL teams was legendary. So it wasn't all that surprising that I didn't have a clue what the older man was thinking, even though my brothers and I had worked alongside the guy for years to get Last Hope to where it was today.

Marshall was an enigma to almost everyone who volunteered for Last Hope. All we really knew is that he'd been injured during a mission while he was active military, which had forced him into retirement earlier than he'd planned.

Jax, Cooper and I had jumped on board with Marshall soon after we'd all left our own Special Forces units, and the military, to take our places as the owners of Montgomery Mining. We'd wanted to help Marshall grow Last Hope, and we had.

In the beginning, my brothers and I had carried out a lot of the rescues ourselves, but Marshall now had way more volunteers than he actually needed for that. Younger guys who were fresh out of special ops.

One of the most important reasons we tried to stay out of doing rescues ourselves was because all our faces had become more and more recognizable since we'd left the military. The press chased Jax the most. I tried to keep a low profile, and so did Cooper, but there were times we couldn't avoid photos, either. Once we'd returned to the civilian world, and put Montgomery Mining back at the top, everybody had wanted a photo of the billionaire bachelor Montgomery brothers.

It had gotten too damn risky for us to be on the front line.

Now, we were much more valuable providing resources and working on the strategic planning—most of the time.

Marshall lifted a brow. "Obviously, the federal government is treading lightly on this one now that we're friend rather than foe to Lania, and everyone has kissed and made up during the last couple of years. They don't want to rock the boat, and any Lanian rebels are considered terrorists. You boys definitely know the U.S. government's position on negotiating ransom with presumed terrorists. They sent in the FBI to assist with the negotiations for Harlow, but Montgomery Mining ultimately was the one who paid the ransom for her release. Any attempted rescue for Taylor, if it happens, would need to be completely covert, and we're on our own."

Fuck! Yeah, I *knew* that. All of the cases we handled were situations that the federal government didn't want to, or wouldn't, take any action on. However, it was a hell of a lot easier to pull out captives when we weren't tiptoeing around politics.

I turned to our lone released hostage again. She'd already told us her story, but as expected from anyone who had been a captive, it had been slightly scattered. I had to make damn sure I was up to speed since I'd only found out about this entire situation a few hours ago. Having the woman show up at Montgomery Mining headquarters not long ago to plead for help for her intern and boyfriend had been the *only* stroke of luck we'd had so far.

I had to give her credit, she *had* gotten my attention, even though she'd *rolled* her way into the upper offices in a wheelchair, completely out of breath from the effort it had taken her to get there. She'd demanded to see a Montgomery in a hoarse but scratchy voice that had somehow carried into my office.

"Dr. Lewis, you were released two days ago?" I asked, trying like hell to use a much calmer tone.

The pretty blonde looked like she'd been through hell, and should be in a hospital instead of here in downtown San Diego. Then again, if someone I cared about was possibly dead, and my friend was still being held hostage, I'd be doing everything I could to get them help, too.

She cleared her throat nervously. "Please, all of you, call me Harlow, and yes, I was released two days ago. It took a day for them to get me back to the U.S., and once I *was* back, the doctors wanted to get me totally hydrated again, run a million tests, and start some physical therapy before they let me out of the hospital. But I couldn't get any information about Taylor and Mark from the medical center since I don't exactly have any of the Montgomery brothers on speed dial. I ended up leaving the facility this morning against medical advice because I *have* to do *something*. I think everyone assumes Mark is dead, and Taylor was my responsibility, a summer intern working under my guidance. She's also my friend, and she's *still* being held. I don't understand why she wasn't let go with me." Her voice was desperate now, and her expression tormented. "Taylor puts on a brave face, but she isn't going to last much longer. We were both in bad shape when I left. And after two more days in that sweltering hot box with no water, I'm not even sure she's still alive."

Harlow looked fragile and haunted, which bothered me much more than I wanted to admit. Even though she and I had never personally met, I felt responsible for every single person who worked for Montgomery Mining, and she'd been on this exploration for *us*. All three of them had. "I'm sorry this happened," I said, not knowing what the hell else to say. "My brothers and I should have been informed immediately, not nine days after the fact. Our management did everything they could to get you released, and *I'll* do everything I can to bring back the other two."

I exchanged looks with Jax and Marshall, because we all knew *exactly* why *only* Harlow had been released. We'd gotten the outrageous demand for Taylor's ransom this morning, along with a proof of life short video clip of the female still in captivity.

As of yet, we hadn't gotten a single word about Mark, Harlow's boyfriend, and the mining engineer who had planned to meet the two women at the dock in Lania. Until her release two days ago, Harlow had been imprisoned with Taylor, but Mark was totally unaccounted for, and hadn't been at the dock when the two women had been taken.

I would have forked over the money for my intern immediately, no questions asked, if I thought it would buy Taylor Delaney's freedom.

But it wouldn't.

I had enough history with Lanian rebels to know that the last ones being held *never* made it out.

Harlow had been lucky. Her release was a supposed act of good faith, but I wasn't buying that bullshit.

"I just want them back," Harlow answered frantically. "I don't know what happened to Mark, and Taylor won't last much longer. We didn't get food at all, and the only water we could get was if and when it rained, which didn't happen often. We could barely get part of our arm through the vents to the outside to gather as much as we could when it was raining. I checked the weather in Lania. It doesn't look they've gotten a drop of rain since I left."

Fuck! If Harlow had been critically dehydrated, Taylor didn't stand much of a chance.

"Other than the lack of food and water, how was your treatment while you were there? Can you give me any more information about where you were kept?" I asked Harlow in a tone that was as gentle as I could manage at the moment.

"It was hot," she answered grimly. "We were kept in a one-room structure with a steel door, and there wasn't much air movement. There were a few openings near the ceiling, which is what we used to try to get water, but the walls were cement. There was nothing we could use as tools to try to break out of there. Believe me, we tried. We were sweltering, and I think our guards wanted us weak. If you're asking if they beat us, they didn't. It was mostly yelling, shoving and most of their communication was in Lanian."

Hell, *that* had certainly changed since she'd left, but I wasn't about to tell the distraught woman about *that*. Taylor had definitely been beaten, and judging by that brief proof of life video clip we'd seen, she was in no shape to try to get water, even if it did rain.

"And there was no….sexual assault?" Jax queried right before he let out an uncomfortable cough.

No matter how many times we'd had to ask the uncomfortable questions, it never got any easier.

"No. Or maybe yes. I'm not sure," Harlow answered as she fidgeted in her chair. "Every night, the rebel leader came to get Taylor. He'd take her away just after dark. It seemed like forever, but she was probably only gone an hour or so before he tossed her back into our prison again. She swore he wasn't hurting her, and that the leader spoke English, so she was trying to get him to release us. She refused to say anything else, and I'll be completely honest, I was half out of my mind. I was so worried about Mark that I believed her at the time. Or maybe I just *wanted* to believe it because there was nothing else I could do. Now that my mind is clearer, I'm not so sure that she wasn't assaulted or raped. No matter how convincing Taylor can be, I don't buy that she was trying to talk the leader into letting us go every single night."

And just like that, the lid I'd tried to slap down on my personal emotions cracked open just a little.

Son of a bitch! My gut started to churn as I thought about some fuckhead rebel using one of my interns as his sexual toy every single evening. And what kind of woman would go willingly, and then come back to Harlow and lie about what had happened to keep her friend and mentor from worrying?

It took some major balls to surrender when all you wanted to do was fight.

"It's possible. I highly doubt that they were negotiating a release plan," Jax told Harlow bluntly, not sugar-coating his response. "Can you tell us anything else that would tip us off to exactly where they're keeping Taylor?"

Before Harlow could answer, Marshall spoke. "I think I have the location for Taylor."

I'd *known* damn well I was going to take on this mission personally from the moment I'd heard Harlow's story, and probably even before that. Like, from the moment I'd heard about this whole debacle a couple of hours ago. The rebels were fucking with two people who were under our protection as Montgomery Mining employees. If anybody was attempting a rescue, it *was* going to be me. Providing resources and tactical planning wasn't going to be enough.

Not this time!

This one, I was determined to carry out *myself.*

The chances that Taylor was still breathing were grim.

Mark's chances were even worse because we'd never gotten a ransom demand for him.

Harlow's intern had recently been beaten up pretty badly. Jax and I assumed she'd tried to escape, and failed. It was a typical Lanian rebel move to pummel escapees so they wouldn't, and physically couldn't, do it again.

"Just out of curiosity, why was one of our summer interns on an exploration mission?" Jax questioned. "It's kind of unusual for that to happen."

Harlow's face completely crumpled into an expression of utter and complete guilt. "It's my fault. That was a bad decision on my part. I met Taylor a year ago, when she was starting the last year of her master's program at Stanford, and I was doing a research lecture there. We kept in touch. She's brilliant, and I jumped at the chance to be her mentor when she was offered an internship at Montgomery. When she heard I was doing an exploration, she really wanted to come, and I thought she'd be a good asset for the team. Really, she didn't *have* to be there. Mark and I could have handled this initial check ourselves."

I shook my head. "We weren't blaming you in any way, Harlow. By all reports, it should have been perfectly safe for her to be there. It should have been safe for *all* of you."

"You don't have to blame me," she said hoarsely. "I blame myself. I've already resigned from my position with Montgomery Mining, but that doesn't matter. I still want to do everything I can to get Mark and Taylor home."

"Why in the fuck did you have to resign?" Jax grumbled. "This wasn't *your* fault."

"We'll discuss your resignation later," I said, shooting Jax a warning look. "Let's focus on the mission to rescue the two who are still in Lania first."

While I didn't agree with Harlow leaving our company, either, it was critical to keep our eye on our mission right now.

"Please do," Harlow pleaded in a voice that was barely more than a whisper.

I quickly explained the basics about Last Hope to Harlow, and told her that we planned to attempt a rescue. While I hated telling anyone *anything* about our volunteer group, Harlow had been through hell, and she deserved to at least know somebody was trying to get her boyfriend and friend out of Lania.

I didn't go into details since we technically didn't exist as far as the federal government was concerned. Okay, so they actually *did* know we existed, and the FBI negotiators sometimes tipped us off about someone who needed help, but their *official* position was total ignorance about our operation.

When I'd finished, Marshall picked up a large envelope and slid it toward me as he said, "Here's the info on Taylor Delaney. She's a twenty-eight-year-old female who just completed her master's degree in environmental geology. She opted to do a summer internship with Montgomery Mining while she hunts for a permanent position."

"She's been staying with me since she's not sure where she'll find a permanent job," Harlow added.

I'd deftly snatched the information coming my direction. I was caught off-guard as I studied the image I'd fished out of the contents.

Taylor Delaney was a beautiful, red-headed woman who had the most stunning pair of green eyes I'd ever seen. She'd been so beaten up in the short video clip we'd been sent that I didn't even recognize her as the same female.

My gut twisted as I tried to stay neutral and just observe.

But it was fucking impossible *not* to be outraged. Taylor *was* my employee. Our interns didn't get paid much, but they did get a wage for their summer work. I felt responsible for *everything* that had happened to her, Mark, and Harlow.

I held the picture a little longer than I needed to in order to memorize her features before I finally shoved it back into the envelope and passed the entire contents to Jax.

There would be plenty of time to study files on the way to Lania.

"Victim number two," Marshall announced as he sent another envelope flying down the table. "Mark Lansdale, one of your mining engineers. He's thirty-five years old, and he's been with Montgomery for almost six years. According to your files, he's got a spotless employee record."

I nodded sharply. "Nice guy. I've met him on a couple of work sites."

"He was getting tired of traveling to remote locations," Harlow mumbled. "He was considering some consulting jobs to keep him in the country, but he didn't want to leave Montgomery because he loved working for your company."

"You two are in a relationship, right?" Jax asked.

She shrugged. "Yes. It's complicated. He's not here that often. We were looking forward to doing the exploration together."

Even though Mark and I had met, I looked at his recent picture, and then passed the file off to Jax.

"I'm all in," I told Marshall sharply. "I'll lead this one myself."

"I'm in, too," Jax said immediately. "This whole situation is so fucked up that I'm not leaving anything to chance."

My brother elbowed me. "What're the chances that they're still alive?" Jax asked in a quiet voice so Harlow couldn't hear him.

I shrugged as I answered in a similarly low tone. "Slim to none on Taylor. She's obviously being mistreated now, and if she isn't getting hydrated or fed while being held in a nearly airless, hot environment, it could very well be a lost cause. Even less for Mark, unfortunately. You know they usually kill male hostages and use the females for leverage."

"But we have to try," Jax said fervently. "We both know just paying them isn't going to work. The bastards only let Harlow go because they were hoping it would motivate a much larger payment for Taylor. You know negotiating and paying her ransom would probably be a death sentence for her if she's still alive."

"I know," I answered harshly.

I had far more confidence in my brother and I as a team getting Taylor back safely...if she was still alive.

I stood up, antsy to get moving. "I'm going to get things in motion. I'd like to be in the air within an hour. Marshall, can you get me the coordinates?"

The older man walked over to me like his slight limp didn't bother him at all, and I knew that meant he wanted to have a short, very private discussion. "You need backup?" he asked.

I shook my head. "We can mobilize and move around better without detection if it's just the two of us. We need to get in and out of there as quickly and quietly as possible."

"Agreed," Marshall answered as he handed me a small envelope that I already knew would contain the woman's location and other sensitive information. "It's just her, Hudson. I got a text during the meeting that Mark's body was recovered by the Lanian government while they were searching for Taylor. His body wasn't far from the same dock Taylor and Harlow used. I think he was probably ambushed just like they were. They'll be returning his remains to the States. I'm sorry we lost one, but I'm glad you boys are taking on Taylor's rescue yourselves. Good luck, son," he said in a firm voice as he slapped me on the back.

"If you found Taylor's location, why aren't you contacting the Lanian government?" I asked him.

Marshall raised a brow. "They've been looking for it for nine days now. I found it in an hour. Lania may be slowly improving, but their law enforcement and military are totally inept. Do you really trust that they'd have any success getting Taylor out of there alive?"

"Hell, no. We're out of here," I grumbled.

I looked across the room at Harlow.

She looked completely destroyed. Now definitely wasn't the time to tell her that her boyfriend was dead.

"Can you get Harlow back into the hospital? She's doesn't look good," I told Marshall.

"I think I can handle that," he answered drily.

Since there was very little Marshall *couldn't* deal with if asked, I nodded to Jax.

He stood and followed me out of the conference room.

Chapter 2

Hudson

"Do you think we should have told Harlow that her boyfriend is dead?" Jax asked as he finished cleaning and inspecting his weapon and set it aside.

I looked up from the file I'd been studying on Taylor since Jax and I had boarded my private jet earlier.

I leaned back in my seat as I replied, "She didn't look good. I think she needs some time to rest before we deliver that information."

Jax kicked back on the comfortable couch in the cabin of my aircraft.

We'd both changed into sweats after we'd gotten underway so we could get some sleep at some point during the long flight.

He shrugged. "You're probably right. Not that I've ever *had* a serious girlfriend, but if I did, I'd probably want to know the truth. I feel a little bit guilty that we didn't tell her."

I looked at my younger brother in surprise. "Since when do you actually feel guilty about anything? And if you'd go out with a woman more than once, you might have a serious girlfriend."

Jax was known as the billionaire mogul who was *never* seen with a woman more than once, and the press had a field day with his playboy antics.

"Seriously?" he said drily. "At least I date, unlike you, who is never even seen with *any* female."

I ignored his comment. It wasn't like I'd *never* had a girlfriend. I just hadn't had one for a long time, and I'd pretty much given up on trying to find a woman who cared about me more than she cared about the status of the Montgomery name and wealth.

Apparently, Jax was still willing to try. Really, really hard. I didn't actually see my brother as a womanizer, but I was starting to think he had a really high tolerance for chronic disappointment.

"Marshall will tell Harlow," I assured Jax.

He nodded. "I know. I'm not sure why, but I feel like I should have done it myself this time. Maybe because they're our employees. This whole thing is just so fucked up. A few days ago, we were watching Mason get his balls cut off in Seattle, and now I feel like we've just entered a different universe."

I smirked. "Mason wasn't getting his balls cut off. He got married, and he's happy with Laura. As he should be. She's a pretty amazing woman."

Jax, Cooper, and my sister, Riley, had just recently met the cousin they hadn't known existed. I'd known about Mason for a while, but until my cousin had been ready to tell his own brothers that he was only their half-brother, and the bastard offspring of my uncle, I'd kept his existence to myself.

My brothers and Riley had not only accepted Mason as their cousin, but treated Mason's brothers like cousins, too, even though they weren't blood.

"I don't get why Mason was in such a big hurry to get married," Jax grumbled. "I like the guy, but he and his brothers act like they can't survive without checking in with their wives at least once an hour."

"They can't," I agreed. "Because every one of them is actually madly in love with their spouses."

Jax scowled. "Yeah. I guess *that's* the part I don't get."

"You don't get it because our family was so damn dysfunctional," I explained. "Unless you haven't noticed, our sister is madly in love with her husband, too."

The youngest in our family, our little sister, Riley, was happily married and living in a small city not far from San Diego. She'd married a billionaire real estate developer, and the two of them were crazy about each other.

I understood Jax's confusion, though. It was hard to comprehend something we'd never seen or experienced.

Our father had been a sociopath, and Riley had recently told us that he'd molested her as a child, a fact that made me wish the bastard was still alive just so I could kill him myself.

Our mother was obsessed only with appearances, and her social status. She'd known what our father had done to Riley, but she'd kept it to herself just to protect the prestigious Montgomery name.

In reality, my parents had hated each other, but had stayed together anyway.

My father had died while my brothers and I had been active military. I'd been in Delta Force, Jax had been a SEAL, and our youngest brother, Cooper, had just been entering the U.S. Army hoping to become a Ranger when the old man had passed away.

We'd attended our father's funeral to support Riley and our mother at the time, but I doubted a single one of us had actually mourned the bastard.

Even though we hadn't known about what my father had done to Riley at that time, or that my mother had covered it up, there hadn't exactly been any tender feelings between us and our parents. Ever.

My brothers and I had hightailed it back to our military duties after the funeral, and for years, we'd let somebody else operate Montgomery Mining. It had taken us years to discover that it wasn't being run the way it should have been.

One by one, my brothers and I had made the painful decision to leave our positions in Special Forces once our contracts were up to save Montgomery Mining from complete destruction.

It hadn't been easy, but we'd put everything we had into getting our company back on top. Not only had we succeeded in putting Montgomery Mining back into its place as the largest mining operation in the world, but our company was bigger and better than it had been under my father's control.

Our mother was still alive, but we'd cut off all communication with her when we'd found out what had happened to Riley. None of us could even stomach being in the same room with her.

"I think Riley chooses to *think* she's in love with Seth," Jax mused. "Not that it's a bad thing, because Seth is a decent guy. But I think being in love is bullshit. We make that choice, whether it's done consciously or not. The whole soulmate thing is crap. I've never met a woman who makes me lose control. I don't think it's possible."

"Never say never," I warned. "You didn't see Mason when he thought he'd never be with Laura. The guy was a mess. If he could have controlled that shit, he would have. He's hardheaded."

In most respects, I agreed with Jax. Although, after seeing how miserable the pragmatic Mason Lawson was when he and Laura had temporarily parted, I wasn't entirely convinced that you could just choose to love someone…or not love them.

Since I'd never been in that position myself, it was hard to say.

Yeah, I'd been temporarily infatuated a few times when I was younger, but that shit had worn off in a hurry once I realized that the woman I was dating was more caught up in my money and status than she was in…me.

"Yeah, well, that's Mason, not me," Jax answered. "Personally, I think it's irrational to think you love somebody that much."

"Does it really matter?" I questioned. "Mason and Riley are both happy with their fates, and I'm all good as long as they're happy."

"I guess not," Jax said. "Better them than me. I just hope you and Cooper never lose your shit over somebody like Riley and Mason have."

"Hasn't happened yet, and since I just turned thirty-four years old, I doubt it ever will. I'd like to think I've gotten wiser as I've gotten older," I joked.

"Right behind you," Jax said, sounding amused.

My siblings and I were all very close together in age. It was like my parents had decided to put their mind to having offspring, and they'd done it...Boom! Boom! Boom! Boom! Just to get it out of the way. Jax was only ten months younger than me.

"So maybe it's time for you to go out with a woman more than once?" I suggested.

Jax grinned. "And disappoint all the gossip reporters who follow us around like puppies? Nah. They'd be bored to death."

Luckily, most of those reporters found Jax a lot more interesting than me, so I wasn't hounded nearly as much as he was, and they'd pretty much given up on the possibility of Cooper doing anything outrageous, too.

We were silent for a few moments before Jax asked, "You up for this mission, old man? It's been a while."

I kept myself in top physical condition, just like my brothers did, so I knew Jax was just razzing me. But I also knew that he wanted to make sure that I was okay with what we were going into. "I'm ready, and so damn pissed that it can't happen soon enough for me."

"Me, either," Jax said in a solemn tone. "I just hope she's still alive. I think it will completely annihilate Harlow if we lose Taylor, too."

I quirked a brow. "You like Harlow," I guessed.

"Have to," he said smoothly. "The woman has been through hell, and all she's worried about is her boyfriend and her intern. She has some balls. We need her to stay with Montgomery, and I plan on doing everything I can to convince her to stay when we get back."

I nodded. "I agree. But you seem...personally concerned. Did you know Harlow before this whole incident?"

"Not really," he hedged. "Yeah, I've seen her a couple of times when I've stopped at the lab, but it's not like we've had a long conversation or anything. Fuck! She's hot. How could I *not* notice her? I suppose I admire her tenacity now, too. I guess I feel like shit because she got hurt while she was doing work for us. We put all three of them in harm's way."

I looked at Jax quizzically. His admission was way out of character for him. It wasn't like Jax didn't have a good heart, but it was usually hidden by his cynicism. Since I was feeling guilty enough for both of us, I said, "This isn't really anybody's fault, Jax. Yeah, I feel guilty, too, but don't let that shit eat you alive. Lania has been considered a safe country to visit for a couple of years now. If it wasn't, it wouldn't have even been on Montgomery Mining's radar. We don't ever intentionally put any of our employees in dangerous situations."

I wasn't sure who I was trying to convince; him or me. Nothing like this had ever happened to any of our crews, the remorse about what had happened was actually eating me alive.

Yeah, shit happened, but my brothers and I had never put profit over safety. Anything could happen on remote job sites, but we kept the risk factor to a minimum.

"How in the fuck did the rebels get a foothold in Lania again?" Jax cursed. "Jesus! I thought I'd never have to go back there again. My SEAL team was in Lania way too much a decade ago. I hate that damn country. Hostage situations there never ended well. The rebels had absolutely no problem lopping off the heads of anyone they considered a danger to their way of life, and they hated westerners."

"I know," I answered, my voice raspy. "I lost a lot of friends there, too. This group was either hiding in a remote area for years, or they were escapees who weren't smart enough to stay gone. Marshall has been there fairly recently, and he swore there wasn't even a hint of violence there. Hell, people are starting to fight over land in that country to build their big resorts. But Lania is a large island country, and some areas are pretty desolate. I don't doubt that this group could have escaped detection for years."

"What's the crown prince's stance on all of this?" Jax questioned.

"According to Marshall, he's put out every force he has to search for the rebels and their hostages."

Jax's mouth shaped into a halfhearted smile. "So Marshall knows where they are, but the prince doesn't?"

"Does that surprise you?" I asked, amused.

Jax shook his head. "Nope. Sometimes I think Marshall likes it that way. He has more faith in Last Hope than he does in some foreign governments."

At the moment, I was glad Marshall had kept the information to himself. "So do I," I informed my brother. "This one is personal for me, and I'd rather not have someone else fuck it up."

"We'll get her out of there, Hudson," Jax said solemnly in a voice that sounded like a vow. "Even if she's not alive, we're bringing her out."

I didn't even want to think about the life in Taylor's beautiful green eyes being completely snuffed out. "She's alive. Until I know for certain that I'm wrong, she's alive. Let's try to get some shuteye so we're as alert as we can be. My plane, my bed."

I rose to head to the only bedroom on my aircraft.

"I have no problem crashing here. It's comfortable," Jax said. "Was there anything in those reports on Taylor that I should know about?"

My gut twisted.

The files hadn't just been employee files. Marshall had included as much history as he could get on short notice.

Taylor Delaney hadn't really had an easy life, and it had felt almost intrusive to read the information about her early years because it didn't make a damn bit of difference in regard to her rescue.

The report had felt personal to me, which was something I'd never experienced before, and for some damn reason, I didn't feel like sharing everything I'd read about a hostage with anyone. Even Jax.

"Nothing significant," I said shortly. "Sounds like she busted her ass to get through Stanford, and I'm not about to let her miss the good parts now that she's finally done with the hard stuff."

"I'm with you on that," Jax said with a huge yawn. "Night."

"Get some rest," I advised as I made my way to the bedroom.

I hit the bed immediately, but didn't sleep as well as I would have liked.

My dreams were haunted by that picture of Taylor during her happier times, and a pair of big green eyes and a mischievous smile that seemed to be begging me not to let her die in Lania.

As I tossed and turned, I just hoped to hell she could hold on just a little bit longer...

Chapter 3

Taylor

The only good thing about being half dead was knowing I looked so bad that the rebel leader wasn't going to come and get me anymore.

He hadn't since the day I'd tried to make my escape, and had been beaten so badly that *nobody* would want to see my face or my body right now.

That had been what…a day ago? Two days ago? Shit! I'd totally lost track of the time, but I knew for certain I hadn't had a drop of water since I'd tried to execute my escape plan.

I'd had a momentary flash of fear when I'd regained consciousness a few moments ago, and it had been completely dark.

It had taken me a minute to remember that nobody was coming to get me anymore.

"What the hell day is it?" I mumbled, the words coming out in a scratchy whisper because my mouth was so dry.

It had been morning when I'd passed out last time.

Was it the same day? The next day? Or a week later?

I had no idea.

I was conscious at the moment, but I knew damn well that death was stalking me.

My heart was racing, and even though I was awake, I was so damn…confused.

Severely dehydrated, I'd been drifting in and out of consciousness, disoriented when I was awake, and too weak to even move a muscle anymore.

I wasn't going to bullshit myself about how close I was to death.

Every single time I felt that big black hole opening up to swallow me, I wondered if I'd ever open my eyes again.

Honestly, I was getting to the point where, each time I lost consciousness, I almost *hoped* I'd never wake up.

I wanted to move. Every muscle in my body was cramped, but I didn't have the strength to try to sit up or roll onto my side.

My appetite was completely gone, but I was so damn thirsty.

Luckily, I hadn't pissed myself, but it *was* a little frightening that I had absolutely *no urge* to pee. Right now, I wished I wasn't a science geek, and didn't know so much about the human body. It would probably be better to be ignorant about what happens when your kidneys start shutting down.

Not a damn thing worked in the human body *without* water.

I grimaced as I tried to move my legs to see if I could get in a more comfortable position, but my leg barely moved an inch, and that small twitch created the most horrific pain I'd ever experienced.

The rebels had landed some pretty hard kicks to all of my limbs, probably to keep me from going *anywhere*. That prolonged beating session, combined with the pain of having my extremities tightly bound in one position, made moving even a single limb pure torture.

I definitely wasn't a crier, but if I could have screamed and cried over the extreme torment my body was suffering right now, I probably would have.

Unfortunately, my tear ducts were bone dry, and my voice was nonexistent at the moment.

All I could do was squeeze my eyes shut, and hope I lost consciousness again.

Soon.

Very soon.

Because there was only so much agony a person could take.

Tiny dots of light appeared as I prepared myself to sink into another dark abyss.

Possibly the last one?

And then, I heard it—that horrible sound of metal grinding against metal as the guards removed the bars and barricades to the door from outside. I'd learned to fear that sound so damn much.

Because it meant they were coming into my prison for some reason, and their purpose had never been good.

My eyes popped open as I listened, not sure if I was just imagining the sound, or if someone was actually coming in.

Except...the noise was a lot more subtle, and not nearly as loud as the guards usually were when they yanked the steel barricades from the door.

I closed my eyes because those obnoxious little pinpricks of light wouldn't stop dancing around in front of me, and I was convinced that I was hallucinating...again.

Just when I thought I was having a moment of clarity, turns out, I wasn't.

I was still hearing and seeing things that weren't real.

At one point, I'd even believed that Mac was here with me, urging me not to give up. To keep fighting this battle until I was rescued.

Obviously, I was hearing all kinds of crazy shit and seeing things that weren't reality.

Just like I am right now.

That scraping sound *wasn't* the guards coming to taunt me.

Or the rebel leader.

Nobody was coming to beat me senseless again.

It was nothing.

Just my brain playing tricks on me.

Nobody was coming.

Ever.

I couldn't even remember the rebels checking anymore to see if I was dead or alive, but hell, I easily could have missed it since I rarely had a moment of reason anymore.

It's time for me to face it. I'm not going to make it out of Lania alive.

Since I couldn't take care of myself, I *was* going to die, and stay here until somebody stumbled over my skeletal remains someday.

Reluctant acceptance washed over me as I felt the blackness rising up to shut down my befuddled brain. Until...

"Taylor, can you hear me? I'm going to get you the fuck out of here."

The voice was deep, harsh, and spoken next to my ear in a low voice that I could barely hear.

I tried to ignore the illusive voice, knowing it was just another manifestation of something I desperately wanted to hear.

It was just a little bit harder to block out a gentle hand on my neck. None of the apparitions I'd conjured up in my brain had ever...touched me. I wanted to swat the delusional sensation away, but I couldn't.

It felt way too real.

"She's alive," the low baritone said.

"She has a pulse, and she's breathing." A second male voice said in a no-nonsense tone.

"Taylor, squeeze my hand if you can hear me," the first voice insisted as he took my fingers into his grasp. "You need fluids, but I don't want you aspirating. I need to know you're with me."

Water? Oh, God yes. I'd do almost anything for *that.*

Phantom or not, I squeezed a little, because there was nothing I needed more than water right now, and I didn't care who or what provided it.

"Good girl," he said approvingly. "We'll stop soon, but we have to get out of this area. Let's move, Jax."

"I'm ready. It's like a goddamn oven in here."

I wanted to scream in pain as I felt myself lifted like I weighed nothing at all, and then settled against a huge, solid object, most likely the guy's chest.

"I've got your six," guy number two said.

I could tell we were in motion, and I recognized the temperature difference as soon as this strong man carrying me had exited to the outdoors.

I relished the cooler air, and took as big of a breath as I could manage.

If this was all a pleasant delusion, I damn well was going to savor it.

"Taylor, my name is Hudson, and me and my brother, Jax, are going to get you to someplace safe," my current captor said in a husky whisper next to my ear. "You're going to be okay. We'll stop and try to give you some water as soon as we get away from this damn camp." He stopped talking for a moment before he added, "Jesus Christ! I hope you can still hear me, Taylor."

The truth was slow to hit my addled mind.

This man isn't a guerilla!

The guy hauling me away from the rebels *wasn't* one of the *them.*

These men were here…for me. To rescue me.

Both of them had American accents.

They were my rescuers, not my enemy.

I willed my eyes to open, but they were uncooperative.

"I…" Dammit, I couldn't get the words out.

I tried again, using every bit of strength I had left to whisper, "I hear you. Just can't talk."

"Good girl," he crooned beside my ear. "I'd feel like a fucking idiot if I were just talking to myself."

If I could have smiled, I would have. It was kind of crazy how calm and confident my rescuer was at the moment, but I was grateful for that cockiness because it made me feel safer.

I had no idea how he was setting such a brutal pace when he was carrying my tormented body with absolutely no assistance from me.

I couldn't move my arms to help with balance.

Nothing.

And God, I really wanted to do whatever I could to assist him now that I knew he was my liberator and not my captor.

Relief flooded over me as I finally digested the fact that I was... going home.

I was going to live.

I *wasn't* going to die in a remote area of Lania and become a pile of bones.

I was actually going to make it out of this.

"Harlow?" I tried to get her name out of my mouth.

Apparently, he heard the scratchy whisper. "She's fine and back in the States. It's all over for both of you, Taylor, I promise. You need some medical attention, but we'll get you that. Hell, at least you're not in a place where you're baking alive anymore."

He had no idea how thankful I was for that. I felt cooler already. It was summer, and it wasn't exactly cool at night in Lania, but at least I didn't feel like I was being roasted while my heart was still beating.

I drifted in and out of consciousness until we finally stopped. I felt myself being lowered gently down to the ground, and if it were possible, I would have bawled like a baby with relief when Hudson cut the bindings on my limbs.

Every muscle in my body still tremored with pain, but knowing I was finally free meant...everything.

"You have to drink for me, Taylor. I can't just dump water down your throat," Hudson said as I felt something wet being pressed against my parched lips. "You have to try to swallow."

My entire mouth was cracked and dry, and as much as I wanted that damn water, it was hard not to flinch from anything that touched the painful area.

My eyes finally fluttered open, but all I could see was darkness. Hudson was nothing more than a shadow, even though he was holding me and tipping the water container up for me.

I was so angry at myself that I wanted to scream because I just couldn't make my throat and mouth work.

It was like dying of thirst in the middle of a clear, freshwater stream.

The water was right there, yet I couldn't drink.

Hudson jerked the water away, and I wanted to protest, until I felt a dripping cloth against my parched lips.

He soothed the dried-up skin while I took a tiny portion of the wet material into my mouth.

The moisture was absorbed almost immediately, but Hudson kept it coming. He wet the cloth over and over again, until I finally began to suck water from it, and then started to swallow awkwardly.

When he finally put the water container to my lips again, I started to drink.

"Hey there, speedy, slow it down a little or you'll end up sick," Hudson instructed.

Once I'd gotten started, I didn't want to stop, even though I knew I shouldn't be guzzling water after being deprived of it for so long.

Unfortunately, my survival instincts were in complete control at the moment, and Hudson had to finally take the water away.

At first, I was pissed that he'd cut off the euphoric feeling of gulping down that precious liquid. After my initial spurt of anger, I was grateful that he'd done it, because my stomach was beginning to rumble.

The last thing I wanted to do was vomit on the guy who had rescued me.

I couldn't explain it if I wanted to, but it was almost like I could feel fluid starting to hydrate my cells. It should have been a pleasant sensation, but it wasn't.

Hudson lifted me into his arms again as he said, "We have to keep moving. There's still a lot of distance to cover before we get to the coast."

I was pretty sure we'd *already* traveled miles from the rebel camp. How was he going to keep going with my weight bogging him down?

Hudson was obviously extremely fit, but how much more could he take before he collapsed from exhaustion?

I put my lips next to his ear. "I want…to walk." It was all I could get out of my mouth.

I heard him chuckle as he started to move again. "Not going to happen, Taylor," he said, his voice amused. "You can't even move your limbs, and you're still severely dehydrated."

Dammit! He was right. But I didn't have to like the fact that he had to lug my ass around like a huge sack of flour.

I hated feeling helpless.

"You're just going to have to deal with taking a little help right now," he rasped, like he'd read my mind.

A sigh escaped from my lips, and I rested my head on his shoulder. Like I had a choice?

I felt the darkness of unconsciousness take hold of me, and this time, I didn't fight it.

For some strange reason, I felt safe with Hudson. I didn't have time to analyze exactly why before I slipped into the blackness.

Chapter 4

Hudson

I t was past daybreak when we finally got to the coast.
Taylor hadn't said a word since we'd stopped for water, and I
was starting to get worried.

I could feel her breath against my skin, and I knew she was still
alive, but I didn't like the fact that she wasn't responding at all
anymore.

Jax and I had remained silent as we'd worked our way through
the woods for the last several hours. The only time we'd spoken was
when my brother had offered to take Taylor, and I'd refused.

She was already confused, and I didn't want her waking up to
being held by a *different* guy.

Honestly, she was a lightweight, and way too thin. It wasn't like
she was exactly a burden, and Jax had both of our packs on *his* back.

I picked up my pace as I heard water, and then stopped at the edge
of the wooded area to survey the shoreline.

Jax halted next to me. "Looks like Marshall came through, as
usual."

There was a man waving his arms as he jogged toward us. "We have the tent set up, mates. Bring the woman over."

Marshall had promised to have a doctor somewhere near our launch point, so I could only assume the guy sprinting toward us in dark jeans and a black T-shirt was that physician.

Who the hell else *could* he be?

"I'm good," I said stiffly as the newcomer tried to take Taylor out of my arms. "Just tell me where you want her."

He nodded sharply and led the way to a tent that looked like it had been rapidly pitched twenty or thirty yards back into the trees.

Yeah, maybe Lania *was* friendly territory for us now, other than the few rebels who had obviously never left, but I hadn't hauled this woman out of one bad situation just to put her into another one.

Taylor was my responsibility until she could take care of herself, and I wasn't letting her out of my sight until I knew she was safe.

"Put her down on the cot so the doctor can have a look," our guide directed.

There was no door on the makeshift structure, so I strode right in and put Taylor onto what looked like a clean, sanitary sheet on a cot. An older man stood inside the tent, apparently waiting for his patient.

"Aren't *you* the doctor?" I asked as I looked at the man who had come to greet us and escort us to the tent.

"Sadly, no," he answered from the doorway. "But I wanted to be here when you arrived. I hate the fact that she was hurt while she was on Lanian soil. I approved that exploration. I thought your team would be perfectly safe."

I stepped away so the doctor could work, but Jax and I watched what was happening from right outside the tent.

I finally studied the man who had brought us here, wondering if he was actually Lanian. The guy sounded like a Brit, but jeans and T-shirt aside, he looked a hell of a lot like... "And who might you be?" I questioned gutturally.

Since Lania was initially made up of a melting pot of people from different countries of origin, not unlike the United States, it was sometimes hard to identify a Lanian strictly by their physical appearance.

However, they *had* developed a native language, and his accent was most definitely not Lanian.

He grinned. "I'm Crown Prince Niklaos, but please call me Nick. I'm not exactly a fan of formal titles."

Okay, so he *was* the Lanian ruler, just like I'd suspected. I'd seen pictures of him, but I'd never seen a live interview.

"It would have been nice if you'd actually gone in to rescue her before she was half dead if you're that damn sorry," I snapped.

"I would have, mate, but it's a big country. We've been trying to locate the rebel camp since we got news of the kidnapping. Unfortunately, we still have to do it the old way, and hunt for them, since we don't have all of the fancy military advances you have in the States. Not yet, anyway. Marshall just called me a few hours ago, and told me to meet you here so we could get the rebel location from you. We'll deal with them now that you have your last hostage out. I certainly didn't turn my back on your team. We just didn't find them soon enough," Nick said tersely. "It makes me ill just to see her in this condition, *and* to be sending a dead body back to the States."

The guy really did sound disgusted, and he was so sincere that I couldn't really argue with his conviction that he would have tried to rescue my team if he could have done it.

"If you're Lanian, why do you sound so British?" Jax asked in a cautious voice.

Nick went on to tell us that he'd been educated in the UK, and had spent most of his life there until his father had become unable to rule any longer.

His dad was still alive, but demented, so Nick had returned to Lania to take up his responsibilities several years ago.

"My father had made my mother a promise before she died," Nick explained. "I was a young child, and she hadn't wanted me to grow up in the middle of a revolution. So I was sent off to boarding school in the UK, and then to college there."

The guy was young, probably a few years younger than I was, and he'd already been in charge of an entire nation for several years? "How did it feel to be back in Lania after you'd been gone for so long?" I asked.

Nick let out a sigh. "Confining," he admitted. "I have to fight against my advisors and the royal council constantly. They were used to working with my father, and most of them still see me as the little prince. My father wanted democracy, but wasn't so keen on progress. His advisors are the same way. There's way too many customs that need to be relegated to the past, and much more progress to make, but that's easier said than done."

"You'll get there," I encouraged. "Maybe it's time to hire new advisors," I suggested.

Obviously, Nick had been responsible for trying to modernize the country. Maybe he didn't have an elite team or the military power that we had in the U.S., but I had to give him some credit for the post-war improvements he'd made.

Nick grinned. "Don't think I haven't tried to shake things up here. Eventually, Lania will become a worldwide powerhouse."

We gave up the rebel location, and told Nick everything we knew about Taylor's captors, which wasn't much.

When we were finished briefing him, he asked, "I'm hoping you can let Taylor know how sorry I am that this happened when she's feeling better? I've already talked to Dr. Lewis, and once Mark's family is notified, I'll speak to them as well."

"Yeah, we'll pass that along," I agreed distractedly as I kept an eye on the doctor and Taylor.

The physician had started an IV on Taylor, done what looked like a thorough exam, and had pushed several meds. He was now cleaning up some of the cuts on her face.

He finally stood up from his stool, and joined us outside. "She'll need monitoring on your way home," he said as he pulled a hand-kerchief out of his pocket and wiped the sweat from his face and his bald head. "There's not much else I can do under these conditions. Some of her lacerations are infected, so I started antibiotics. She'll need more as soon as you arrive in the United States. Taylor's muscles are deteriorated, bruised, and badly strained from being bound in the same position for so long, but they should slowly improve once she can walk. And as expected, she's severely dehydrated, which is affecting every system in her body. She's getting fluids, but the bags will need to be changed once they're empty."

"I got it," Jax said abruptly. "Do you have extra bags?"

Between the two of us, Jax had the most medical training, so I let him handle getting supplies with Nick as I asked the doctor, "Is there anything else we should know?"

"She'll need comprehensive lab work and x-rays to make sure all her systems are functioning normally again. Expect her to be confused and extremely weak while her body is trying to hydrate. I couldn't find any obvious fractures, but I could only do a cursory exam. I suspect her main issue is her critically dehydrated state."

I frowned. "Taylor wasn't talking to me. Is it normal for her to be unconscious?"

He nodded. "Her body was shutting down. She did wake for a moment for me. I don't think she liked the IV or the exam. She's not really unconscious. She'll rouse to physical pain, but it's better just to allow her to deep sleep until she gets some hydration. I'm sending some pain and anti-anxiety medication in case she needs it when she's more awake."

"Hell, I can't blame her for waking up during that IV, and all that poking and prodding," I muttered. I wouldn't exactly enjoy having a needle shoved into my arm, either.

"Since she wasn't awake for more than a few seconds, I couldn't access her mental state, but I imagine she's going to need time to recover. Luckily, she was only held for a short period of time, but her treatment by the rebels was incredibly harsh."

I nodded, my gut wrenching from thinking about just how much abuse this woman had suffered. "I know. I'll make sure she gets everything she needs."

After the doctor finished his instructions for the ride back home, we loaded Taylor into the transport boat, making her as comfortable as possible in the cabin.

"Be safe," Nick instructed as the captain who had ferried us over pushed off the dock. "Let me know how Taylor and Harlow are faring," he called out.

I lifted a hand in goodbye and entered the cabin as we departed.

"He's likable enough, I guess," Jax grumbled as he hung the IV bag. "But I still don't trust the bastard."

"Doesn't matter," I said gruffly. "At least we're on our way home with Taylor."

"I'm not sure if it's *her* that smells so bad, or *us*," Jax said as he raked a hand through his hair.

We'd trekked for miles carrying a lot of extra weight. "Probably a little of both," I answered, noticing how tired my brother looked now that we were actually facing each other. "The clothes that Cooper designed worked out great, but I'm sweating my balls off."

Since we didn't do military issue anymore, Cooper had developed special protective clothing for Last Hope, and Marshall had distributed it to all of his members.

We'd opted to use the black outfit for this particular mission, and although comfortable, the long sleeves had gotten hot.

Jax shrugged. "He said he had to give up some things to keep us safe. Long sleeves are necessary to protect your arms, and to stay undetected. It can't be any worse than military issue."

I shook my head. "It's not. It's a lot lighter and less confining, I guess I just feel like bitching."

Jax grinned. "Then bitch away. It was a long damn hike."

We'd nixed the black masks once we'd gotten away from the camp, and had just kept our high-tech night googles on, but it wasn't cool in Lania in the summer, even at night.

I was pretty sure every one of us in the small cabin right now was responsible for stinking it up.

"Since it's my jet, I'm getting the shower first," I informed my brother. "Taylor needs to get cleaned up, too."

"I'll wrap up her IV, but otherwise, that task is all yours. You better make it short; I'll be right behind you," Jax grumbled. "I'm not going to sleep until I wash this stench off me."

"I'll be as quick as possible, but she comes first right now," I reminded him shortly.

My eyes drifted to Taylor's face, and I felt my temper rise all over again.

I'd been infuriated from the moment I'd found her, weak and close to death.

Son of a bitch!

Nick had better deal with the rebels, or I'd come back and kill the bastards myself.

Taylor's bruises weren't as bad as they'd been in the proof of life video, but they were still there, and the big lacerations on her cheek and the one over her brow looked infected. The doc had done some hasty sutures, but they were probably going to leave a mark.

I let out a long, pissed off breath. Everything that had happened to Taylor, Harlow and Mark was just so damn wrong on so many levels.

They'd gone to Lania to do their job, and all three of them had gotten shafted.

They were geologists, not warriors. They were in Lania to check out a possible new site for Montgomery Mining.

I leaned closer, and took Taylor's hand in mine. "You're going home, Taylor. We're out of Lania," I said next to her ear, hoping she could hear me, even if she didn't respond. "And I'll make damn sure that you're okay after we get home, too."

For some reason, this whole mission had been different for me, and I wasn't able to distance myself from the victim like I usually did.

It *felt* personal.

It *was* personal.

Fuck! I knew I was throwing the rulebook out the window, and taking a mission way too personally.

Taylor Delaney was going to make everything complicated because she was *my* intern, but for once in my life, I didn't give a damn if I didn't follow the rules.

Chapter 5

Taylor

When I came out of the darkness, I came out swinging. Well, at least I *tried* to throw punches, but they were pretty ineffective.

It was pitch black, and I fought against whatever was wrapped around me, which, as it turned out, was simply a blanket.

But I didn't know that at first, so I tried to fight my way out of the cocoon I was in.

"Hey, Taylor," a deep voice said in the darkness, right before strong hands pinned my wrists gently to the bed. "Stop. You'll pull out your IV. You're okay. You're safe. You aren't in Lania anymore. You're on your way home."

Just that short burst of energy caused me to totally deflate, and I stopped trying to fight…because it was *him*. The same voice that had given me hope when I'd had none left. "Hudson?"

My voice was hoarse, and my throat was dry, but at least I could talk.

"Yeah, it's me. Everything is okay, Taylor. I'm glad you're awake, even if you did try to deck me," he said as he released me.

I panted for a moment, exhausted just from trying to move my arms. "Why is it so dark? Where am I? And who are you?"

"Hold on," he told me. "Don't get crazy. You have an IV in your arm."

I blinked as the room became bathed with a soft glow from a bedside lamp.

Logically, I knew it wasn't a bright light, but it was way more than I was used to, so I squinted as I tried to get my bearings.

"Right now," Hudson drawled. "You're on my private jet and on your way back to the U.S. We're only a few hours into the flight, so we have a long ways to go. And it was dark because we were sleeping. As to your question about me, my brothers and I all belong to a volunteer hostage rescue organization. My full name is Hudson Montgomery. My brothers and I own Montgomery Mining."

Oh, God. It's the big boss. What in the hell is he doing here?

I gaped at him as my vision cleared, and I could see exactly who I was talking to at the moment.

Sweet Jesus!

I got my first good look at the man who had hauled my ass for miles to rescue me.

Hudson Montgomery was breathtakingly gorgeous. His coal black hair was short, but slightly tousled from sleep, and his jawline and chin were covered with a dark, short beard. He was dressed in a pair of dark sweatpants, but his upper body was bare, every inch of tawny skin that covered all those tight muscles of his on display. Hudson was completely ripped, but not in a bodybuilder sort of way. He looked more like the type of guy who did physical labor all damn day, but I already knew he *didn't*.

I knew exactly who he was, and what he did all day.

When I finally tore my gaze away from his powerful chest and six pack abdomen, I met a pair of gray eyes that sucked all the air out of my lungs.

I shook my head as I took a deep breath in. "Am I hallucinating, or are you really Hudson Montgomery who owns Montgomery

Mining? Why in the world would a billionaire be rescuing people from Lania? It doesn't make sense."

I wanted to tell myself that it was just another crazy dream, but I didn't feel like I was hallucinating anymore, and the man claiming to be Hudson Montgomery seemed much too...real.

I was a peon at Montgomery Mining, a summer intern. I'd never met any of the big bosses, but never in my wildest dreams had I imagined that *any* of them looked like this.

Or that they spent their spare time rescuing hostages. According to Harlow, the Montgomery brothers were in the local papers, and the sensational gossip publications a lot. But I'd been in northern California for years, and I'd definitely never had the time or inclination to paw through the gossip rags.

"You recognize me?" he asked.

"Not really. I mean, I didn't recognize your face, but I *am* an intern with your company. I know *who* you are."

"I'm so damn sorry about what happened," Hudson informed me.

"So, do you go rescue people as a hobby?" I asked, wondering if Hudson had all of his marbles.

Or maybe it was *me* who wasn't all there. At the moment, it was hard to tell which one of us was delusional.

He shrugged. "I guess you could say that. My brothers and I got involved with Last Hope because we were Special Forces in the military before we took our places at Montgomery Mining, and we still wanted to help where we could."

My brain tried to take in exactly what he was saying, but it was no use. My mind was too scrambled. *"Last Hope? That's* pretty appropriate in *my* case, I guess. Where is Harlow?" I muttered.

"She's being taken care of back in the States. She's safe, Taylor."

Had he already told me that? I seemed to remember him telling me that before. "And Mark? Did you find him? Is he on his way back home, too?"

The pleasant look on his face crumbled, and was replaced with a far grimmer expression.

He stood, walked to a little mini fridge, and brought me back a bottle of water. Hudson handed it to me after he unscrewed the cap. "I think we should wait to discuss all the details," he said huskily. "You're being hydrated by IV, but it will help if you drink that." He nodded at the bottle.

I took a small sip of the water, my eyes trained on his face.

My mouth was still parched, and drinking the chilly liquid was one of the best sensations I'd ever experienced. I took a bigger sip, and let it go down slower this time, before I questioned, "He's dead, isn't he? I still might be a little bit out of it, but *no* answer is worse than a *bad* answer, and since you haven't said *anything*, I have to assume it's even worse than bad. You don't have to sugarcoat anything, Mr. Montgomery. I'd rather know the truth."

His intense gray eyes searched my face before he slowly nodded. "His body was recovered, and it's being sent by the Lanian government back to the U.S. And please just call me Hudson. I think we're way beyond formalities, Taylor."

"Oh, my God. Getting kidnapped was horrible enough, but this is going to be so hard for Harlow," I said, my voice already scratchy since I wasn't used to talking. "Does she know?"

I wasn't convinced that Harlow had been head over heels in love with Mark, but she'd really cared about him. She'd been hoping this trip would bring them closer together since Mark was traveling most of the time.

Hudson let out a long breath and planted his ass on the other side of the bed. He reclined against the headboard. "By now, I'm sure she does know. The director of Last Hope was waiting for her mother to get to the hospital before he broke the news when I talked to him earlier. Did you know him well?"

"No," I said quietly. "I only met him twice, and those encounters were very brief, and via video chat when he and Harlow were talking remotely, but he seemed really nice. I'm glad Harlow's mom is going to be there. They're pretty close. She's going to need her mother right now."

I laid back down, and put the water I'd been slowly consuming on the bedside table.

"Don't think about all of that right now," Hudson said in a soothing voice. "You need to rest."

I turned my head and studied him.

Hudson was probably one of the most gorgeous men I'd ever seen, but he was looking pretty rough. Closer up, I could see that his jaw was covered in dark scruff, but I wasn't sure whether that was his usual beard, or if he just hadn't shaved for a while.

I could see the weariness in his beautiful gray eyes, and the tension in his strong features.

"No offense," I said. "But I'm not so sure that you don't need the sleep worse than I do right now."

He put a hand to his jaw, and rubbed the dark hair on his face. "Do I look *that* bad?" he asked, sounding slightly amused.

"Yes. I suppose it's not the best thing for an intern to tell the big boss, but you look like you hiked for miles carrying a half dead woman through the woods of hostile territory," I said drily. "Get into the bed, Hudson, and get some sleep."

His eyes finally met mine, and my heart skittered as he gave me a long, slow smile.

God, the man was wickedly handsome, even if he did look dog-tired.

"You don't mind?" he asked as his eyebrow lifted. "Sleeping here was the best way to keep an eye on you."

"It doesn't bother me as long as you're aware that I could end up injuring you if I wake up in a fighting mood again," I joked weakly.

He chuckled as he moved his body until his head hit the pillow. "You're so weak right now that I doubt you could even get in one decent punch."

Hudson might be surprised. I actually had some pretty good moves, although he was probably right. I was doubtful I could do him much harm since I was so debilitated.

"I kind of want you to stay, anyway," I confessed. "I-I don't really want to be alone right now."

It was strange for me to say that because I was more than accustomed to being by myself.

"I'll be right here, Taylor," he said in a husky, reassuring voice.

I let out a sigh. "Just tell me one thing. How did I manage to get so clean, and what in the hell am I wearing?"

"I took you into the shower with me, and you're wearing one of my clean T-shirts."

If I was capable of letting out a long groan, I would have. "That must have been disgusting," I observed. Not only had I stunk from not showering for so long, and being held in a sweatbox, but I could tell I'd lost a lot of weight. Not to mention the fact that I was bruised up everywhere.

He laughed as he reached out and turned off the light. "I wasn't looking. I promise. Okay, maybe I *had* to look to get you clean, but that was it."

I'd felt an instant surge of panic the moment he'd plunged the room into darkness, and I tried desperately to fight it.

Suddenly, I was back in Lania, and all of the bad stuff was like video clips playing on a loop over and over again in my head.

Worse yet, I couldn't stop the accompanying emotions from rising to the surface.

The fear.

The pain.

The endless thirst.

The incessant thoughts of dying.

I reached my hand out, and it landed on Hudson's rock-hard abdomen.

Fight it, dammit! I can't panic every time it's dark outside!

Hudson's big hand enveloped my smaller one, and he threaded our fingers together. "What's wrong, Taylor?" he asked, sounding worried.

There was something about that simple human touch that made me feel more grounded, more connected.

Now that I knew what Hudson looked like, his image had replaced the horrific memories the moment he'd taken my hand, and his presence assured me that I *wasn't* going back there again.

"I'm sorry. I think I've developed some sort of…fear of the dark," I answered, trying not to sound as apprehensive as I'd felt a few moments ago. "I'm better now."

"Fuck! I really should have thought about that. I'll turn the light back on."

"Don't," I requested as I squeezed his hand. "I really am okay now."

Hudson started to circle my palm with his thumb, and I deescalated a little bit more.

"You sure?" he questioned skeptically.

"I'm positive," I insisted. "Just…don't leave."

"I'm not going anywhere, Taylor. I promise."

My breathing slowed, and for some reason, I wasn't really embarrassed because Hudson saw my fear. Probably because I sensed that he completely understood it. "Thank you," I mumbled as I closed my eyes.

I fell asleep just like that, clinging to Hudson's hand like he was my lifeline to sanity.

Honestly, right now, maybe he was…

Chapter 6

Taylor

When I woke again, it wasn't pitch black anymore .

Not that the bedroom on the aircraft was exactly flooded with light. There was some kind of blackout glass on the window, but I *could* actually see the room without any lights on.

"You're awake," Hudson said huskily from the door.

I sat up slowly, and sighed.

Seriously, the guy looked the main character in some kind of sexy female wet dream, and I couldn't force myself to look away.

If I'm still hallucinating, or dreaming, I'm going to get every second of pleasure I can get before I wake up again.

Hudson had one shoulder resting on the doorjamb, and a very large mug of coffee in his hand. There was a small smile on his lips, and God, those eyes! He was surveying me like he wanted to know everything about me with a single glance.

He'd shaved, and I couldn't decide if I was thrilled or disappointed about that. On one hand, the short beard and the scruffy wild look

had suited him, but on the other, he looked equally amazing without
it. He had a strong, perfectly sculpted jawline and face.

My eyes quickly scanned his body. He was dressed in a pair of
well-worn jeans, and a navy-blue T-shirt that hugged all of those
glorious muscles in his upper body.

Well, good morning to you, too, handsome!

He swept those gorgeous eyes over my body, like he was trying
to make sure I was all in one piece. His smile broadened a little in
approval. "You look better," he observed.

"I feel better, but I have one small problem."

He grinned as he asked, "You have to piss?"

I nodded hard. "I think it's all those IV fluids."

While I definitely wasn't shy, I was a little embarrassed to ask
him to help me get to the bathroom to pee, but rationally, I knew I
wasn't going to make it on my own steam.

He sauntered into the room, put his mug on the side table, and
grabbed my IV bag from the small stand. "It's *definitely* the IV
fluids," he confirmed as he lifted me in his arms. "I'm actually surprised you didn't have this little problem earlier. You've been pumped
with fluids for hours now."

I didn't realize how close to naked I was until I had to yank my
borrowed T-shirt over my upper thighs as he'd lifted me up. I'd
forgotten that I wasn't sleeping in shorts and a tank, and I felt even
more ridiculous as my cheeks flushed *after* I'd briefly flashed him.

*When in the hell had I become the kind of woman who blushed
about anything?*

When somebody needed to see a bathroom as much as I did
right now, it shouldn't matter how, or under what circumstances, I
got there.

Normally, I probably wouldn't care, but there was something about
Hudson that made me feel a little…off-balance.

I reminded myself that it was nothing he hadn't seen before, but at
least when he'd taken me into the shower, I'd been out. I was awake
now, and perfectly aware of how bizarre my situation with Hudson
was at the moment.

I didn't really know him, but he was the most important person in my life right now because he was *all* I had, the *only* thing that had stood between me...and dying.

I couldn't exactly call him a stranger.

But he wasn't a friend, either.

We shared some kind of weird intimacy because the guy had literally saved my life.

I was finally able to get my arms around his neck for balance, and I clung to him, finding it almost impossible *not* to think about how good it felt to be cradled against his chest. Hudson was big, warm, and solid, which was pretty damn comforting after what I'd been through.

It was a short trip from the bed to the attached bathroom. Hudson sat me down on the toilet, and hung my IV bag on a hook that was actually meant for clothing. "Call me when you're done," he demanded. "I'll be right outside. And don't be embarrassed, I didn't see a thing this time, either."

I rolled my eyes. Just the fact he mentioned my discomfort told me that he *definitely* saw me flash him, *and* noticed my silly pink-cheeked reaction to it happening.

I sighed. "Does it really matter? You took off my clothes and dragged me into the shower at some point, so I think you've pretty much seen it all anyway."

I could have sworn I heard him chuckle a little as he closed the door.

I shook my head a little. Hudson *had* seen me completely naked. Worse yet, he'd had to scrub ten days of filth off my body and out of my hair, too.

I cringed as I examined my legs and all the other areas I hadn't been able to look at before, noting all the bruises I'd gotten during my beating.

No wonder every muscle in my body hurts!

I finished my business, and then tried to test my legs, hoping I could get a look at my face in the vanity mirror above the sink. Every muscle protested when I tried to stand, and I ended up leaning over to the sink from a sitting position on the toilet to wash my hands.

It was probably a good thing that I *couldn't* see my face if it looked as bad as the rest of my body.

"I'm done," I called out, hating the fact that I couldn't even walk out of the bathroom on my own right now.

I was used to doing *everything* by myself. Mac had always encouraged my independence, even at a young age. I didn't ask for help with much of anything, but Hudson had already saved my life, literally, and then had taken care of me when I couldn't take care of myself. The man acted like it was a perfectly normal situation, but it was far from *my* usual. The details of what had happened *after* we'd stopped for water right after his rescue was a blank spot in my memory, but he must have hauled me for miles to get back to the coast.

It was frustrating as hell that I was now free, but unable to deal with even my simplest needs on my own.

It bothered me that I was still totally dependent on Hudson, but what choice did I have?

Suck it up! It wasn't like my physical state was in my control right now, so I really had *no* option but to live with what my body could and couldn't do at the moment.

"I'm really sorry," I muttered as he effortlessly hefted me back up. "My legs aren't working right yet."

"Don't even try to walk," he warned me. "Not after all the abuse your body has taken. You need further medical testing and treatment before you do anything except stay in bed and get rehydrated. You'll walk when your body is ready to do it. It's going to take time, Taylor."

His voice was stern, a tone that most people might find almost scary, but somehow, I knew it was coming from a place of concern, and not from irritation or impatience.

On the surface, for most people, Hudson Montgomery probably seemed pretty intense, and a little beyond intimidating, but I just couldn't see him that way.

Not after all the things he'd done for me.

In fact, to me, it was almost endearing that he gave a damn that much about my welfare, no matter how grumpy he seemed when he was doing it.

"Do you have any idea how weird it is to have somebody physically carry me around?" I murmured as he put me back in the bed and covered me with the sheet and blanket.

He was quiet as he took my nearly empty bottle of water, strode to the fridge, and brought me back a fresh one, along with another bottle of something that looked familiar.

He screwed the cap off and handed me the mystery container along with a couple of pills that he pulled out of his front pocket. "Breakfast," he stated in a rough voice.

I wrinkled my nose as I took a good look at the liquid nutritional supplement. I'd tried it before, and it was nasty. Mac had needed them when he'd gotten sick, and he'd loved them so much that I'd taken a tiny swig of his once just to see what he liked about it. "This stuff is horrible," I said as I made a face. "Even if it *is* supposedly chocolate flavored, it doesn't taste very good. I'd much prefer some of that coffee I smell."

I had no problem with taking the pills he'd given me. He hadn't risked his own life only to poison me hours later, but I hated the nutritional supplement.

Not only did it *not* taste good, but it brought back some very bad memories during my last year with Mac.

Hudson leaned his ass on the short, built-in dresser only a foot or two away from the bed, his coffee back in his hand, as he shot me a warning glance. "Drink it, and take the damn pills," he insisted. "Doctor's orders. Since you've had no solid food for a long time, we're starting with that."

I lifted a brow. "I suppose that means the big, medium-rare steak, and the really huge loaded baked potato I'm craving is a no-go?"

He nodded, a small smile on his sensual lips. "For now. But I'll let you have a very small amount of coffee if you down those. We'll see how it goes. I know you're starving, Taylor, but you'll have to take a raincheck on the steak dinner. I promise that you'll get it, and anything else you want once you can handle it."

He was right, of course. My digestive system needed to restart before I fed it an entire pizza, a steak dinner, any of the other things I was madly craving.

"I'm going to hold you to that, and I take my coffee with cream, no sugar," I said matter-of-factly, and then popped the pills in my mouth, and tipped the container up.

I'd learned that the best way to get something done that I didn't want to do was to plow right through it. The pills went down awkwardly, and I drank until the liquid was gone, and the container was empty. My throat was still sore, and it wasn't easy to swallow, but there was no sense in prolonging something unpleasant.

"Here," I said, holding out the drained container to him. "It's gone. Where's the coffee?"

Hudson looked amused as he obligingly took it without a word, and left the room.

He came back moments later and handed me the smallest cup I'd ever seen. It looked even tinier than an expresso mug. Honestly, it was probably more suitable for a doll than a human. "When you said *small*, you really meant it," I grumbled right before I caught the aroma of the contents.

I held it up to my nose, closed my eyes, and just took one long breath after another. I felt my eyes water with happy tears that were threatening to fall, but I blinked them back.

A few days ago, I thought I'd *never* catch a whiff of good, freshly made coffee again.

Now, I savored every damn second that I could relish the scent.

"Are you planning on drinking that, or snorting it?" Hudson asked, sounding entertained by my actions.

I opened my eyes slowly. "I didn't think I'd *ever* smell good coffee again," I informed him. "I'm taking my time."

"So you demolish the unpleasant stuff in seconds, and take forever when you like something?" he asked, like he was trying to figure me out.

I raised an eyebrow as I lowered the coffee to my mouth. "Life is a whole lot better when you approach it that way, and I'm a coffee lover. What can I say?"

I started to enjoy the tiny amount of coffee as he said, "Do you want to talk about what happened, Taylor?"

I got exactly three sips from the miniature cup before it was gone. My hand shook just a little as I finished the last drop in the cup, set it on the bedside table, and grabbed the water.

I wasn't sure I *wanted* to discuss the last ten days, but I knew I *needed* to do it. Not to mention the fact that Hudson deserved to know the details after risking his own life to save mine. "I want to, but my head is a little scrambled. Can you catch me up on how I got here first? My memories are so scattered. I remember you, I remember your voice, and I know that you hauled me out of there, and that you gave me some water. After that, there's a...huge hole until I suddenly woke up here."

And you comforted me, holding my hand so I wasn't afraid of the dark.

Nobody would know that Hudson was that sweet by looking at his face right now, but I could never forget that part of him existed, no matter how hard he tried to hide it.

He nodded sharply. "It's normal, considering your physical state, for none of your recollections to be clear. You were in bad shape, Taylor. I'm not sure you would have lasted another day without water. Honestly, I'm surprised you were still alive and able to comprehend *anything*, but I was pretty fucking grateful that you were still breathing. Jax and I hiked our way in, and took you out the same way. So you do remember stopping for water, but nothing after that?"

I nodded slowly. "I remember wanting to drink until I couldn't do it anymore, and how damn hard it was to take in that first bit of water. I even recall being glad you took the water away, so I didn't throw it up all over you. I couldn't see you, but you were there for me, and I'm more grateful for that than you'll ever know. You saved my life, Hudson."

"Don't," he said with an irritated growl that I hadn't heard before. "You were in that situation because of me and my company in the first place. So don't thank me for saving you from a situation you should have never been in to begin with, Taylor."

I took the cap off the water, and downed a sip before I answered, "It wasn't your fault. It was something *nobody* could anticipate, and I'm going to be grateful whether you want me to be or not. I'm happy to be alive, Hudson, and if you hadn't gotten me out of there when you did, I know I would have died."

God, he had no idea.

"You're stubborn," he muttered. "But that's probably what kept you alive."

"Then don't complain about it," I suggested, trying to give him a smile, and mostly failing because of a painful crack on my lip.

Hudson let out an exasperated breath. "I definitely can't complain about your tenacity, and I won't, because it most likely kept you breathing until we got there. I'll catch you up on what happened while you were out." He drained his mug and sat on the dresser. "Jax and I didn't stop again after I got some water into you. Not until we got to the coast. Our only objective was to put as much space between us and the rebels before they woke up. We were met by a physician and Prince Niklaos when we got to the coast of Lania where the boat was waiting. The doctor did all that he could for you from inside a small tent and on a cot. After that, we took the boat to a mostly uninhabited island that has an airstrip. Jax and I had landed there, and my pilots were ready for takeoff when we got back. We were in the air almost immediately. We stopped on the Portuguese coast to refuel, and right now, we're currently over the Atlantic Ocean. We'll be flying over the East Coast of the U.S. in a few hours, but since you're awake, and have your vital needs covered, we're heading straight for San Diego. If we don't have to risk having the general public become aware of this entire incident, we'd rather not. There are several ex-military physicians on staff at the best medical facility in San Diego who know what we're doing with Last Hope, and who know how to keep the media away." Hudson took a deep breath before he concluded, "Honestly, you didn't miss a whole lot after you conked out. It's mostly been a scramble to get you back to the States, and out of Lania as soon as possible."

My mind was about to explode from trying to follow his expla-nation. I wasn't even going to ask how he knew about the so-called *mostly uninhabited* island with an airstrip big enough to land and launch a sophisticated private jet. "Did you have to confront the rebels at any point? Were you or your brother injured?"

"Not at all," he said, brushing off my concerns. "Our goal was to get you the hell out of there, and back home. Jax and I know exactly how to get in and out of almost any area without detection. None of the bastards even opened an eye. Personally, I would have loved a confrontation, but that wasn't the plan. We were in and out quickly while they slept."

Hudson sounded highly disappointed about the fact that he couldn't shoot every single one of the rebels, but I was relieved. "Do you think the Lanian government will catch them?" I didn't like the fear I could hear in my own voice.

Instinctively, I reached for the dragon pendant I'd always held onto when I needed an emotional boost, only to come up empty-handed.

Even though the jewelry hadn't had that much monetary value, those bastards had taken it from me anyway.

I lowered my hand back to my side.

"They already have," Hudson informed me. "Prince Niklaos sent me a text that the job was done. I gave him their location before Jax and I left, and he sent his people in after he received it. They're locked up, Taylor. I promise. None of those assholes will ever see freedom again. "

I let out a sigh of relief. "Thank God. They're all completely insane, Hudson."

"Yeah, I pretty much got that when I realized they'd executed Mark for no other reason than their warped brains," he drawled. "Did I fill in all the missing areas of your memory?"

"Yes," I said after hesitating for a moment. It wasn't like Hudson could give me any information about what had happened during those last few, mostly lost days when I'd drifted in and out of reality before he and Jax had gotten there. "I wish I could have been awake to meet Prince Niklaos. What was he like?"

I'd seen an occasional picture of the young crown prince, and I knew he was responsible for many of the changes taking place in Lania, but it would have been interesting to meet him in person.

"Helpful," Hudson said carefully. "He worked with the director of Last Hope to get a doctor and medical supplies to our location before we boarded the boat, but I can't say I completely trust him after what happened. It's hard to say whether or not he suspected that there were still guerilla forces in Lania, but I certainly hope he didn't when he allowed my team to enter his country on an exploration. My brothers and I don't exactly have a great history with Lania since we had to do multiple missions there to rescue hostages when we were in Special Forces. But like everyone else, we *did* think the country was safe now. And he was supposedly trying to find you, but that wasn't good enough in my opinion. It will be a very long time before any of *my* employees puts a single foot in that damn country again, if ever."

He went on to explain about the delay in him finding out about the kidnapping, and how Harlow had gotten released.

I watched Hudson's face as he spoke, and it was impossible not to see the haunted look in his eyes. Somehow, I knew he was taking the entire responsibility for what had happened onto his very broad shoulders. I sensed that it wasn't easy to gain this man's trust because he'd seen far too much, experienced way too much of the ugliness in the world.

If there was anyone who would get that, it was me, which is probably why I could see it in Hudson without really knowing him that well. "Do you think it was just a one-off incident by a bunch of crazy, leftover rebels?" I asked.

"Christ!" he cursed as he raked a hand through his dark hair. "I hope so."

"Tell me more about Last Hope," I requested. "How is it that nobody really knows they exist?"

Now that my head was more together, I believed every word he told me about Last Hope. I just had no idea why a billionaire mogul like Hudson would be involved. Actually, why in the hell had he gone into the military in the first place?

Montgomery Mining had been the worldwide leader in mining for a long time, probably way before he'd been born. I knew at one time, the company had mined just about everything profitable, but had become pretty focused on gems and minerals over the years, and the cutting-edge technology to do it without creating an environmental disaster. If his father, and possibly generations before him, had already been outrageously wealthy, hadn't Hudson been born with a solid gold spoon in his mouth?

I waited patiently for him to answer, but judging by the troubled look on his face, I wasn't quite certain that he actually would.

Chapter 7

Hudson

I struggled with how much to tell Taylor.

The reason she knew *nothing* about Last Hope is because we all worked hard to make damn sure nobody knew we existed.

Marshall was a master at bullshit, and all of the other guys who were actively involved were required to be previous Special Forces for several reasons.

One, because they had the skills needed.

Two, because they were mentally tough, and physically capable.

Three, because they knew how to keep their mouths shut about covert missions because they knew lives could depend on their silence.

Eventually, we'd have *the talk* with both Taylor and Harlow, and try to make sure they knew how important it was for them to keep our existence a secret.

No doubt Marshall had *already* spoken to Harlow. He made that a priority before anyone who was not a member of Last Hope could get the chance to expose us. Marshall had probably pounced on Harlow about it right after I'd been obligated to mention it.

I knew that the Montgomery Mining security team that had picked Harlow up in Lania had asked her not to talk about any of her experiences in Lania, for reasons of national security...blah, blah, blah.

But it was *our* responsibility to make sure that Last Hope's involvement never came out when a non-member had to know what we were doing.

Last Hope worked on a *need to know* basis, and we didn't say any more than absolutely necessary. Yeah, we had to tell victims enough for them to trust us, but not so much that it jeopardized future missions.

We'd walked that fine line for years now.

And I'd *never* had a problem with that...

Until now.

Taylor was my goddamn employee, and after what she'd been through, she deserved to know whatever the hell she wanted to know.

In fact, *because* she was an employee, she already knew much more than she should know.

Okay, so maybe we could have the talk...right now.

I raked a frustrated hand through my hair as I started to talk. "Here's the thing, Taylor. If everyone knew about us, it could very well compromise future missions," I explained. "We try extremely hard to avoid *any* type of news media and general public knowledge about what we do so we can keep helping future victims. We ask every single hostage we rescue not to out us, and so far, we've been lucky enough to get their promise that they won't. Usually, they don't have enough information to completely blow the whistle anyway. No last names, no personal info on their rescuers. No one has outed our group yet, and I hope they don't. It could destroy the entire organization, and the work that we do. Our best weapon is ignorance about the fact that we even exist. Do you understand?"

My cousin Mason's brother, Jett, had once been part of an operation similar to Last Hope, but on a smaller scale. When Jett's helicopter had crashed during an attempted mission, one single leak had demolished the entire organization.

Now, since PRO had gone down, our group was the last of its kind, and we *had* to stay covert. If we didn't, hostages would die because we were all they had in some instances.

Taylor shot me earnest look. "Of course I understand. I'm not an idiot. Maybe I've never been in the military, but I totally get how important it is for Last Hope to stay a secret, and why. But if you saved someone's life, why *wouldn't* they keep your secret?" she asked. "That's definitely not much to ask after you've risked your own butt to save theirs. I'll never tell a soul about anything regarding Last Hope or how you rescued me. I promise, Hudson. I'd never do anything that could jeopardize you, your teams, or someone in trouble like I was."

I nodded. "Some people will at least have to know about the kidnapping, and what you went through. Most of our previous victims simply say they were taken out of their situation by a private party if asked, and refuse to disclose anything else. Medical professionals and counselors are bound by their own code of ethics not to reveal anything you tell them except things they're mandated to report. Over the years, we've learned who takes those obligations seriously."

"Okay, so you have your own doctors, and your own professionals?" she asked, and then immediately put up a hand. "Wait! You don't have to answer that."

"No, but I will, because it's something you're going to know anyway," I assured her. "None of those professionals are part of Last Hope, and we can't force you to see the professionals we know are safe. A few do know the basics about Last Hope, and are...sympathizers, if you want to call it that. Others are just damn loyal to their profession and ethics, and when you ask them not to share your information, they don't. If we've dealt with them before, we know that. If you choose somebody we don't know, it's basically a crapshoot, but it's your right to do whatever you think is best for yourself."

She tilted her head in an adorable way that I was starting to think only happened when she was turning things over in her head. "So really, you're always vulnerable? Especially you and your brothers since at least *some* people would recognize your faces."

I shrugged. "We have been since the beginning, and we knew that when we signed on. My brothers and I have been backing away from doing the actual missions over the last few years because we could be recognized. So we mostly do the strategic planning and provide resources. We've just gotten lucky so far, but if Last Hope takes on a rescue, we see it through. It's not like we just get you away from the bad guys and dump you in a hospital. You won't see the last of this organization until you're completely healed, emotionally and physically."

"That's actually a benefit for you, right?" Taylor mused. "If somebody is always there to guide a victim through the rough patches, and they always have somebody to talk to about it, then they're way less likely to talk to somebody on the outside. They already have people who completely get what they're going through."

Jesus! This woman was bright, and her reasoning ability had to be off the charts if she could pick up on that immediately, even though her brain wasn't fully functional yet. That was *exactly* why we took our aftercare duties so seriously. It's not that we didn't give a damn what happened after a victim was rescued, but most of the benefit was on our side. "Pretty much," I answered simply.

"So if you and your brothers don't take on rescues yourself anymore, why are you doing it this time?" she pondered.

"Jax and I knew that every moment was going to count, and we didn't have time to pull another team together. Plus, this one was personal for me because every one of you were *my* employees." It was the most honest answer I could give her. Had I taken the time needed to get another team together, she would have been completely screwed.

She met my gaze with those big green eyes of hers, and the sincerity in that look made my gut ache as she said softly, "Babysitter or not, I'd never do anything that I knew would put you at risk, Hudson."

For some reason, I felt it in my bones that she'd die before she'd reveal any information about us. I wasn't sure why my instinct was to trust her this early on, but generally, my inklings were never wrong. "So ask me whatever else you want to know, and I'll tell you what I can," I grumbled, irritated with myself because those forest-colored eyes could get to me so damn easily.

I watched as she tilted her head again, and looked at me like she had a thousand burning questions, but was trying to narrow that number down.

"I think my biggest question is...why?" she mused. "I don't need to know how you operate and where, or who carries out the rescues. None of those details really matter to me. But *you're* Hudson Montgomery, billionaire, genius, and the head of one of the most successful companies in the world. Why the military in the first place, and why are you part of Last Hope now? It didn't make sense to me before, and I guess it still doesn't. Not completely. Weren't you groomed to take over Montgomery Mining?"

Very few people could catch me off-guard, but Taylor did. It was the last thing I'd expected her to ask. Most people would want to know about other rescues, or how many countries we operated in, or how many guys were in the organization.

All the questions I'd rather not answer.

But not...her.

Jesus! Taylor Delaney was...unexpected. She had been from the start. I'd had a feeling she was going to play hell with my psyche, and she did. I just hadn't realized how much.

She'd held onto life a lot longer than she should have been capable of without food or water, and sheer stubbornness and the unwillingness to give up had been her only survival tools.

How the hell she could wake up and still have a sense of humor, the ability to appreciate the smell of coffee, and lightning quick rationale was a damn mystery to me.

She had to be hurting.

She had to be emotionally messed up, and scared.

She had to be angry for fuck's sake.

Most people we rescued were only concerned about things that involved their own wellbeing, and rightfully so.

But *her* one burning question was about…me? Personally?

Holy fuck! She was completely unlike any rescued hostage I'd ever dealt with before, and I had no goddamn idea how to deal with her.

I was the kind of guy who was always wary of the unknowns. And *she* was like uncharted territory.

The woman threw me off my game, dammit, and *that* didn't happen to me. *Ever.* I was the guy who was *always* one step ahead, and ready for anything.

"I was," I started to explain, not particularly comfortable with talking about myself. "And I wasn't. I honestly don't think my father thought he was ever going to die. My brothers and I were all educated in business, and we all had our college degree by the time we were twenty, but I'm not really sure how to explain my family except to say it was highly dysfunctional. My father wasn't a pleasant man to be around, so my brothers and I decided to do our own thing. Maybe we thought he'd never die, too, so we pursued our own goals. Every one of us had always wanted to do something that made a difference, and the military was it for us. I was recruited from a Marine company into Delta Force, and I never looked back. My younger brother, Jax, ended up in the SEALS, and my youngest brother, Cooper, was in the Rangers."

"Blackhawk Down," she said, her tone awed.

"That was a little before my time in the unit," I told her. "And I think they used a lot of creative license in that movie."

She shrugged. "Can I help it if I like some of the pulse-pounding action films, even the old ones?"

I tried to stop myself from smiling because Taylor sounded so defensive. Hell, I'd seen the movie a couple of times myself. I was just surprised that *she* had. The film had probably come out around the time she was in grade school. "Hey, I'm not judging. I've seen it. In real life, being in any Special Forces unit pretty much consumes your life, but I was okay with that since I felt like I was part of something bigger than myself."

"Then why did you leave?" she queried curiously.

I was relieved that she *didn't* ask me anything else about Delta Force, because there wasn't much I could tell her about my years there. However, trying to talk about myself wasn't exactly a picnic for me, either. "After my father died, Montgomery Mining faltered. My brothers and I were gone, out of the country most of the time, so it took years for us to realize that the man in charge was a crook, and that he'd brought in an entire upper management team who were systematically killing the company that had been in our family for several generations. We had to make a tough decision. My brothers and I all chose to save our legacy. We came back to San Diego permanently to make Montgomery thrive again."

"You did well," she acknowledged. "I never knew it was even in trouble."

I shrugged. "Obviously, we didn't want anyone to know. It wouldn't have been a good company image if people had known we were on the verge of bankruptcy. Luckily, we were able to turn it around, and Montgomery is better than it was during my father's time."

She sighed, and the longing in that sound made my damn chest ache as she said, "It's an amazing company. It's my dream job. Honestly, Montgomery is probably every new grad's hope for future employment. You've made such enormous strides in protecting the environment during the mining process, and you've done it through technology, research, and ingenuity. Your lab is mind-boggling. I'm grateful for every minute I got to spend there with Harlow."

I grimaced. "She resigned, but I plan on convincing her to stay with Montgomery."

Taylor's eyes widened. "She did? Oh, God, she can't leave. I know she's probably upset, but she can't blame herself for any of this, and she has a lot of important research going on in the lab."

"She's not going anywhere," I assured her, hating the fact that I'd told Taylor about anything that would upset her right now. "I'll convince her to stay. Or better yet, I'll send Jax to do it. He's a hell of a lot more charming than I am. We'll keep her at Montgomery. None of this is her fault."

My brother had a way with women, which was probably why he was always surrounded by a lot of them, and I…didn't possess his easy charm.

"It's not yours, either. It's nobody's fault, Hudson," she said gently. "It's not like anyone sent any of us into something obviously dangerous. We're geologists, and it should have been fine. We were there to look at samples, not to fight a war. We just happened to be there at the same time as a bunch of crazy people. Every location in the world has mentally-unbalanced people in it. There's no way anybody could have predicted what happened."

Fuck! I found it totally surreal that she was trying to make *me* feel better after what *she'd* been through. "It will all be thoroughly investigated to see exactly where the fault lies," I informed her. "And if something happens while any employee is doing something for my company, it *is* my goddamn fault!"

"Really?" she answered drily. "I had no idea you were *that* powerful, Mr. Montgomery. I mean, I know you're filthy rich, mentally gifted and all, but I didn't know you were capable of predicting a future freak incident *before* it happens." Her voice was dripping with sarcasm by the end of her statement.

I glared at her. Was she actually…making fun of me?

I couldn't remember the last woman who had gotten this sassy and sarcastic with me.

Come to think of it…well, *no one* ever had, male *or* female.

In my world, my employees said, "Yes, Mr. Montgomery." Or, "I'll get on that right away, Mr. Montgomery."

The women I'd dated in the past never would have rocked the boat. All they'd *ever* been interested in was my money, the Montgomery name and the power it carried. They'd been awed by the very idea of changing their last name to Montgomery. They sure as hell had *never* made fun of it, even if I'd never been on board with changing *any* of their last names to mine. None of my past relationships had ever gotten that far.

I was pretty much an *all* business, *all* the time, kind of guy. The only time I *wasn't* like that was when I was with family or a close friend, and I didn't have all that many friends I could completely trust.

My business associates respected me, so I never got anything except compliance in that arena, either.

And I pretty much liked it that way.

I lifted a brow as I glared at Taylor. "Are you messing with me?"

"Probably," she confessed. "Don't you know?"

"No," I answered unhappily.

"You just seem like the kind of guy who really needs somebody to mess with him once in a while," she informed me. "I get that you've had a lot of responsibility your entire life, and that you can handle that, but I think you need to cut yourself a break. You saved my life after the unthinkable happened, with no real thought about the risk to yourself. I find that incredible, yet you're still blaming yourself for what happened in the *first place*, even though it was unavoidable. Nobody is *that* all-powerful, Mr. Montgomery. Not even you. You might be incredibly rich and ridiculously smart, but you're still just one man. Even *you* can't stop anything bad from happening if it's a fluke incident."

"I don't know for sure that it *was* a fluke," I rasped, uncomfortable, yet fascinated by the fact that she saw me as anything other than the head of Montgomery Mining. Most people didn't, and I wasn't sure how I felt about the fact that she apparently did. "Maybe we missed something? What if Lania really *isn't* all that safe? What if there are still more rebels there, and Prince Nick doesn't want the world to know that?"

"Paranoid much?" she asked in an innocent voice that I instantly knew was completely fake.

"I'm careful," I growled. "I've always had to be."

"I give up," she said in a completely genuine tone this time. "It wasn't my intention to piss you off. I'd never be a bitch to you after everything you've done for me. I guess I just…wanted to help. I wanted you to understand that it's not always possible to control everything in your world."

And then, just like that, I felt like a total asshole.

I saw something that resembled hurt in her beautiful green eyes, and it made my fucking chest ache with regret.

She'd been trying to help...me?

Taylor had been through hell, and honestly, it showed. Her pretty face was marred by fading bruises and lacerations, and her voice was still hoarse and raspy from disuse and deprivation. Taylor was small-boned, so the weight she'd lost was obvious, and she was way too thin. I didn't even want to think about the fact that she was so weak she couldn't stand on her own two feet. I hated the fact that she was vulnerable in any way, and it completely pissed me off that she'd ended up like *this* while she was doing something for *me*. After all, my brothers and I *were* Montgomery Mining. I didn't hide behind company bullshit when it came to personal responsibility. None of us did.

However, the last thing I wanted to do was hurt this intrepid female, and for some reason, it really bothered me that I had.

"Stop calling me Mr. Montgomery," I rumbled. "I've seen you naked for fuck's sake. Maybe I'm just not used to anybody messing with me or trying to help me," I confessed honestly, and then quickly changed the subject. "Taylor, do you want to tell me how in the hell you got so banged up? Harlow said she was never beaten. What happened *after* she left?"

I wanted to know.

I needed to help Taylor any way I could, and surprisingly, that instinct wasn't coming from a place of obligation or responsibility this time.

The raw need to protect this woman was actually burning in my gut for some odd reason that I didn't really understand.

Hell, I knew I wasn't the psychologist she actually needed, and I sure as hell didn't have Jax's charm, but for now, I was *all* she had.

Chapter 8

Taylor

I t was perfectly obvious to me that Hudson Montgomery wasn't comfortable talking about himself, and that he much preferred to be the one asking the questions.

I took a small sip of my water, still stunned by Hudson's confession that he wasn't accustomed to anyone joking around with him or trying to help him.

He seemed like the kind of guy who deserved a hell of a lot more than he'd been getting.

God, didn't he know that most billionaires didn't even actively work at their own companies every single day?

Didn't he get that most guys with his kind of money and power didn't risk their own life for anyone, much less a peon intern like me?

Most ultra-rich guys didn't go into the military to make a difference, and I could guarantee that very few people, wealthy or not, were going to participate in a group like Last Hope.

Hudson Montgomery was probably the most intriguing man I'd ever met, but he didn't see *himself* that way.

Okay, so he *had* gotten a little crabby when I'd tried to tease him out of his own head about being hyper-responsible for something that wasn't his fault. My guess was he'd been defending himself because he really *didn't* understand that sometimes shit just happened, and there *was* no explanation as to why it happened, or who caused it.

I had a feeling that Hudson liked to think he could control *anything* that happened, that he could solve any problem, make anything that he thought was wrong be right again.

For God's sake, he'd saved me when I had no hope of living another day. And *that* wasn't good enough for him?

He had a fortune at his disposal, and could have been living it up on a yacht somewhere instead of being so determined to help other people in trouble.

Strangely enough, I was pretty sure that the whole secrecy thing worked out well for him when it came to Last Hope. The guy didn't seem to want anyone to thank him, or even recognize what he'd done for them in any way.

"I tried to escape in the middle of the night, right after Harlow left," I said, finally answering his question. "Apparently, that's a harsh punishment offense for the rebels. After they caught me, they took turns trying to beat me into submission. When one of the guards looked in for his late-night check to see if I was still alive, I'd already managed to get my legs free, so I just made a break for it. Unfortunately, my hands were still tied, literally, I was really weak, and I could barely walk, much less run, so I was pretty much screwed from the second I made a run for it. I had no way of taking a single one of them down once they caught up with me." Actually, in hindsight, it probably wasn't the greatest plan, but it was all I had at the time.

"No offense, but how would you take any of those guys down, even if you were healthy?" he asked, looking confused.

I rolled my eyes. It wasn't the first time that someone scoffed at me when I said I could take a guy twice my size to the ground. "I'm a Tai Chi master. I've been studying the art since I was thirteen, and I started working as an instructor while I was working on my master's at Stanford."

I could see the wheels turning in his brain before he asked, "Tai Chi. Isn't that kind of like meditation in motion? It looks like a slow dance."

Okay, it wasn't the first time somebody had said *that*, either. "It is, but it's a lot more than that. It's a martial arts form, and I wasn't trained in the gentler type of Tai Chi. There's a lot of that being used for relaxation and meditation lately, and it's popular these days. My first teacher was a Chen master all the way, and he fought dirty. Anyway, I *didn't* succeed in escaping. So I was beaten up, and tossed back into the lockdown hotel from hell after it was over. They tied my legs so tight that it probably impeded my circulation, not that I was exactly in any shape to try another self-rescue anyway. I think I used up most of the energy I had left during that failed attempt. After every rebel used me as their punching bag, my physical condition went downhill a lot during those last few days."

He paused a moment, his expression broody as he answered, "I would have done the same damn thing, Taylor. I would have figured it was better to try than to lay there and die. You had no way of knowing whether anybody would try to rescue you, and the Lanian rebels aren't known for letting their last hostages, or single hostage in your case, leave alive. That's why we didn't just pay your ransom when they demanded it. The only reason they let Harlow go free was to try to get more money for you. Historically, if the ransom is paid for those final captives, they'll take it, kill the hostage or hostages, and then stall everyone on the release information, using that time to escape."

My head started to spin as I tried to comprehend what he was saying. "So I was a dead woman, anyway? They would have killed me even if I was still alive when the ransom was paid?"

He nodded slowly, like he was reluctant to admit the truth. "That was our best guess, and since they've done it many times in the past, we didn't want to take that risk. Jax and I figured *we* had a better chance of getting you out of there alive. If we'd had *any* reason to believe they would have released you, we would have paid the ransom in a heartbeat to get you back, but we didn't want those actions to be your death sentence."

My hand started to shake as I set my water bottle on the bedside table.

It wasn't like I hadn't *known* my chances were slim anyway, but knowing that, had Hudson paid my ransom, one of those bastards would have finished me off, was mindboggling and terrifying.

The enormity of just how bad my previous circumstances had been was just starting to hit me. *Hard.* I'd managed to compartmentalize everything so well when my fear factor had been high, but the walls of separation were obviously getting weaker. "I knew I was dying," I told him in a monotone voice. "After my escape attempt, I was never really in my right mind for more than a few minutes. I lost a lot of my reasoning ability, and I started to hallucinate. I wasn't always sure exactly what was going on. But during those brief moments of clarity, I knew I wasn't going to make it, and every time I felt the darkness coming for me, I wondered if it was the last time. There wasn't a damn thing I could do to save myself, and I really hated that."

Hudson moved and sat on the end of the bed, close but not too close, like he was worried that he'd scare me. "I'm not going to even try to tell you that I know how you felt," he said grimly. "I don't. I've been in a lot of life and death situations, but I've always had the means to defend myself." He paused before he asked tentatively, "Did they injure you before you tried to escape in any way? Harlow mentioned that the rebel leader came to get you every night. Did he hurt you?"

Holy shit!

Hudson knew the truth.

I wasn't sure how I'd come to that conclusion, but I *knew* that he *knew*, no matter how mildly he'd asked the question. I could hear it in his voice, and sense it by the tension in the air around us. "You can never tell Harlow the truth. Promise me that first, and then I'll tell you," I insisted.

Our gazes locked, and my breath caught when I saw the bleakness in the depths of his gorgeous eyes as he shook his head. "I'll never tell her. You've agreed to keep our secrets. Everything you say right now will never be shared with anyone. You made some kind of deal with him, didn't you?"

"I did." The two words that came out of my mouth were barely a whisper. "My willing body in exchange for no one touching Harlow. It made sense. He was going to rape me anyway. The guy had some kind of weird fascination with my red hair. By subduing me, I think he thought he was conquering some kind of demon or devil. So I decided to get something out of all that weirdness. What would be the point of fighting? All *that* would have gotten me was the horror of watching my friend and mentor go through the same thing I did. And it *was* horrible, because everything in me wanted to fight and try to scratch his eyes out, but once it was over, at least I got to go back to our prison and see Harlow untouched. She was already frantic over Mark, weak from no food or water, and I didn't know what would happen if she had to go through a sexual assault every damn night. I knew the asshole couldn't break me. I wouldn't let him. Every night, I had to let him use my physical body, but I let my mind go somewhere else, if that makes any sense."

"Yeah, I get it. You try to detach," Hudson answered hoarsely. "But I still wish I would have killed the bastard for you anyway while Jax and I were in that camp. Had I known then what I know now, I *definitely* would have."

I could honestly say I hadn't had anyone who'd wanted to defend me in a very long time, so his words made my heart ache. "You got me out of there," I said softly. "That was more than enough. I feel like it's a miracle that I'm actually sitting here talking to you. I'm afraid I'm going to wake up in Lania again and realize this is all one huge hallucination incident."

"It's real, Taylor." He grimaced. "And I *think* it's a goddamn miracle that you're still relatively *sane*."

I shrugged. "I'm not sure I completely have my head together. I think that I was so focused on survival that I couldn't allow myself to think about *anything* else. Now that I have way too much time to think, I might be starting to crumble," I answered with a tremor in my voice.

He shot me a concerned look. "Still scared?"

"A little," I confessed.

Okay, maybe more than just *a little*. I couldn't seem to stop the images or the brief flashbacks of some of the really bad things that had happened to me.

Maybe talking about it *hadn't* been such a great idea, but I knew that I was going to eventually push through it. Pretending it never happened, and not acknowledging the pain and fear would just keep me stuck in the past.

Been there; done that.

When I'd been confused and angry, Mac had always told me that the only way to get to the other side of it was to acknowledge the way I was feeling, and then leave it behind.

"Being afraid is completely normal, Taylor. Most people come out of a hostage situation a lot worse off than you are right now, even if they haven't been sexually assaulted," Hudson said gruffly. "The flashbacks of what happened will probably stay with you for a while, and the fear, but you're going to be okay. Is there..." I watched as he did some kind of inner struggle before he asked in a calmer tone, "Do you think you could be pregnant?"

I wasn't the kind of woman who got freaked out about openly discussing medical stuff. Especially not with a guy who had seen as much as Hudson.

I firmly shook my head. "Highly doubtful since I've had a hormonal IUD since I was twenty-two. I had horrible periods, and they tried other stuff, but that worked the best. I knew I was protected against pregnancy, which is another reason I offered myself up rather than seeing Harlow used, too." I shuddered. "Obviously, that IUD won't protect me from other nasty stuff, but getting pregnant is the least of my worries."

I *was* concerned about STDs, HIV, Hepatitis, and any other disease that I could get through sexual contact, but I'd have to deal with that if it happened.

If I let myself think about that too much, I'd be completely overwhelmed.

Hudson looked relieved. "We'll deal with most of that once we get to San Diego. It will take time to get all the medical test results on the rebel leader, but everything will get done. The doctor told Jax that he started PEP treatment because every hour counts, and he'd rather be safe than sorry. I'm not a doctor, but I know it's some kind of antiretroviral medicine that helps prevent getting an HIV infection." Hudson released a frustrated breath. "Everything will get better. We'll fix all this, Taylor. I fucking promise we'll work everything out. I won't let *anyone* hurt you like that again. Just don't stop...talking to me. We'll get through it together."

The fierceness, the utter conviction in his tone broke me.

A single large tear plopped onto my cheek.

Then another.

And one more.

Suddenly, like a dam in my tear ducts had burst wide open, those droplets formed into a river of tears that were coursing down my face.

I felt like an idiot, but no matter how hard I tried, the raging river wasn't going to stop until it ran dry. "Why am I crying?" I asked in a desperate tone. "I'm alive. I should be happy right now."

The problem was...these *weren't* happy tears. They were tears of pain, fear, and incredibly painful sorrow.

I was crying for Harlow.

I was crying for Mark.

And I was crying for myself.

Mark was gone, and I knew that Harlow and I would never be the same after this experience.

Hudson rose, lifted me up like the weight of my body was next to nothing, and then sat back down on the bed with his back against the headboard, cradling my body on his lap as he pulled the covers around me. "Cry all you want, Taylor. Get it all out. I don't give a damn if you're still bawling when we get to San Diego if it will make you feel better," he said roughly.

"I-I never cry," I said with a small hiccup as I let my arms creep around his neck.

God, he *felt* good.

He *smelled* good.

Hudson wrapped his powerful arms around my body, and used his hand to guide my head gently to a comfortable place on his shoulder. "Make an exception this time," he suggested.

There wasn't even a hint of judgment in his voice, although I knew he was obviously a guy ruled by reason.

I was upset, and like it was the most normal thing in the world to do, Hudson was giving me a soft place to fall.

I felt accepted.

I felt protected.

I felt sheltered as I melted into his warm, hard body.

I finally felt…safe.

Hudson was there for me, muttering nonsense to comfort me, rocking me and holding me close when my walls finally went tumbling to the ground, and I sobbed out all the emotions that were threatening to consume me.

Chapter 9

Hudson

"I don't give a shit whether it's *practical* or not," I said to Jax in an irritated tone. "I'm a billionaire. It wasn't all that difficult to make it happen. Taylor hates hospitals, and after what she's been through, I'm *not* going to make her stay here one damn second longer than she has to. We got Harlow set up for home treatment with her mother in Carlsbad, and Taylor is coming home with me. End of story."

I took a slug of bad hospital coffee, and grimaced.

We'd landed in San Diego yesterday, and Taylor had gone through rigorous testing to make sure there were no underlying injuries that the Lanian doctor had missed.

Now that all the tests were nearly completed, and everything was negative, I was taking her home. *My home.*

There wasn't a single thing they could do here that I couldn't do for Taylor at my house.

It sure as hell wasn't like I didn't have the space for her. I owned an enormous house in Del Mar, on the beach. It was the perfect location for Taylor to recover.

Harlow had already been discharged to her mother's care early this morning,

Yeah, I could have gotten Harlow's key so Taylor could stay there, but she'd be *alone*.

That *was not* happening.

The woman could barely stand on her own, much less take care of herself.

Something had happened to me while she'd sobbed her heart out while I'd held her on my lap. I'd promised that I wouldn't let anything, or anyone hurt her again, and I was keeping that damn promise. I was going to stay close to her until she was completely over this whole incident, emotionally and physically.

Holy fuck! I never wanted to see her cry like that ever again.

I glared at Jax, who was sitting across the table from me in the hospital cafeteria, as he shook his head. "Uh, no offense intended, bro, but you look like shit. Have you been here since we landed?"

I raked a hand through my hair. He was probably right. I needed some sleep, a shower and a shave. "Of course I have. What was I going to do? Leave her all alone after everything she's been through?"

"There's about a dozen people Marshall could have gotten here last night that *hadn't* been through an entire rescue situation already," Jax pointed out. "And it's not the whole homecare thing I'm worried about. We set it up all the time. With family. Nursing care—"

"She doesn't have any family," I barked back at him, hating the fact that Taylor had no close family that gave a damn about her. Not because I minded taking care of her, but she should have…someone. "As her employer, I'm stepping up to the damn plate."

Jax had stayed until it had gotten late the night before, but he'd gone home once Taylor had gotten situated back in her room.

He'd just come back about fifteen minutes ago, and dragged me down to the cafeteria for coffee while Taylor was in radiology for one last x-ray.

"She's going to need physical therapy, and other treatment," Jax said reasonably. "Not only that, but somebody is going to need to help her out for a while. Until she's back on her feet, she needs a nursing assistant or a homecare professional. What the hell, Hudson, are you planning on making your multimillion-dollar beach house into a hospital? I get that Taylor is currently homeless because Harlow is in Carlsbad now, and that she also gave up her apartment in Stanford when she came to San Diego as our intern for the summer. But the hospital is perfectly willing to put her in a transitional unit while she recovers, or we can get her a place fully staffed with medical personnel round the clock—"

"Not. Happening," I growled.

During a moment of weakness, Taylor had confessed that she hated hospitals because she'd spent a lot of time watching someone she cared about die in one of them.

The last thing she needed was to recover in a goddamn institution that heightened her discomfort, or a furnished apartment with only strangers to take care of her.

She needed a place to rest. To relax. To wind down. Somebody around who was actually familiar to her.

Right now, that recognizable person was *me*.

Marshall had already offered to set everything up, and have a nursing assistant with her every hour of the day in addition to a crew member from Last Hope.

That shit wasn't going to cut it. Taylor needed...me.

And damned if I didn't *have* to be there in case she wanted *me*.

It would drive her crazy to have somebody she didn't know hovering over her all the damn time. I got that, even if she hadn't mentioned it. It would make *me* uncomfortable. The woman needed to breathe, and for some idiotic reason I didn't understand, I *knew* what she needed.

"So you really plan on taking care of her *yourself?*" Jax said skeptically.

"I have a housekeeper."

"Who comes in once a week to clean," Jax reminded me.

"Taylor will get back on her feet," I argued defensively.

According to the doctors, Taylor would be able to walk better once she was fully nourished, and her body got back in balance with hydration. Yeah, so she was going to need a physical therapist. It wasn't like I couldn't bring someone in for that, and my assistant had already arranged for Taylor to get therapy at my place to get her through this ordeal mentally, too.

In my mind, we were all good. Taylor just needed time…

"You'll never be able to stay away from the office that long," Jax warned. "You know how you are, Hudson. Work is your whole life. It's not like Cooper and I can't handle everything, but you'll be itching to come in and see what's going on yourself."

Nope. I wouldn't. My obsession to make sure Taylor got well trumped *everything* else in my life right now, including Montgomery Mining.

"I have a home office. I'll do my share," I informed him.

"I'm not worried about that," Jax answered sharply. "You've always done *way more* than your share. You were the first one to get back to San Diego when the company was in trouble, and you had things well in hand by the time Cooper and I were discharged. Maybe I'm just worried that you're taking this whole thing a little too…personally."

I raised a brow as I scowled at him. "She works for us, Jax. She's our employee."

He stared back at me, his gaze never wavering. "Why do I have the feeling that there's a lot more to this whole thing than Taylor being our intern? Hell, I want to make sure she's taken care of, too, but I know there are a lot of people who could do a better job at it than me."

Jax might be an asshole sometimes, but his instincts were spot on most of the time, and he was way too intuitive sometimes. "Okay," I said reluctantly. "Maybe I just *want* to help her."

"Why?" he asked calmly. "She's not our first rescue, Hudson, and we both know it's a mistake to get sucked into any of our missions emotionally. We lose our ability to be objective if we do."

Luckily, we were the only ones in our area of the cafeteria when I slammed my hand down on the table in utter frustration. "I like her, goddamn it. I know I shouldn't get involved, but I can't fucking stop myself because Taylor is *different*. She's *not* just another victim to me. She's hurting. I like her. She's probably the bravest, smartest woman I've ever known. I want to be there for her. Just her. It's not like any rescue has ever gotten personal for me before, and I've done way too many to count. I can't explain why *she's* different. She just…is."

Christ! It wasn't like I hadn't told myself over and over that Taylor was just another rescue among many, and that I didn't need to personally take care of her. Unfortunately, I didn't believe a single word I'd said to myself.

Jax's eyes widened. "No, you don't just like her. You *like* her. Holy fuck! You really *like* her. This doesn't have a damn thing to do with her being our employee, and it's not some misguided sense of guilt or obligation. You just…*like* her."

"I already admitted that I did," I said, irritated. "Why are you making a big deal out of it?"

Jax snickered. "You *like* her."

"Will you knock that shit off," I insisted, completely annoyed now.

"Damn, Hudson," Jax drawled. "I never thought I'd see the day when you started acting like Seth does with Riley. Why didn't you just tell me you had a thing for Taylor?"

"Because I don't," I said adamantly. Okay, so maybe I'd denied that a *little* too strongly. Probably because I wasn't just trying to convince Jax, but myself, too.

He smirked. "You're so full of shit that your eyes are turning brown. Don't even try to tell me that somewhere deep inside, you aren't hoping that once Taylor is recovered, this will turn into something more than mutual admiration. I don't buy it."

"She's weak, and she's fragile," I growled. "Do you really think I fantasize about tearing off her clothes, bending her over the nearest available surface, and screwing her until we're both completely satisfied?"

Jax shook his head. "No, man. I think it's even *worse.* I think you might fall for her, and *then* you'll want to bend her over," he said in a serious tone.

"Now you're being totally ridiculous," I scoffed.

He shrugged. "Don't say I didn't warn you in a couple of months. It's there."

"What's there?" I asked shortly.

"That same crazy protective look that Seth gets when he thinks something might hurt Riley. Mason, too, and his brothers. I can see it in you because I've seen it in them. Hell, *all* of them get this strange look in their eyes that says they'd move mountains if it would make their woman happy. I see *that* look in *your* eyes right now, and to tell you the truth, it's scaring the hell out of me."

"I'm not thinking about moving any mountains," I grumbled, disgusted with Jax.

"Not yet," he answered wryly. "But I kind of think you will if she sends you some pleading look with those big green eyes of hers."

Fuck! I'd already seen that vulnerable look from Taylor when she'd admitted that she hated hospitals.

Not that she'd done it on purpose, and she hadn't been trying to manipulate me in any way.

But *dammit!* My gut had ached with the need to make damn sure I could erase that apprehensive expression in any way possible.

Even if it meant moving that fucking mountain from one country to another.

"I want to protect her. She's vulnerable right now," I confessed. "I'll get over it once she's feeling better."

"I gotta wonder how many times Seth told himself that," Jax mused.

"I am not *Seth*," I ground out.

"I guess I don't get why it has to be a big issue," Jax said in a perplexed voice. "It's been a long time since you've had an interest in any female, Hudson. You work too damn much. Why can't you just let things happen, and keep it real. Taylor doesn't seem like a woman who is going to make your money her first priority, and she isn't like most of the females we grew up with in our status-obsessed circles."

"She's not," I said flatly. "She's not the least bit intimidated by me, my name, *or* my money."

"Well, damn, that must be painful," Jax ribbed me. "But seriously, isn't it nice to just talk to somebody with no ulterior motives for a change."

Honestly, when Taylor treated me just like any other guy, it *was* nice. "I'm not sure. It's been a while," I muttered.

"Just relax, man. Help her recover and see what happens. I get why you want to do this now, and I'll handle stuff at the office. It's way beyond time that you take a break."

I gave him a skeptical look. "So you're over trying to talk me out of it?"

Not that anything my brother might say would change my mind.

"Definitely," Jax answered. "I guess I was just worried that you felt motivated by guilt because Taylor's our employee and our rescue. I didn't want you to get caught up in that. You blame yourself for way too much shit already. But now that I know your real motivation, I'm all good. You could use a lady friend who isn't intimidated by you, and God knows you really need to get laid."

I glared at Jax. "I told you that I'm not—"

He held up a hand as he interrupted, "Hey, you can't blame a guy for hoping. I have to work with you every day."

"Speaking of work, I really need to reach out to Mark's relatives, and to Harlow," I told Jax grimly.

"I got it," Jax informed me. "Mark's parents have been gone for years, but I contacted his brother this morning. Needless to say, he's devastated. I can't say I blame him. He mentioned that he didn't see Mark much in person because he was always out of the country, but they stayed in touch. Of course, we're covering all the funeral expenses, and doing a settlement in addition to Mark's life insurance. It won't bring him back, but I want to do right by his family."

I nodded sharply. "I completely agree. What about Harlow?"

"She was insistent about not coming back to Montgomery Mining, but I'm working on that. I think she just needs some time," Jax said, his voice remorseful.

"Give her all the time she needs," I suggested. "Not only does she need to heal from her trauma, but she has to mourn someone she cared about, too."

"I planned on waiting until she comes back to San Diego to start working on her, but I'm sure as hell not letting her just walk away. The projects she has going on in the lab are important to her, and Montgomery Mining. I think once she's feeling better, she'll realize that," Jax explained. "The woman is wicked smart."

"Then you should be able to relate to her," I said drily.

My brothers and I had been sent to a boarding school for the gifted when we were young, and had advanced to college courses by the time we'd hit fifteen.

I wasn't quite sure if our paths in life had been good or bad.

Yeah, it was great as businessmen to have lightning fast brains, but it was highly possible that we'd gotten robbed of our childhood, and had grown up way too fast.

I didn't have any fond childhood memories that I could recall, but I wasn't sure if that was because my family was so dysfunctional, or the fact that I'd been in a boarding school heavily focused on academic advancement as far back as I could remember.

I rose, anxious to get back to Taylor's room before she did. "Anything else we need to discuss?"

Jax got up with a troubled look on his face. "Just one thing," he answered.

"Tell me," I instructed.

His jaw was tight as he said gruffly, "Don't get hurt. Anything worthwhile is usually a risk, but don't give anyone your damn heart until you know for sure that you can trust that person with it."

We stared at each for a second before I replied, "It's not going to go that far. No worries," I assured him and clapped him on the back as we started walking toward the cafeteria exit.

I was close to all of my siblings, but it was a rare moment when Jax got deadly serious.

It was during those very infrequent instances when I truly realized how damn glad I was to have him watching my back.

Chapter 10

Hudson

"There's no fucking way you're getting into the shower
by yourself." I tried to make my voice firm, but gentle.
Unfortunately, the words had flown from my mouth
before I could achieve either of those tones.

Is she out of her mind?

I'd just gotten Taylor home from the hospital a few hours ago.

I'd made good on my promise to give her the medium-rare steak
and loaded baked potato I'd vowed to get her as soon as she could
handle it.

My assistant had picked up an order from the best steakhouse in
San Diego, and had left it in the warmer for us to consume when
we'd arrived at my home.

Since the hospital had started her on solid foods, and she'd handled
it well, I didn't need to hold back on anything she wanted to eat.

Thank fuck!

I was learning that I was completely unable to *not* give Taylor
anything she wanted when she looked at me with that trusting green-
eyed gaze of hers.

But this…

Hell, no…

The woman could break her neck while trying to take a shower on her own. She could barely stand up.

After dinner, she'd looked so damn tired that I'd brought her upstairs, showed her the big bedroom with an attached bath that she'd be using while she was here, and put her down on the bed.

She'd scrambled into a sitting position, her feet on the floor, and had immediately decided she needed to utilize that enormous shower in her bathroom.

Taylor glanced up at me as I stood right in front of her. Like blocking her view of the bathroom was really going to help her forget that crazy idea?

"I need…to feel clean," she said in a hoarse, wavering voice that revealed just how tired she was at the moment. "I didn't get to shower at the hospital. I can at least manage that."

I saw her shudder, and I knew all the hot water in the world wasn't going to help her scrub away the memories that were haunting her right now. "No," I said in a calmer tone this time. "Be reasonable, Taylor."

"I am," she assured me. "There's a huge bench in the shower, Hudson. I can sit down. I haven't cleaned up since you scrubbed the first few layers of dirt off me when we first got onto your jet. I shower every day, sometimes twice a day if I work out later in the afternoon. I guess I just want to do something…normal."

Shit! My damn chest hurt as I watched her rub her upper arms like she was chilled to the bone.

Everything was foreign to her right now.

The hospital.

My home.

The hospital gown she was still wearing.

Her inability to move around on her own.

Her mind that kept going back to everything she'd been through.

I was a guy who kept a rigorous schedule, all day, every day.

So it wasn't like I couldn't imagine what it would be like to be in her shoes right now.

I'd just never experienced some of the traumatic events she'd suffered.

Bottom line: She felt like she'd lost complete control of her life, and she needed me to give her some of that power back.

Truth was, I didn't want to see her like this, feeling like she was helpless to make a single decision in her life.

I'd observed her long enough to realize that she was used to being organized and focused.

And right now, everything she knew about herself was…shaken.

"I'll help you," I conceded. "No walking. I'll help you get to the shower and back in bed. And I'm not leaving you alone. I'll wait for you until you're finished."

If she was going to fall, I was going to be there before she hit the ground.

Her face fell. "I don't want this to cause you more work. I can do it on my own. I'm sure I can make it—"

"No deal," I interrupted curtly.

"So it's your way or the highway?" she asked, not sounding the least bit upset. "Because you're afraid I'll hurt myself?"

"Pretty much," I shot back. "I want you to be able to do exactly as you please. I wish to hell you could just do whatever you want, but that's not even reasonable right now, Taylor. You need help doing anything right now, but this isn't going to last forever."

She looked away from me, and paused for a moment before she finally said, "You're right. I can live without the shower right now. If I was in your position, I'd probably say the same thing, but these sheets are so clean." She ran a hand over the pristine, crisp bottom sheet that matched the room décor.

Her voice was so damn melancholy that I couldn't stand it. "We can do it; you're just going to have to put up with me helping you during the whole process."

She let out a squeak of surprise as I scooped her up and carried her toward the bathroom.

They'd pulled her IV right before she left the hospital. As long as she was drinking the required amount of fluids every day, she wouldn't need it anymore.

"I said I could go without it," she scolded as I set her down on the large marble seat in the shower. "You've put that strong back to work quite enough for me over the last day or two."

I lifted her chin, forcing her to look at me. "Taylor, have I ever complained about that?"

Eyes wide, she whispered, "No. I don't think you're the complaining type. But don't you dare think that I don't see everything you're doing to help me, even if you don't bitch about it. But I'm telling you right here, right now, that when I'm feeling better, ask me for anything, and I'll do it. At least three big favors, and nothing is off-limits, Hudson. I doubt I'll ever be able to do anything that saves your life like you've done for me, but if you need something done, I'm your go-to-woman for anything. Promise me."

Her expression was so fervent that I diverted my gaze. "I can pay someone to do almost anything I want. I think you can reach the shower controls. Toss your gown out when you're ready. I'll be waiting right here in the bathroom when your done. You need me, you call me."

"Well, that was a total brush-off," she sniffed testily as she crossed her bruised-up arms over her chest. "Promise me, Hudson."

"Fine!" I said, sounding a little impatient. Really, I wasn't mad at her. I just wasn't accustomed to anyone offering to do me a big favor free gratis, much less three of them. "I promise."

Did it really matter what I promised if I was never going to cash in on that promise anyway?

"Thank you," she murmured softly.

I shook my head, "For what?"

"For everything," she said, her voice completely sincere.

"I told you not to thank me," I said gruffly as I closed the shower door.

"And I already warned you that I was going to do it anyway," she reminded me as she tossed her hospital gown over the shower door.

I caught it before it hit the ground, and tossed it into the hamper.

I'd already noticed that my assistant had left a stack of new pajamas and panties on the long bathroom stool like I'd asked.

I hadn't known Taylor's size, but after telling my assistant that she was a little shorter and leaner than Riley, I noticed that most of the sizes were small, with a few medium thrown into the mix.

That should work.

The shower turned on, and I straddled the bench so I could make sure the stubborn woman didn't nosedive to the hard tile flooring in the shower stall.

The entire enclosure was made of glass, but there was embellished scrolling etched into the design, so I couldn't see Taylor clearly, but well enough to know if she was plummeting toward the ground.

I heard a small moan, but I knew the sound wasn't a distress signal. It was a noise thrumming with pleasure.

"This shower is amazing," Taylor said, lifting her voice enough to be heard over the sounds of the water. "I can't wait until I can stand up and turn on all the jets. I hope it's okay for me to use the sponge in here."

"It's fine. It's new," I told her.

"And the shampoo and body wash?" she asked in a hesitant tone. "I never did ask if you had a girlfriend or an important significant other in your life. All of this stuff is Chanel. I didn't even know they did bath and body stuff."

"There's nobody," I said nonchalantly. "Whatever is there is all yours. My housekeeping leaves every bedroom guest ready."

"Oh, God. It smells amazing, like citrus and lily. You have no idea how good it feels to get myself clean with something that smells this good."

She sounded so damn happy that I was glad we'd compromised on the shower, and I made a note to give my housekeeper a huge bonus for stocking the extra rooms with something that apparently delighted a female guest.

Okay, maybe some people *wouldn't* be this ecstatic about the shampoo and body wash, but Taylor obviously took a hell of a lot of joy from anything she liked.

She let go of another moan as I saw her figure dip forward, probably to wash her hair. "Oh, God," she crooned.

Holy fuck! If she got this damn orgasmic over sweet smelling body wash, shampoo, and hot water, I could only imagine…

Nope! I wasn't letting my mind go *there*.

Okay, maybe I *had* gone there *briefly*. I'd seen a picture of a completely healthy Taylor, and it hadn't been hard to imagine…

Shit! I really needed to end this entire line of thought.

"You doing okay?" I called out.

"Fantastic," she answered, sounding slightly out of breath. "Almost done. Can I just take another minute or two?"

"As long as you want," I said amiably.

Hell, if she was feeling better, I'd sit on this fucking bench all damn night.

A few minutes passed.

And then five minutes.

By the time it got to almost ten minutes without a word and almost no movement inside the shower, I finally asked, "Taylor, everything good in there?"

When I got no response, I stood, strode to the shower, and opened the glass door.

Her eyes were closed, but there was a faint smile on her lips.

I grinned as I stepped into the enclosure, shut off the water, scooped up her naked body, and carried her to the bench where I could dry her off.

She was completely out, probably so tired from her efforts that she hadn't been able to keep her eyes open any longer.

Taylor let out a faint protest as I put her into new pajamas and panties, but she settled back down as I carried her to her bed.

I could smell a hint of oranges and flowers clinging to her skin, and in the hair I'd just brushed and detangled. I tucked her body between the sheets.

"Please don't go," she whimpered suddenly as I started to straighten up.

I frowned. Her eyes were still closed, but she was thrashing around restlessly.

Now what in the hell am I supposed to do?

Taylor was obviously dreaming, and I doubted that she was talking to me, but I'd still feel like a dick if I left her.

Just leave. She's perfectly safe here.

As I walked to the bedroom door, I heard one more pitiful cry.

Shit! I hit the light switch to shut them off, and then strode back to the bed.

I'd left the light on in the bathroom, so she didn't wake up scared because the room was completely dark.

I can't do this. Jax was right. I shouldn't be getting this attached to a rescue, even if she is my employee.

I could see her face because of the light from the bathroom, and when she flinched, like she was terrified of whoever she was dreaming about, I finally gave up my internal war.

Nobody ever had to know, not even her. I'd leave before she ever woke up.

I crawled into the bed from the opposite side, and shifted my body close to hers. Wrapping my arms around her waist, I spooned in behind her, and said quietly, "You're okay, Taylor. I'm here. Sleep. No more bad dreams."

"Hudson," she whispered, sounding relieved as she melted into my body with an enormous sigh.

That one little word, my name on her lips, her instinct to trust me—was like a knife to my damn heart. I tightened my arms a little around her defenseless body.

Taylor had been through so damn much in rebel hands that it was a miracle the woman could trust anyone right now.

Part of me said that she was a fool to trust a guy like me, then again, maybe she wasn't.

Yeah, I could be an asshole sometimes, but I *knew* that I was going to do everything in my power to make sure *nobody* would ever hurt this woman again.

Just the thought of *anybody* putting a hand on her made me see red right now.

So maybe I *was* the best person for the job as her temporary protector at the moment.

I stayed with Taylor for a couple of hours—a hell of a lot longer than I needed to—before I finally left her sleeping peacefully, and got into my own bed where I belonged.

Chapter 11

Taylor

"Dinner was fantastic, Hudson. Thank you," I said as I put my hand on my distended belly. I'd eaten way more than my share of the scrumptious chicken and noodle casserole he'd fixed for dinner.

I sighed in contentment from my place in one of his outdoor loungers, feeling incredibly lazy and totally spoiled.

Tomorrow, it would be two weeks since Hudson had brought me home from the hospital, and he'd been feeding me almost continually since the moment we'd arrived at his ridiculously large, luxurious home on the beach in Del Mar.

We'd gotten here on a Sunday, and on Monday morning, the parade of professionals had started to march in and out of Hudson's place, and had kept right on coming every weekday after that.

Physical therapists.

Physicians.

Psychologists.

Personal assistants who had brought my clothes and my vehicle from Harlow's apartment to Hudson's home.

To tell the truth, it had been an exhausting few weeks, but at least I was on my feet with the help of my physical therapist, and getting my head together with a very good psychologist who specialized in trauma.

Yeah, I still had a few nightmares about my experience in Lania, but the constant flashes of memory every time I heard or saw a trigger were beginning to slow down.

I had no idea how to thank the man sitting next to me, and if I did try to thank Hudson, he'd just blow it off. I'd tried many times with very little success. It wasn't all because of the support people he'd brought in, either. My gratitude was more about *him* being a constant companion and confidante.

If I was having a bad day…he was there.

If I was having a good day…he was there.

If I just wanted to talk…he was there, too.

Honestly, he'd been the biggest support system I could have asked for after what had happened, and because he'd been so understanding, there wasn't much I couldn't tell him.

Okay, so maybe I *hadn't* mentioned much about the nightly sexual assaults, and he didn't know much about my past, but we'd talked a lot about how it felt to be a hostage in general.

Hudson shrugged from the lounger next to mine. "Dinner was nothing fancy, but I do have several containers of ice cream for later. You did mention that you really liked cookie dough ice cream."

I groaned. "You have to stop feeding me."

"Why?" he asked, sounding confused. "You have some weight to gain back."

I laughed. "But I don't have to gain it all in less than two weeks."

I *had* lost a lot of weight, more than I'd even anticipated. Some of those pounds had returned once I was well-hydrated, and well-nourished. I'd packed on plenty of pounds since then, too, because I'd been eating like a pig. I could use another five, maybe six pounds or so to get back to my normal weight, but I'd put that back on naturally, over time. What I really needed was to build more muscle by getting back into my daily routine, but my physical therapist had wanted me to wait on getting back to my Tai Chi.

I smiled. When my appetite had returned that first week, it had hit me with a vengeance. I'd eaten anything and everything Hudson had given me, appreciating every bite. I'd slowed it down after the first week, when I'd finally realized that I didn't have to eat like every bite I took was going to be my last.

"Honestly, I've never seen a small woman like you put away as much food as you did last week," he said, sounding slightly amused, and strangely awed. "It was pretty incredible."

"Horrifying, you mean?" I corrected, not wanting to think about the constant, ravenous look that had probably been plastered on my face.

"It's good for you. You missed a lot of meals," he answered.

My body relaxed to the sound of the waves hitting the shore. For some reason, Hudson and I had made it a habit to head outside every night after dinner, and we generally stayed on his patio until after the sunset.

He had amazing views, and enough privacy to make it an ideal way to spend the evening.

Sometimes we talked a lot, and sometimes we didn't, but if there were silences, they were never uncomfortable.

Granted, he'd had to physically haul my ass out here the first few days, but I could step outside on my own two feet now. I wasn't about to win any races, at least not until my leg strength was built up again, but at least I could walk reasonably well.

Thank, God! I don't have to rely on poor Hudson to lug me around!

I still wasn't certain what had prompted Hudson to carry me out here that very first day. It was almost like he knew I really needed to breathe in the fresh air so I could truly believe I was free...

Sitting outside was still like therapy for me, and I was always anxious to get outdoors, so Hudson's instincts had been spot on.

I *did* need the fresh air to chase away some of the lingering shadows.

Harlow and I talked every morning. She was dealing with a lot of grief, remorse, and anger. Really, the only thing I could do as a friend was listen to her, but maybe that was all she actually needed from me right now.

"I'm not quite sure what happened," I tried to explain to Hudson. "Don't get me wrong, I love my food, and I can eat a lot of it. But I was starving every single moment of the day for that first week."

"You're healing," he said huskily. "Your body needs the nutrients. You need to keep eating well, Taylor."

I snorted. "Not like that. I don't feel as desperate for food anymore, so I'm just listening to what my body is telling me."

"I hope it's saying we can scarf down some ice cream later." His tone was hopeful.

Like he can't do that without me?

Hudson didn't need my permission or participation to do any damn thing he wanted, but for some reason, he did seem to like company whenever he gave into his love of desserts.

"Maybe I can manage a small bowl once dinner wears off," I teased, knowing Hudson had the same sweet tooth I did.

From what I'd seen so far, he ate pretty healthy most of the time, and he had a workout routine in his home gym that would probably leave most men crying in pain halfway through it. But when it was time for dessert, he rarely passed on anything sweet.

"You better eat some," he said in a fierce tone.

I smiled at his bossy demeanor. I'd gotten used to it, and mostly just ignored it. Underneath his somewhat intense, fierce exterior, the guy had an amazing heart. Yeah, maybe he preferred not to reveal it most of the time, but I knew it was there.

What other man would bring a woman he barely knew back to his Del Mar mansion to recover from her injuries just because he knew she hated being in the hospital? Or cater to her every need as she healed?

I suspected his actions were somewhat motived by some kind of misplaced guilt. Hudson was willing to take on way more responsibility than he needed to, so I'd been doing my best to be a good guest.

It wasn't easy being unobtrusive when there was a gaggle of medical professionals visiting me every single day, but I tried not to bother him while he was working in his home office.

Oh, we'd definitely argued about me coming here in the first place. I had a key to Harlow's place, and I would have been fine there, but I was forced to admit that he'd had a point about my ability to get around on my own back then.

And somewhere, deep down inside, I really hadn't *wanted* to be alone. Since being by myself was rarely an issue for me, I'd been surprised enough by that unfamiliar urge to have somebody with me that I'd made an agreement with Hudson.

I just *hadn't* planned on him arranging every single thing I needed while I was his guest, or having him wait on me so damn much.

As of yet, he hadn't taken me up on his promise to let me do some things for him in return, but I planned on making sure that he did.

I could probably never be as in-tune with what he needed as he seemed to be with me, but he wasn't an easy man to know. Even though he'd let me see more of him, he was still basically an enigma.

Incredibly, Hudson Montgomery could actually cook, and didn't seem to mind doing it.

I definitely hadn't expected *that*.

Didn't most billionaires have a chef?

Not that I minded since there was something incredibly sexy about a man who knew his way around a kitchen, and managed to make meal prep look easy.

However, now that I was on my feet, I was starting to feel guilty—especially since watching *him* had become one of my favorite activities. I was starting to feel like a sex-starved voyeur with a fetish for men who cooked, but I couldn't make myself *stop* watching him.

Even after spending some time with him, Hudson still fascinated me.

Really, it was probably time I started thinking about what I was going to do now that I was feeling better physically. The bruises had faded, and I'd probably have a few small scars on my face, but when I looked in the mirror, I was actually starting to see *me* again.

"I need to start looking for a job, and I think I'm well enough to go back to Harlow's place. She's going to stay with her mom for now, but she told me to feel free to use her apartment," I told Hudson. "I can't be a freeloader forever."

"You're not a damn freeloader," he said gruffly. "You're my guest, and you'll be here until you're completely healed. No arguments. That was the agreement."

I *had* actually told him I'd stay until I was fully recovered. "I'm going to need a job, so I know where I'm going to end up living. Once I have a position, I can find a place." I argued. "I need to start sending out more resumes."

I certainly couldn't go on with the rest of my internship. Harlow was gone, and by the time I was able to go back to work, summer would be almost over anyway.

"No, you don't," he grumbled. "You *already* have a job. Here. In San Diego. Montgomery Mining needs brilliant geologists like you."

I rolled my eyes. We'd already had this argument, and I knew damn well I didn't have the kind of experience I needed to work in his lab. That was the kind of job I could dream about once I had more experience under my belt, but it was no place for a new grad to even consider. Eventually, I'd love to go back to school for my doctorate, but my resources were completely tapped out, and I could find a good-paying job with my masters, and work toward that in the future. Right now, I needed some serious income in my bank account, which was why Harlow had offered to let me stay at her place for my summer internship. Since I'd already had the internship offer, and a place to stay, I'd decided I could survive a few months on the pay I was getting as an intern to get the experience from Montgomery.

All the same, I'd learned that arguing with Hudson about my career path was useless. I'd just shoot out more resumes and see what happened, but I'd be sending them for positions that were actually *realistic*.

"God, you're cranky sometimes when you're not getting your way," I scolded, trying my best not to laugh.

"It's rare that I don't get my way, except when it comes to you," he said unhappily. He was silent for a minute before he asked, "You're messing with me again, right? I find it hard to believe that you're actually afraid of me."

"I'm not," I assured him. "Bark all you want. I'm used to it."

"Still messing with me?" he asked.

My heart ached because I knew it was a serious question. Did the guy joke around so little, and get exactly what he wanted without question so much that he couldn't tell when someone was actually razzing him?

"Yep." I quipped.

"I thought so," he said as he let out a long breath. "It's not like I'm an asshole all the time."

"You are *never* an asshole," I said, feeling the need to reassure him, even though he was a powerful billionaire who didn't have to give a damn what he said. "I think you're actually pretty sweet. Nobody has done something this nice for me in a long time, Hudson."

"Why?" he asked curiously. "I don't get it. Why *isn't* there some-body special in your life, Taylor? You must have had plenty of guys all over you at Stanford. You're beautiful, and highly intelligent. Yet there's no adoring male wrapped around your finger."

My heart started cartwheeling inside my chest, even though I knew I was far from beautiful.

I was a redheaded wild child, complete with all the freckles that had never entirely faded away when I'd become an adult. "I'm not beautiful, Hudson. And have you actually *looked* at my face? I'm a mess. I did date a little while I was at Stanford, but I guess I just never found that…spark. No connection. And I was really busy. Things were pretty tight for me. I had a part-time job and my Tai Chi classes to help pay the bills, but most of my energy was focused on getting through my master's program. Stanford isn't cheap."

I was a realist, and my initial reaction to his comments settled down in a hurry.

My flame-colored hair had a mind of its own most of the time, so I usually just hauled it back in a ponytail like it was right now. I'd accepted that some of my freckles were *never* going to disappear, and that my less-than-impressive breast size was never going to change. I was even okay with the fact that most makeup made my face break out in hives, so I had to avoid the majority of them. I certainly wasn't going to have some kind of growth spurt at the age of twenty-eight, so I'd never have long, sexy legs that made me look elegant and graceful, but I could live with that, too.

Luckily, I'd never really been a "girlie" kind of girl, and I wasn't one as an adult, either.

His comment that men should have been chasing me all over Stanford was ludicrous.

Yeah, I'd gone out with a couple of guys, but mostly, I was that woman who plenty of men wanted as a *friend*, but didn't exactly look at me with any kind of passionate intentions.

I sighed as one of Mac's many statements ran through my mind. Something he'd said to me not long before he'd closed his eyes for the very last time.

Someday, you'll meet a man who is worthy of you, Tay. You'll know he's the right one because you'll recognize him with your entire soul, and you'll see the same longing when you look into his eyes. Wait for him, and don't settle for anything less.

So far, *that* guy had been nothing more than a fantasy, then again, I hadn't been that eager to leap into anything, either. Maybe because I was still waiting…

"I have looked at your face," Hudson finally said in a throaty, deep voice. "I thought you were pretty damn gorgeous even *before* I met you in person. Maybe you're still a little banged up, but you don't look all that different from your picture now." He halted for a second before he continued, like he was dreading whatever it was he needed to say next. "Marshall puts together a dossier on every victim so we know what they look like, and he also includes as much history as he can get so we know what kind of person we're dealing with before we go into a mission. I think the picture I viewed was from the day you graduated from Stanford."

My body tensed, and I turned my head to look at him. His gaze was still facing the water, but his jaw was tight.

Oh, God, he knows.

At that moment, Hudson turned his head, and our eyes locked.

The ferocity in his gaze made my heart stutter as he said hoarsely, "It was just facts, Taylor. Words on a page, and a picture so we could recognize you. The only thing I really got out of reading that whole dossier was the fact that you're a survivor. It gave me some hope that you'd be stubborn enough to still be breathing once we found you. It's mostly just a history so we can anticipate any problems we might have."

I relaxed a little, but I couldn't manage to tear my eyes away from Hudson.

God, the man was intense, but the apprehension in his gaze was very, very real.

Obviously, he was worried about how I'd take the fact that he'd studied me before he'd ever met me.

"I get it," I said softly, and really, I *did* comprehend why they needed some info on people they were going to risk their lives to rescue. "I understand that it was probably necessary."

I saw Hudson visibly relax as he said, "Nobody saw it except me, Taylor. Marshall put everything together, but I'm not sure how much he actually read. Like I said, it was just words on paper. If you ever want to tell me what it was really like for you as a child, that will be *your* choice."

I looked away from him to watch the last few moments of a gorgeous sunset, and because I needed time to get my head together.

If I'd spent one more minute looking into those sexy, empathetic eyes of his, I might have started to believe that he'd understand.

I wasn't ashamed of my past.

And I'd had Mac to help me fight through my emotional turmoil.

It wasn't that I didn't want to share that information with Hudson, I just wasn't sure how to do it, or if he could ever understand. Yeah, his childhood had been dysfunctional, but we'd been raised in two different worlds, and because mine would probably seem totally foreign to him, I wasn't sure he'd be able to relate.

Once it was dark, Hudson rose from his lounger. "Time for that ice cream," he said in a much lighter tone.

I shot him a dubious look, but I took the hand he'd offered, letting him pull me gently to my feet.

I stumbled forward a little after I got up, and crashed into his massive chest.

"Sorry," I said breathlessly as I looked up and saw him watching me.

Any time I was this close to Hudson, my body reacted instantaneously.

My heart would start to race, my brain shut down, and all I could do was surrender to the way he made me feel.

I started to drown in his masculine scent, and the feel of his warm, hard body.

I wanted to move closer, wrap my arms around his neck, and jerk his head down so I could taste those sensual lips of his.

Instead, I backed away a little before I made a complete fool of myself.

"Taylor?" he queried in a graveled voice.

"Yes?"

He took my hand and started leading me slowly toward the French doors, like he was still afraid I'd fall and break my neck. "If I'd been your classmate at Stanford, I would have been all over you. I have no idea what's wrong with the idiots you went to school with, but it's highly possible they were intimidated by the fact that you could probably kick their asses."

If his statement had been uttered for my amusement, it worked. I laughed like I hadn't done in a very long time.

Young, hot billionaires like Hudson Montgomery would *never* have to seek a woman out for a date. *Women* found *him*, and I had no doubt he had a lot of eager females panting just to get his attention.

Honestly, *I'd* probably be one of those panting women if there was a chance he might be seriously interested. Not because he was rich and gorgeous, but because he was an absolutely amazing guy.

I smiled up at him as he opened the door to let me enter in front of him, and I kept my mouth firmly closed. I *knew* a guy like Hudson Montgomery could never be sincerely interested in an ordinary woman like me.

Chapter 12

Hudson

Jax has absolutely no idea he's going to get his ass kicked.

Three weeks after I'd brought Taylor home from the hospital, I was on my patio, carefully watching my brother and Taylor play what my brother had termed "a friendly game of chess." They were sitting across from each other at the small patio table, and I was surveying them from a lounge chair.

Of course, he'd called it *that* hours ago when Taylor had mentioned she played, and Jax had suggested the two of them have a friendly game.

Right about now, or at least in the next ten minutes, I had a feeling Jax wasn't going to feel the same way he had right after dinner.

Serves the bastard right since he dropped in for dinner unannounced.

Not that I didn't know *exactly* why Jax had casually dropped in just in time for dinner.

Number one, he was a lousy cook.

And number two, he couldn't wait any longer to check up on me.

I'd been pretty evasive when I'd talked to him every day on the phone about work. Maybe because I'd had no idea what to tell him. I learned something new about Taylor every single day, every reveal more surprising than the last, but I didn't want to discuss that stuff with Jax. I'd never hear the end of it, and he'd start all that crazy shit again about me *liking* Taylor.

I didn't really want him to know that there wasn't a single thing that I didn't find attractive about her, and no, my instinct to protect her *wasn't* getting any better.

It fact, it was becoming fucking unbearable.

And now that she wasn't as defenseless and vulnerable as she'd been right out of the hospital, my goddamn dick wanted in on that obsession, too.

I knew if I told him that, Jax would start crowing about how he'd been right, and I wasn't in the mood for his bullshit.

My balls were starting to turn blue, and if Jax knew, he'd have a damn field day with *that*.

But dammit, Jax *had* been right about me wanting to bend her over the nearest object and fuck her until we were both sweaty and satisfied.

Christ! Taylor was still recovering, and all *I'd* been able to think about for the last few days was getting my painfully hard dick inside her.

Maybe if it was simply a bad case of lust, I could handle it better, but it wasn't. I refused to bullshit myself about *that*.

I was attracted to Taylor in ways that I didn't understand, but I was past trying to figure out *why* she was the gnawing pain in my gut that wouldn't fucking go away.

I just didn't care about the *whys* anymore.

All I wanted was to satisfy this damn carnal obsession.

Honestly, what guy *wouldn't* be enchanted by Taylor Delaney? She was alive with warmth and energy that seemed to exude from every pore in her body, and I was a chilly guy who wanted to wallow in all that vibrance. I wanted to make it mine.

I wanted to make *her* mine.

I wanted her naked, writhing in the throes of a powerful orgasm, screaming my name while she came so hard that her pleasure was almost too much to handle.

Not. Happening.

Her body still had healing to do, and I'm sure her mind needed that, too.

Nope. I wasn't going there.

I tried to jerk my lurid thoughts from my brain, shaking my head a little to get a grip on myself.

I'd been fighting that fight for a couple of days now, and even when I had control, it slipped pretty damn quickly.

The only thing that kept me reined in now was my concern for her physical and emotional state.

Taylor didn't need a man who wanted to fuck her. She'd been sexually assaulted over and over, so that was probably the last thing on her mind. If she ever thought about sex, it was probably with revulsion, and I certainly couldn't blame her for that.

Luckily, every medical test Prince Niklaos had gotten done on the rebel leader had been negative, and Taylor had the file of results to prove it.

She was getting healthier every day, but I knew she still had a ways to go before she'd physically be where she was before the kidnapping.

I tried to focus on what Taylor was doing, and the game that was in progress.

Jax and I were both really good players, but I was better, so he almost never suggested that we play against each other.

He only asked Taylor because he was cocky about the fact that he easily beat her.

He didn't ask Cooper for a game, either, because *neither* one of us could beat my youngest brother.

Jax wasn't a good loser. Never had been, which was why he tried to excel at *everything*.

At the moment, I was transfixed by what Taylor was doing. Honestly, it had taken me a while to figure it out, but Jax was apparently *still* clueless.

Where in the hell had she learned to play chess like this?

I watched her face, her gorgeous green eyes intent, but giving up absolutely nothing.

She looked perfectly serene, just like she had earlier when I'd found her in my gym, going through her Tai Chi routine in a pair of yoga pants and a skimpy tank top that had done nothing to hide a pair of perfect breasts.

Taylor had moved like poetry in motion, every movement precise, but so free flowing that I'd wanted to be lost in the same peacefulness with her.

The physical therapist had agreed that Taylor could go back to her Tai Chi practices, as long as she didn't do anything combative that would strain any of her muscles before they were strong enough to handle it.

Fuck! I probably could have watched her for days, leaning against the door of my gym like an idiot, awed by how much gentle power resided in that petite body of hers.

In the end, my thoughts had, of course, gotten carnal, so I'd *had* to walk away.

Her breasts were small enough that they hadn't needed to be confined, but so round and pert, the outline of her nipples so well-defined through the thin material of her tank, that I'd nearly lost it. Add in one shapely ass well worth watching, and I'd been so close to the edge that I wanted to lay her down on the mat that my brothers and I often used for kickboxing, and fuck her until she was screaming my name. Loudly.

I clenched my fists, forcing myself to keep my eyes on the chess game, but mostly, I just watched Taylor's face because she was so damn adorable that I couldn't tear my eyes away.

I started to grin as I realized that Taylor was going in for the win.

Okay, it's about to happen.

Right.

Fucking.

Now.

"Checkmate," Taylor said grimly as she made her final move.

She wasn't gloating.

Or arrogant.

Taylor wasn't triumphant about winning. She was just stating a fact.

Jax was, in fact, checkmated, and I knew he'd figure that out for himself soon enough.

"Not possible," Jax grumbled as his eyes frantically searched the board for a way to free his king.

I knew the second he realized there was no escape. A brief look of disgust crossed his face.

Jax being Jax, he got over his defeat fairly quickly since he wasn't the type of guy to start badgering a female, especially one who had recently been through hell and back.

Like it or not, he *had* to be a graceful loser this time.

"How in the hell did you do that?" Jax asked as he studied the board carefully.

"Sneak attack," I informed. "One of the best ones I've ever seen, and nothing I've ever learned."

Taylor shrugged, looking almost embarrassed. "Just something I learned. You're a really good player, Jax."

God, the woman was intuitive. She knew exactly how to stroke Jax's ego after she'd kicked his ass. Taylor was so…inherently kind, that it would be incredibly hard for anybody *not* to like her.

My brother shot her a wry smile. "Thanks." He leaned back in his chair after he'd figured out exactly how Taylor had won. "Where in the hell did you learn to play? There aren't that many people who can beat me up like that."

She smiled at Jax softly as she stretched her back. "My very first Tai Chi instructor was an amazing chess player, too. He started teaching me chess when I was twelve. I didn't win a single game against him, even after years of playing with him, but I learned a lot."

"What was his name?" I asked curiously.

"Mac Tanaka," she answered in a gentle tone. "He was a truly amazing man."

"Shit!" Jax cursed. "He wasn't just an excellent player; he was a Grand Master. The guy was a legend. If *he* was your teacher, I probably never stood a chance," he ended good-naturedly.

Like Jax, I was completely familiar with Mac Tanaka's name, even though I'd never had the pleasure of meeting him in person. Anyone who knew chess would recognize it.

I watched as Jax folded his arms over his chest, a teasing grin on his face as he asked, "So tell me, my Obi-Wan of chess players, where did I slip up?"

When Taylor shot Jax a teasing smile, I suddenly realized that I really didn't like her sending that mischievous, cheeky grin toward anyone...except me.

For fuck's sake, Jax is my brother. It's not like he's flirting with her.

"Do you really want to know?" Taylor asked.

"Tell me," Jax encouraged.

Taylor let out a sigh. "One of the most important things Mac ever taught me was to *never* underestimate your opponent. I think you allowed yourself to think that I wasn't a particularly good player, and with that assumption, you opened yourself up to an unusual attack. You weren't looking for something you didn't believe I was capable of doing. Always go into a game with the belief that your opponent is better than you are, no matter how unlikely you may think that is, or how unassuming that person might seem, and you'll always be on your toes."

I grinned as I watched her advice roll around in Jax's head for moment.

Taylor was spot-on in her analysis, but I wondered if Jax would be willing to admit that.

It was evident to me that Jax liked Taylor. I couldn't remember the last time he'd asked *anyone* for advice, not even me, and I was his older brother. He rarely let his guard down at all.

"I think," Jax said slowly. "No, I *know* you're right, dammit! It was a rookie mistake."

"It's not," Taylor reassured him. "There are some people who play the game their whole life and never understand that they can't go into it with any preconceived ideas. Especially when they get good enough to beat everyone they play."

My brother's grin grew wider. "Lesson learned, Obi-Wan," he said. "Are you as good at Tai Chi as you are at chess?"

"No," she answered, deadpan. "I'm better. But I do it every single day."

"I'd like to see your moves," he told her with a playful wink.

And...I lost it.

I got up from my chair. "Speaking of *moving*, it's getting late. Time for you to be going, Jax," I said in a raspy, warning voice.

My brother frowned when he glanced at his expensive Patek Phillipe watch, but he stood up. "It's just after midnight. It's not that late."

"Time to go," I insisted.

Rationally, I knew my brother hadn't meant anything lascivious toward Taylor, but I'd had about all I could take for one evening.

Jax was a charmer on the surface, and he liked women, but that didn't mean he wanted to screw every one of them. Hell, I'd seen him wink at women of all ages, and some that I knew he *definitely* didn't want to get naked.

But for whatever reason, his growing friendliness toward Taylor was hitting a nerve.

I just needed...a break.

Jax watched me, assessing me for a moment with a puzzled expression as I strode to the patio door and opened it for him.

He followed, stopping when he was out of Taylor's hearing range before he asked, "You don't really think I was hitting on Taylor, do you?" Jax sounded slightly wounded.

"I don't," I said honestly in a low voice. "Christ! I guess I'm just a little...edgy."

He smiled wryly as he replied, "She's pretty, and I have a thing for intelligent women, but she's been off-limits from the second I knew how *you* felt about her, Hudson."

I heard the scrape of her chair as Taylor rose from the table.

"I know," I said to him hurriedly before Taylor joined us.

"I really enjoyed our game, Jax," Taylor said guilelessly as she joined us.

"Me, too," Jax replied earnestly as we all made our way to the front door. "Will I see you both on Friday?"

"Friday?" I asked. "What's on Friday?"

"Your little sister's annual barbeque," Jax reminded me.

Holy hell! I'd been so damn distracted that I'd forgotten all about Riley's party.

I turned my gaze toward Taylor. "You up for it?"

"I'll be fine. Just go. I can take care of myself," she urged.

I balked at the idea of leaving her here while I took off for the whole afternoon and evening to Citrus Beach.

"You should come, Taylor. It's always a good time, and I think you'd really like Riley and Seth," Jax said encouragingly.

"I want you to come with me," I added.

Taylor's cheeks flushed. "Then I guess...I'll go. It will be nice to get out for the first time."

She sounded perfectly cheerful, but her tone was way too bright.

Something's wrong with her.

Jax said his goodbyes, and departed.

I realized that I'd put Taylor on the spot as I watched Jax depart, and I was sorry I had.

I'd made her uncomfortable, and as I closed the front door, I was determined to find out exactly why, so it never happened again.

Chapter 13

Taylor

"Ice cream?" Hudson asked mildly as he moved toward the kitchen.

"I'll get it," I answered as I hurried to the fridge before he did.

If I let *him* scoop it up, I'd end up with a pile of ice cream a mile high.

If I kept eating like he wanted to feed me, I'd end up as big as this monstrous house.

I pulled the carton out of the freezer, and reached into the cupboard for bowls while Hudson leaned his gorgeous ass against the kitchen counter a few feet away.

"I made you uneasy. I'm sorry," he said gruffly.

It was rare for Hudson to sound so contrite. "It wasn't your fault," I assured him.

"Then what exactly is it?"

"I'm not exactly a dress up kind of woman," I explained.

What I really meant was that I had no money to spend on clothing. Not the kind of money it would take to go designer label for a billionaire sort of event. I'd been a thrifty student for a long time.

I could see him studying me from the corner of my eye, his gaze sweeping over me from my cheap summer peasant blouse to my cutoff denim shorts. "You look beautiful," he concluded.

I smiled as I started scooping ice cream. "I look *okay* for a woman who is just knocking around the house. I'm definitely not dressed for a fancy party. I'd stick out like a sore thumb. It's just…not my thing."

"You're still not comfortable," he observed. "Taylor, what the hell is wrong?"

"I can't afford to buy expensive new clothes right now," I said in a rush, completely unable to beat around the bush or lie to Hudson.

Maybe there were some things I *hadn't* told him about my past, but I cared about him too much not to tell him the truth when he asked.

Dammit! I was lousy at hiding my feelings with him.

Maybe because I knew him well enough to know he'd never intentionally hurt me.

"Are you under the impression that this is some kind of elite gathering?" he asked.

"You're a billionaire. What else would I think? Even a casual party for you is way out of my league," I said, exasperated.

He moved closer, so close that I could feel his body heat, and smell his delicious, musky scent.

Hudson always smelled so damn good that it made me crazy.

Being this close to him was a torturous kind of pleasure, but I couldn't move away this time.

I was startled when he put his hands on my shoulders and turned me to face him. I tilted my head until our eyes met, and then, I melted.

For a moment, I got lost in his beautiful gray eyes.

"It's just family and friends, Taylor," he said roughly. "You are *not* going to feel out of place. Most likely, my sister will run around the beach squealing in a bathing suit while her adoring husband chases her in the sand until she lets him catch her. The two of them are almost embarrassing the way they play around like teenagers who can't get enough of each other. Anyone else there will be exactly the same way. None of us are pretentious. At all. Admittedly, Riley *does* like her clothes, and shopping, but I think she does it mostly because she wants to drive her husband crazy with lust. She's also an attorney, so she has to look professional sometimes. But you won't see a single ballgown or tux at this party. You'll get hamburgers on the grill, potato salad, and beach volleyball."

I raised a brow skeptically. "Seriously?"

He nodded. "If you want to go see a bunch of people make fools of themselves, you'll enjoy it. My sister's husband wasn't born rich, nor were any of his siblings. In fact, he was dirt poor for most of his childhood and adult life. His newfound wealth was a fairly recent occurrence. He's turned into a very successful businessman, but his heart is blue-collar, and probably always will be."

"And you like your sister's husband?" I asked, wondering how he really felt about his little sister marrying a guy who wasn't born into the same social circle.

He nodded sharply. "I do. I'd like any guy who makes my sister as happy as Seth makes Riley. Is that really what you think? Is that who you think I am? A guy who does useless parties in his spare time?"

I swallowed hard when I saw a flash of hurt in Hudson's beautiful eyes.

I felt horrible as I realized that I'd judged Hudson and his family without really knowing any of them. I'd just assumed that since they were outrageously rich, and had been born that way, that they'd have lavish parties. "I'm sorry. I shouldn't have assumed—"

He put a finger to my lips. "Don't," he said harshly. "I'm not saying that we don't all love the conveniences of being wealthy. Our private jets, our ability to buy whatever we want without thinking about the price, our nice cars, and expensive homes. I'm just saying that every one of us works our asses off like normal people, and there isn't a single one of us who hasn't had our own challenges that money can't fix. I just want you to give us a chance. Give *me* a chance."

My heart skittered as I saw a hint of vulnerability in Hudson's expression.

He was asking me to accept him as he was, just like he'd always been willing to put up with me and any weird quirks I had.

He knew I hadn't grown up rich, and *he'd* never judged *me*.

What in the hell had I been thinking?

He hadn't made a single judgment about me, no matter what I said.

I'd let my own insecurities rule me, and I'd hurt someone who had done nothing but help me during a very difficult time.

Hudson Montgomery was asking me to see *him*, and not all the superficial things that surrounded him.

And God, somebody needed to see this man, because I was pretty sure very few people did.

Not really.

"I think I'd like that," I said in a hushed voice, feeling overwhelmed by his humility because I knew that being the least bit vulnerable didn't come easy to Hudson Montgomery.

God, wasn't I the one who had told him that he was just one man?

My breath caught in my lungs as he lowered his head, his eyes on my mouth, his gaze...hungry.

In an instant, Hudson had gone from slightly pleading to predatory, and my heart started to race.

He'd *never* looked at me the way he was right now, but I'd sure as hell fantasized about seeing a Hudson Montgomery who *did*.

Every damn night.

I just never thought I'd experience it with my eyes open.

I'd tried so damn hard not to let Hudson see exactly how much I wanted him, because I was sure that carnal desire didn't go both ways.

Okay, so maybe I was wrong?

I started to drown in his masculine scent, and then his smoldering heat as he shifted even closer.

He *was* going to kiss me, and my body was wound tight with anticipation.

Needing to get closer to Hudson, I lifted my arms to wrap them around his neck, but before I could complete that move, I felt a very cold sensation on the bare part of my upper arm.

"Crap!" I hissed, realizing that I was still holding the ice cream scoop in my hand, and that the residual ice cream in that utensil had started to melt, dropping in a big blob onto my skin.

And just like that, any hint of the carnal desire I'd thought I'd seen in Hudson's eyes disappeared—if it had ever *really* been there at all.

Hudson dropped a lingering kiss on my forehead as I put the stupid scoop into one of the bowls.

I'd been so dazed that I'd completely forgotten what I'd been doing just moments before, and I felt like a complete idiot as I turned back toward the counter, searching for something to wipe the offending frozen treat from my arm.

Had I really been ridiculous enough to think Hudson Montgomery had been about to give me a toe-curling, passionate embrace?

He hadn't.

Had I really thought that what I'd seen in those mesmerizing eyes of his was really some kind of out-of-control hunger for...me?

It hadn't been.

All he'd meant to do was thank me sweetly for offering to be his nonjudgmental...friend.

I moved to the sink, wet a washrag, and scrubbed the sugar from my arm way harder than I needed to simply remove it.

Honestly, I should be grateful that the incident had happened.

If it hadn't, I would have felt like an idiot moments later for literally throwing myself into Hudson's arms.

"Hey," he said in a husky tone. "It's just ice cream."

I took a deep breath, put the rag neatly back in its place, and turned toward Hudson. "I know. It was just a really...dumb thing to do."

Apparently, one perceived look of passion from Hudson, and I completely lost my intellect.

He turned his head for a second, and shot me a mischievous grin that I knew was meant to cheer me up. "It wasn't dumb," he argued. "I find it very hard to believe that you've done a single dumb thing in your entire life, Taylor Delaney, and it was just a little...ice cream mishap."

I lifted a brow. "An ice cream mishap?"

He nodded as he handed me a bowl. "Exactly. Now stop kicking yourself and eat that before it's completely melted."

The awkwardness between the two of us just wasn't there like I thought it would be. Most likely because he still had no idea how much I wanted to get him naked.

Thank God!

I looked at the bowl, and as usual, Hudson had stacked it.

I pushed my way to the carton, forcing myself to ignore the way my body reacted when we were shoulder-to-shoulder, and scooped half of the pile of ice cream back into the container.

He grabbed my wrist. "Hey! What are you doing?"

"You don't have to feed me like I'm starving to death anymore, Hudson," I said in an amused voice, easily breaking his grip, and backing away once I had a *reasonable* amount of ice cream in the bowl.

"I want to make sure you're well fed," he grumbled. "I want you as healthy as you were *before* the kidnapping."

I took a small bite as I watched him put the container away. Hudson was big and solid, but his movements were efficient, purposeful, like he didn't have a single second to waste.

And God knew I liked nothing better than to watch that scorching hot body of his move.

Okay, maybe I was pathetic, but if I couldn't touch, it wasn't like I was going to *stop* looking.

I'd never been attracted to a man the way I was to Hudson, so it wasn't like I went around drooling over men's bodies every day, but for some reason, I couldn't help myself when it came to Hudson.

"I'm on my feet, and I'm eating well," I reminded him. "I'm so much better than I was in the beginning. I feel pretty normal."

"Not good enough," he said in a guttural voice as he picked up his bowl and turned toward me.

The two of us ate in silence for a few minutes before he spoke again. "Once we discuss the settlement and get it into your bank, you won't have any financial worries. Not that money is ever going to make up for what happened, but at least you won't be so damn obsessed about working before you're healthy again."

I swallowed a huge mouthful of ice cream before I asked, "What settlement?"

Hudson stopped eating for a moment as he replied, "The compensation for this entire incident. You and Harlow were on the job, so obviously we're going to compensate you for what happened."

He was making absolutely no sense. "You already have. I know you paid my hospital bills; I'm still getting my intern pay, and you've covered every single expense I've had since I've been here."

"Our workman's compensation handled that," he scoffed. "I'm talking about a *personal* settlement."

I looked at him, confused. "Why in the world would I need that?"

"Because you deserve it after what happened," he responded matter-of-factly. "We already gave Mark's family his payout, and our life insurance company paid them as well. I know that money isn't going to bring him back to his family, but it should help them financially for the rest of their lives."

"Mark is dead," I said flatly. "In case you haven't noticed, I'm still alive, and have absolutely no intention of suing you. Ever. So this conversation is irrelevant."

I took the last bite of my ice cream, rinsed the bowl, and put it into the dishwasher.

Hudson finally spoke as he dropped his own bowl into the dishwasher. "It's not like a lawsuit. Think of it as an apology from us for what happened."

"No," I said firmly. "Absolutely not. I already told you that this *wasn't* your fault, and I'm declining your offer."

"You can't decline," he rasped. "We already paid Mark's family."

I could see the stubborn look on his face, and I knew he wasn't backing down. Unfortunately, I couldn't ignore him this time. Not about this.

"No!" I said adamantly. "I don't *want* your money. Not as some kind of payoff or guilty conscience payment, not from a lawsuit, nothing. You've done more than enough already, Hudson. You'll just have to trust me when I say I am *never* going to sue the very person who ended up saving my life. If you want me to sign something that says I'm never going to sue you, I will, but first you have to promise not to *pay* a single dime for that signature. I'm heading to bed since you refuse to be reasonable. Goodnight, Hudson. This discussion is over."

"You promised me that you'd do three things for me, no questions asked," he reminded me in a hoarse, frustrated tone.

I stopped right before I exited the room, but I didn't look back as I said, "Don't. Don't you dare use that against me. I would do anything for you, Hudson, but please don't force me to do something that I feel would be morally and ethically wrong."

I left the kitchen and started up the stairs, feeling more than a little disappointed that Hudson would ever assume I'd take that kind of payment after he saved my life.

It wasn't just the act itself, the rescue, that had saved my life. It was *him*. Everything he'd done for me *after* he'd pulled me from that hellish situation, too.

His concern about my wellbeing. His patience. His thoughtfulness. Even his constant need to supply me with large quantities of food touched my heart. His ability to put himself in my shoes and instinctively understand what I'd needed was priceless to me, as was his ability to empathize.

And he *still* thought he needed to *pay me* for what happened?

Is that *really* what people expected from him?

And did they *really* take it when he offered it?

When was the bullheaded man going to understand that there were some things that money couldn't buy?

Standing by me, supporting me emotionally, listening when I had a rough day had meant *everything* to me.

Hudson was a workaholic, and Montgomery Mining was his life. Did he think I didn't know how hard it had been for him to work at home with limited work hours? How difficult it had been for him to give up what little free time he had to spend it catering to me?

Well, I knew, and I wasn't taking his damn money, too.

I had no idea if anybody had approached this subject with Harlow, but she certainly hadn't mentioned it during any of our daily phone calls. I couldn't begin to presume what *she* would do, but I had a feeling she wouldn't take it, either.

I was able bodied, educated, and I was *alive*. I wasn't about to say I was *completely* fine yet. Everything that had happened had been traumatic and painful, but that was pretty much...life.

Hudson Montgomery owed me nothing. If anything, I owed him.

"You're right!" he bellowed from the bottom of the stairs. "That comment was out of line, but this discussion *isn't* over, Taylor."

I turned to look behind me near the top of the steps. I couldn't really see the look on his face because the staircase was long. "It is over," I said firmly. "To be quite honest, you hurt me. I have no idea why you'd even, for one moment, think I'd want something like that. But since you *did* think I'd accept it, that doesn't say much about what kind of person you think I am, does it? Now, goodnight."

There were so many things I ached for when it came to Hudson Montgomery, but a huge influx of cash didn't even make the list.

I didn't look back as I climbed the final few steps, and went to my room.

Chapter 14

Hudson

"She wouldn't take a goddamn penny of our settlement," I growled into the phone to Jax. "I talked to her last night, and she completely refused. Said I've done enough for her already. What in the hell did I do?"

Jax and I had only been discussing business for a few minutes, but I really needed to get what happened with Taylor off my chest.

I'd had to force myself not to go after her gorgeous ass once she'd fled upstairs, and I hadn't slept worth a damn last night.

At breakfast time, she'd come into the kitchen, grabbed some coffee, and had headed to the gym.

I hadn't seen her since.

And it was almost noon.

Not that we generally spent much time together during the day. She had appointments. I had business. But she could have at least stuck her head into my office since things hadn't ended very well last night.

"Was that her final word?" Jax asked. "Or do you think she'll come around?"

"No, I don't think she'll come around at all. She offered to sign something that says she won't sue for God's sake, but she won't take money for it. It's a damn good thing she's a geologist because she'd make a terrible business negotiator," I griped.

"Now is probably *not* a great time to tell you this," Jax said, his voice cautious. "But I spoke to somebody in legal, and apparently, they got the same answer from Harlow. One of our attorneys called her this morning. He didn't tell me what she said word-for-word, but she told him not to call her again, and that she didn't want any money. Essentially, it sounded like she told him to go screw himself, and hung up, but he's way too nice of a guy to say it quite that way. Sounds like she needs more time than I thought before I approach her."

I raked a hand through my hair as I leaned back in my office chair. "I don't get it. All I want to do is make Taylor's life easier. She wouldn't have to stress over going to work if she didn't want to, or if she wasn't ready. Her financial worries would essentially be over."

"Maybe she doesn't *want* to become an instant millionaire," Jax mused.

"I don't think her refusal has anything to do with her bank account," I told him.

I could still hear her telling me that I'd hurt her, and dammit, that was killing me. I wasn't going to see her as a money grubber if she took that settlement. Hell, I *wanted* her to take it because she deserved it, and not because I saw it as some kind of payoff. I wanted her life to be easier, and I didn't want her to suffer ever again.

Granted, if we were paying a large sum, we usually *did* want a legal agreement signed so we didn't get slapped with a lawsuit the second that enormous check hit their bank. But I hadn't even thought about that with Taylor. I didn't give a shit whether she signed anything. I just wanted her...safe.

"I think you should try approaching her about it again. Let me know if she changes her mind and I'll send the paperwork to legal," Jax said.

"If she takes the money, it will be a gift from me, no paperwork necessary," I answered in a clipped tone. "But I doubt that's going to happen. She's too damn stubborn."

Yeah, so, maybe I *had* said that I wasn't going to question her bullheadedness because it had saved her life, but now that she was fighting *me*, I wasn't so sure about that statement.

"She's also incredibly smart. I don't know if those two qualities are a good combination," Jax mentioned drily.

I grimaced. "She's not usually like this. Usually, she's more than willing to compromise, but not on this one. I could see a never-going-to-happen glint in her eyes last night. She really *was* offended."

Jax cleared his throat. "Has it even occurred to you that maybe you should just tell her how you feel? I'm assuming she has no idea that you want to be more than a friend who's helping her out."

"Hell no, I haven't told her that I want to get into her panties. She's been through too much, Jax. It's too damn soon," I said remorsefully.

"She looked pretty together when I saw her last night," he commented. "Maybe she's not exactly like she was before the kidnapping, but she was probably in amazing physical shape since she was a martial arts teacher. It will take some time for to recover that kind of strength, but there's nothing wrong with her, Hudson. She can handle knowing that you're attracted to her, and what you hope will happen."

"Maybe I have no fucking idea *what* I want," I said, frustrated.

"Please don't even try to tell me that you're okay with just being a casual friend once she's fully recovered."

I thought about that for a minute. Could I handle just being a guy she considered a buddy? Watching her date other men? Hearing about those relationships? Knowing that some other guy was touching her, but not…me. "I can't," I answered hoarsely. "It would kill me."

Bottom line: I wanted Taylor way too much to watch any of those things happen and to be relegated to the category of a casual friend.

"Then I think it's way beyond time the two of you had that discussion," Jax said rationally. "Have you made a single move to let her know what you're thinking?"

"Almost," I confessed. "Last night before the argument, but I was saved by a little ice cream mishap. I got my shit together before I even had the chance to touch her. I came damn close to losing it. I don't think she had a single clue what was going on in my head, thank God."

"Maybe that's not such a good thing, Hudson. Maybe it's better if you find out if there's a spark...or not."

"I already know," I answered gruffly. "And for me, it's more than a spark. It's a whole damn forest fire consuming more and more acreage every damn day."

Jax chuckled. "Don't you want to know if she feels the same way?"

"No," I said adamantly.

"Why?"

"What if she doesn't? Then what in the hell am I supposed to do? Be her brother figure, her friend? I don't even want to think about that shit."

"I doubt very much that's the case," Jax drawled. "It's pretty hard to hurt someone if there aren't some tender feelings involved. It's not like you two have known each other long enough to have an established friendship that's in jeopardy here. She's touchy because you two are dancing around the way you really feel. I guess I just don't see the problem with you letting her know that you'd like all of this to end in the bedroom."

The bedroom?

Hell, I wasn't picky.

In *my* bed.

The kitchen.

The patio.

The living room.

The gym.

I didn't really give a damn about the location. Wherever we were, I always felt the same damn way: pathetically desperate to make Taylor mine.

"Truthfully, I doubt I can make it much longer *without* her knowing," I said in a raw voice. "And I'm not sure how to handle that."

"Because you aren't used to *not* being in total control," my brother said smoothly. "You're used to being a workaholic who always has the upper hand. Before that, you were a highly regimented Special Forces officer. None of us really had a childhood, but we sure as hell weren't encouraged to openly express any kind of emotion. Ever. We were miniature robots, Hudson. We weren't supposed to *feel* anything. We were just expected to excel. Do you even remember crying once as a child? I sure as hell don't. And I doubt very much that Riley and Cooper remember doing it, either. Hell, our own sister hid being molested by our father for years. She couldn't even tell *us* that it happened, much less somebody she didn't completely trust," Jax finished in a disgusted tone.

I let out a breath of frustration. "You're right," I admitted grimly. "Taylor and I are almost total opposites. She lives every day when it comes, and she does it wholeheartedly, while I'm trying to shape that day into what I want it to be. Maybe the fact that we're so different is what attracted me to her in the first place, and I wouldn't change a hair on her head to be more like…me."

"I think you two are much more alike than you think," Jax said in a contemplative tone. "You just show the world different faces."

"I'm not completely following you," I mumbled.

He let out an exasperated sigh. "I mean, maybe you show things differently, but deep down, you want the same things. Hell, I'd probably be willing to cut off one of my damn balls to have a woman stand up to me the way Taylor did with you. To say that I actually *hurt her*, instead of just ruined her chances to be with a billionaire Montgomery. Because that would mean she actually gave a damn about *me*, Hudson. If you have the ability to hurt Taylor, what she's really saying is that she cares what you think about her character, whether she realizes it or not. Fuck knows I'm no expert in relationships. Maybe because I've never had anything real. But ultimately, I think you and Taylor want the same damn thing: she wants somebody to care about her, and so do you."

"I do care about her," I rasped. "Probably too damn much."

"Well see, there's a problem with that situation," Jax commented. "*She* doesn't know that. I know you, Hudson. You're a damn master at playing the game, and not letting anybody know what's really going on in your head. While that makes you an excellent business-man, and before that, a great Special Forces member, it isn't working so well in your private life."

"I don't have a private life," I informed him.

"Now, you do," Jax snapped back. "You have Taylor, and I think she wants to care about you, so start communicating and let her know exactly what you're thinking. This isn't business, Hudson. Not anymore. I think she was disappointed because she thought you had more faith in her ability to take care of herself. Yeah, maybe she needed somebody to take care of her for a short period of time when she couldn't do it herself, but she's highly intelligent, educated, and perfectly capable of running her own life."

"I know that," I growled. "I see how smart and together she is every single day. I've never seen somebody who has been held hos-tage bounce back as fast as she has, and to tell you the truth, it scares the hell out of me." I wasn't about to share the fact that Taylor had been forced into allowing the rebel leader to use her body every damn night. I was fairly certain Jax knew about that anyway since Harlow had mentioned it, but he didn't need to know the details. I couldn't say I had any specifics to share anyway. That was the one thing Taylor hadn't discussed a whole lot with me.

"It was a short duration, Hudson. Her body is almost healed, and if she had her head straight in the first place, maybe she is okay. I'm not saying that going through something like that isn't going to cause some lingering issues, but hell, don't we all have some of those?"

"Maybe," I said noncommittally, not ready to admit all the short-comings I had.

Not to Jax, anyway. We were too damn much alike having come from the same background, so that would be kind of like telling him he was a hot mess, too.

"I will tell you one thing," I offered.

"What's that?"

"There's not a single *choice* for me in this situation," I admitted, referring back to the conversation we'd had on the way to Lania. "If I could have talked myself out of wanting Taylor, I would have done it by now."

Jax snorted. "I kind of figured *that* out already."

I intentionally shifted the conversation away from me, and into the rest of our business.

After thirty minutes or so, we were done catching up for the day when Jax asked, "What do you want me to do about Harlow?"

"Nothing," I said flatly. "She needs time to grieve and get her head on straight. As her employers, we owe it to her to give her all the time and support she needs. *I'm* not accepting her resignation, even if some supervisor or department head did. As far as I'm concerned, she's going to be on an extended leave of absence, a paid leave. You on board with that?"

"Definitely," Jax said emphatically. "I'll handle payroll and the lab chief. What about Taylor?"

"She stays a paid employee, too. The woman already gets a ridiculously low wage for her education, intern or not. I think that's something we need to look at in the future. Her internship isn't over until the beginning of September, and by that time, she damn well better accept my job offer and get her ass into a permanent position with us," I said unhappily.

"She doesn't want that?" Jax asked, sounding perplexed.

"Doesn't think she has the experience to work for us," I replied.

"With an average person, that's probably true," Jax considered. "But it's not totally unheard of to see an intern go into a permanent position with us if they're really exceptional. It's happened before. It just doesn't occur frequently, but I'd more than agree that Taylor is one of those exceptions. She's one of those rare interns I'd rather *not* lose to another company. Anyone who has the brains to kick my ass in chess is somebody who's dangerous on the outside," Jax said, sounding like he was only *partially* joking. "I'll have a word with her at the barbeque, let her know what I think. Maybe she assumes you're doing her a favor or something. Just try not to slug me because I'm talking to her at Riley's place," he requested.

"I already told you I regret the way I acted," I answered. I'd mentioned it at the very beginning of our conversation. "No winking, no flirting, no charming, and I'll be fine."

"We'll see," Jax said, drawing those two words out longer than needed.

Much to my annoyance, I could have sworn I heard the bastard laughing right before he ended the entire conversation.

Chapter 15

Taylor

"I think it's time for us to get a few things straight," Hudson said ominously from his lounger.

I shuddered. Usually, that growly tone didn't bother me at all, but things had been incredibly tense since our disagreement last night.

I took a larger than normal gulp of the white wine I was drinking, and hastily swallowed it.

Tired of feeling helpless, I'd made dinner, and had let Hudson know it was ready. We'd pretty much eaten in silence, which had been pretty damn uncomfortable.

All of my anger had disappeared long before I'd called him for dinner.

I'd totally made a snap judgment about *him,* so I couldn't really feel devastated that he'd done the same thing with *me.*

Hudson and I had a strange bond, but really, we didn't know each other all that well.

We were judging each other on our previous life experiences, and on my part, *that* was going to stop.

I was going to learn more about him and his family, instead of trying to measure him beside every other rich guy I'd ever known.

Yeah, there had been a lot of trust fund pricks in Los Angeles who had looked down on the poorer kids while I was growing up, and more than enough attending Stanford, too. Maybe Hudson had more money than any of them could ever dream of having, but that didn't mean the level of snobbery went up exponentially because Hudson was a billionaire. I couldn't put every filthy rich person into the same mold.

"I'm sorry if I misjudged you," I blurted out. "You've done way too much for me to deserve how I acted. I guess I was hurt, so I just...retreated."

"So does that mean you'll take the money?" he asked hopefully.

"Absolutely not," I retorted.

"I was afraid you'd say that," he answered, sounding disappointed. "It wasn't some kind of payoff, Taylor. I want you to understand that. I didn't expect or want you to sign a release, and it wasn't meant to satisfy my guilt, either. All I really wanted to do was make your life easier. In my mind, you've had enough to deal with, and you don't need financial worries. If I could take that off your plate for you with nothing more than a damn signature to wire the funds, why not do it? Everything else aside, you *were* working for Montgomery when it happened, so if we can ease your mind in some way, we owe that to you."

I sighed. "Look at this from my perspective, Hudson. I'd be dead right now if you and Jax hadn't shown up exactly when you did. You went way beyond what any company would do for an employee, and you're still doing it. I know you meant well, but I can't look at this as all business. It's personal to me. I can't keep taking from you. And really, I've had to watch my pennies my entire life. That's the way I've *always* lived, and why I pushed my ass through school. I'm *temporarily* strapped because I made the decision to do an internship that I knew would give me invaluable experience before I took a permanent position, but I'm in a lot more of a powerful position than I've ever been in my entire. I can get a good job that will eventually lead to the extras I've never had, and I've done it on my own. Probably the most important thing to me is that all of this will happen while I'm able to work in a field that means something to me. I'm no different than you are. I want to make a difference in the world, too. If you go plop some five or six figure amount of money into my bank account, that pretty much disregards everything I've been working for all these years."

"Seven figures," he grumbled.

I rolled my eyes. Did Hudson *always* have to do everything in a big way? "I'm not taking it," I warned him.

"I want to be assured that you're safe, Taylor," he said in a tight voice. "That's all I've ever intended."

My heart melted just a little. "And I appreciate the fact that you care as a friend now. Just knowing that you do is more valuable than any amount of money. But as your friend who never wants you to be taken for granted, it's nauseating even to think about taking that kind of payment from you. Give me a chance to give back for God's sake. This friendship has been all one-sided so far."

"I'm not your *friend*, Taylor," he answered abruptly. "I think that's one of the most important things we need to get straight right now."

My eyes widened as I turned my head to look at him. The sun was starting to set, and Hudson's gaze was set on the horizon, but the tension on his face was all too clear.

Shit! Had I been way too presumptuous in considering Hudson Montgomery a friend?

"I'm sorry, I guess I just thought—"

"Don't," Hudson cut me off. "This is my issue, not yours, and you haven't done a damn thing to encourage me, but understand that I'm never going to see you as some kind of buddy of mine."

Tears sprang to my eyes immediately. It wasn't that I didn't know that the two of us were very, very different, but I cared so much about Hudson that it was excruciatingly painful to hear that he didn't feel the same way.

Maybe the majority of men *weren't* dying to go out with me, but it was the first time I'd ever had a *friendship* with one of them completely tossed back in my face.

Unfortunately, it was also the first time I'd wanted to be close to somebody so damn much.

"Understood," I mumbled because I couldn't get any other response out of my mouth.

"No, I don't think you do understand," Hudson rasped. "If I could possibly treat you like a friend, I would, but I can't. I've never in my life wanted to fuck a single one of my *friends* or *buddies*. My dick doesn't get rock-hard the second one of *them* walks into the room. And I sure as hell don't think about bending *them* over a kitchen counter while they're scooping ice cream. I know I don't fucking obsess over *their* safety, whether they're well, or if they're happy every goddamn minute of the day until I'm half crazy. I've never jerked myself off thinking about what it would be like to hear *them* screaming my name while they were coming so hard that it seemed like that pleasure was never going to end." He stopped abruptly, and sucked down the entire tumbler of whiskey in his hand in a single large gulp.

Holy shit!

I watched him, my entire body tight with shock, as he visibly tried to get his emotions under control.

He clenched his fists and then released them, and he did it over and over again until some of the tension on his gorgeous face started to ease.

I didn't know what to say, so I kept my mouth shut until I could wrap my head around what he'd just said.

He put the tumbler down on the small table beside him, and added, "I've never felt this way about anyone. It's. Just. You. So don't ask me to try to act like you're a friend when all I really want is to get as intimate with you as two people can get."

My hand was shaking when I took a sip of my wine this time.

My emotions were probably even more chaotic than his at the moment.

My heart was racing, and I could barely catch my breath.

I'd wanted Hudson Montgomery almost the same way since the beginning.

At first, he'd been my rescuer.

Then, the person who had been beside me at one of the worst times of my life. The guy who didn't seem to mind hauling me from one room to another, and wasn't embarrassed even when I needed help to pee.

After that, Hudson had been my safe place to fall while I was getting my shit together.

But truthfully, I'd *always* wanted him.

I'd wanted to lick every inch of his powerful body since the first time I'd seen it.

Intimacy wasn't really something I was completely comfortable with, but God, I'd wanted it. I'd craved it with this man. Just like him, I'd gotten myself off to carnal fantasies about him.

But I'd never, not in a million years, thought he'd felt the same way.

Maybe I had hoped I'd seen desire on his face last night, but it hadn't been difficult to discard the entire idea of somebody like Hudson wanting...me.

I wasn't sophisticated.

I wasn't beautiful.

I didn't really know how to be flirty.

I didn't know how to be a woman Hudson might be attracted to, but he was. It was written all over his face tonight, and it *wasn't* my imagination.

Last night's perceived desire *had* been real, too.

A large tear dropped to my cheek, but I didn't give a damn.

Hudson had just made himself so vulnerable to me that it ripped me up inside.

He wasn't the kind of guy who just blurted out the way he felt, or gave someone all the ammunition to destroy him if that was their goal.

Luckily, that wasn't my ambition.

What I really wanted was to get him naked, and satisfy every dirty fantasy he'd ever had.

I'd savor every second of this man's fierce, raw passion greedily, and then, no doubt, I'd beg for more.

Truthfully, I'd never felt like this before, either, but I was beyond willing to find out what it felt like to wallow in those desires rather than hide them.

"Son of a bitch!" he cursed. "You're crying. I didn't mean to upset you, Taylor. I just needed you to know the truth. Forget what I said. I'll try to be your damn friend if that's all you need."

It wasn't.

It wasn't even close to being what I needed.

For once in my life, I wanted somebody to really know me, every part of me.

Like I'd done many times since Hudson had rescued me, I reached for my dragon pendant for a little boost of confidence, but it wasn't there.

"Why do you do that?" Hudson asked in a husky tone.

"What?"

"Put your hand up to your neck like that. I've seen you do it before?"

"The rebels took all my jewelry, which wasn't much," I explained. "But I had a pendant that Mac Tanaka gave me when I was a teenager, a dragon with a cage tail that wrapped around a pearl. I never took it off. I miss it, I guess."

Hudson rose and held out his hand. "It's dark. Let's go in. We don't have to talk about this shit anymore. I won't even mention it again. You're not fully recovered, and you're dealing with enough right now."

I took his hand because I wanted to touch him. I didn't really need help anymore.

I looked up at him when I was on my feet, and I was disappointed when all I saw was concern in his eyes.

He'd obviously managed to conquer his previously out-of-control emotions.

Hudson's expression was careful, closed off, but I *knew* what I'd seen early. It was still there, somewhere, but could I really blame him for needing to defend himself?

It wasn't like I'd said a single thing to help him.

I held his gaze as I said, "I feel the same things you do, Hudson. I guess I'm just not quite sure how to give you what you want."

He nodded sharply, and looked away. "I understand."

I followed him into the house with a sigh. Just like I hadn't understood him earlier, he didn't understand me now.

How in the hell could I explain that even though I had the same desires that he did, I had no idea what to do with them?

Chapter 16

Hudson

I couldn't sleep later that night when I finally went to bed.

Instead, I kept cursing myself for being a coward, and running off to my home office after I'd confessed to Taylor that I couldn't see her as a friend.

I'd wanted to end the conversation once we'd stepped inside, even though I'd known that Taylor had more to say.

She hadn't been ready to hear my bullshit because she'd told me straight out that she didn't know how to give me what I wanted.

Fairly certain she was just trying to let me down easy by claiming she felt the same way, I'd muttered some excuse about needing to get some stuff done in my office, and I'd walked away from her.

Fuck! What if she was confused? What if she *hadn't* just been trying to politely blow me off?

What if…

What if…

What if…

I should have given it more time, and told her later if I thought there was a chance we could become lovers when she was completely recovered.

Maybe I didn't want to be relegated to the friend category in her mind, but I could have been a lot more subtle about it.

I could have waited until she felt more comfortable with sex in general after being assaulted.

And I definitely hadn't needed to be a dick when she had more to say.

Problem was, I hadn't wanted to hear her say she didn't know, or that she wasn't sure if she could ever be more than a friend.

I didn't want to be that guy who was suffering from unrequited lust.

I also hadn't wanted to be that man who had threatened to use something she'd promised me as a damn tool to get exactly what I wanted.

But I had, because I'd wanted to know that Taylor would always have enough money to get whatever she wanted, whatever she needed.

Fuck knew she had to replace her older model vehicle. The ugly blue compact looked like it was ready to take its last breath any day now.

No doubt she had student loans to pay as well, and she could wipe those out in a heartbeat if she'd just take the damn money.

That's what I want.

Does it matter what Taylor wants, how she feels?

Hell, yes, it mattered, but like an idiot, I hadn't been listening to her. I'd been too damn concerned about relieving some of my own concerns about her wellbeing, so I'd bulldozed right over what she wanted, or what felt right to *her.*

I was just rolling over in bed for the millionth time when I heard the first bloodcurdling scream.

I sat up, my heart thundering, as the next one nearly stopped my heart.

"Taylor," I rasped as I hauled ass to get out of my bed and race the short distance to her room.

Jesus Christ! Her cry had sounded so desperate and terrified, that I didn't even bother to knock.

When I saw her small figure in the large bed, I was relieved to see that she was sitting up. On closer inspection as I neared the bed, I wasn't all that sure she was okay.

The moonlight filtered in through her open shutters. I could see her body trembling, and she was rubbing her upper arms like she was cold. She was still whimpering with fear as she rocked her body.

Every protective instinct in my body was screaming at me to hold her, comfort her, but I had no fucking idea what had scared her in the first place. Maybe my earlier confession had triggered it, and maybe she didn't want to be touched, so I held back.

"Taylor?" I said, trying to stay calm. "What happened? You screamed, and it scared the shit out of me."

"I'm sorry I woke you. I had a bad dream," she mumbled, and then took a deep breath like she was trying to pull herself out of the paralyzing fear she'd been experiencing. "I guess I woke up so quickly that I panicked."

I watched as she crawled out of the bed and added, "I think I need something to drink. You can go back to bed."

Like hell I will.

She's acting like she's unphased, but I knew damn well Taylor was still shaken up.

She strolled toward the door in a pair of pajamas that probably weren't meant to be sexy, but on her, they were. The tank top was thin, and the matching shorts barely covered her ass.

I followed her, even though I wasn't exactly covered, either. But the boxer briefs I was wearing concealed enough.

When we got downstairs, Taylor went directly to the kitchen, grabbed a huge glass, and filled it with filtered water and ice from the fridge.

She leaned against the counter as she downed half the glass before she said, "Seriously, Hudson, I'm fine."

"You're not *fine*," I grumbled as I opened the fridge. I pulled out a pitcher of fruit infused water, and filled a glass for myself.

I held out the pitcher, and she nodded, so I filled the glass she'd just emptied.

"Let's go sit," I suggested as I moved toward the living room, turning on the lamp instead of flooding the room with overhead light.

Taylor took a seat on one end of the comfortable leather sofa, so I flopped down on the opposite side.

I looked at her as I asked, "So is this the first nightmare you've had? It *was* about the kidnapping, right?"

She'd told me she had occasional dreams about the kidnapping, but she hadn't described them quite like this.

She shook her head. "No. They started several days after you brought me here, but this one was the worst. I told you that I pretty much zoned out while I was being sexually assaulted by the rebel leader, and for the most part, that was true. Now, it's like I'm experiencing all the things he did in my dreams, and I can't detach anymore."

I took a gulp of my water, wishing I'd added a healthy amount of vodka to it.

"Did you talk to your counselor about it?" I asked.

"I did. She thought my brain would eventually calm down, and the dreams would stop. And they did. I haven't dreamed about the kidnapping for almost a week now, until tonight." She took another sip of her water and set it on the side table.

"Do you think it was because I told you that I wanted to fuck you?" I asked hoarsely.

Taylor shook her head firmly. "No. I'm not afraid of you, Hudson. I never could be. I told you I felt the same way. In fact, I'd really like to sit closer to you if you don't mind. I think I'd feel better."

I plunked my glass down on my side table and opened my arms. "I'm all yours, sweetheart. Come as close as you want."

She scrambled across the distance separating us so fast that I was almost surprised when she burrowed into my body. "You're so warm," she murmured as she pressed her body against mine, drilling into my side like a heat-seeking missile.

I wrapped my arm around her shoulders and pulled her into me until her head rested on my shoulder. At that moment, I didn't give a damn if she just needed me to be there as a warm body she trusted.

The only thing I wanted was for her to feel safe.

I threaded my hand into her gorgeous, fiery mane of hair and stroked it, trying to get her to calm down.

She sighed in contentment before she said, "I'm not sure why I'm dreaming about being sexually assaulted now. Maybe because I couldn't think about it before. I told you it was horrible, and it was. But now that I can feel every emotion, see every action, I'm so angry, and so terrified. The man had the coldest eyes I've ever seen, dead and lifeless, like he had absolutely no soul. Honestly, I'm not even sure why he bothered to rape me, because it was obvious that he saw me as some kind of evil he needed to banish. I think he felt that if he could conquer me, it would make him more powerful."

I dropped a kiss to the top of her head. "Tell me," I encouraged. "I'm never going to judge you for something that was totally out of your control."

She nodded. "I know. It was the same thing every single night. He'd only undress me from the waist down, and then he'd pull my bound hands over my head and attach them to a long stake near the head of his cot. It never lasted long, but it seemed like an eternity. He'd always rant for a few minutes in Lanian, and then he'd spit in my face before he violated my body. I tried to meditate my way out of the whole experience during that tirade, trying to detach as much as possible."

"What did you think about?" I asked tightly, trying not to fucking lose it.

This was about Taylor, not me, but I'd kill the bastard slowly and painfully if I could get to the rebel leader right now.

"Mostly the good times with Mac Tanaka. Or I'd try to think about beautiful places all over the world that I haven't had the chance to see yet," she said softly. "Anything positive to replace the bad things. I was absolutely terrified, but I didn't want him to see that. I knew he hated me so much that I was afraid he'd end my life right after he was done." She paused before she continued. "In my dream tonight, he did kill me. He pulled out a knife and slashed my throat. I woke up just as the dagger made contact, which was probably why I was screaming. When I first opened my eyes, I thought I was dead."

I closed my eyes for a moment, hating every second of pain and degradation Taylor had been through. "You had every right to be horrified, and scared," I grunted. "You were so damn brave, sweetheart."

"I wanted to be courageous, but I wasn't always," she said in a shaky voice. "I feel like my nightmare was a manifestation of every fear I had while I was their prisoner."

I tilted her chin up until I could look at her face.

Her eyes were wide and glassy from the tears I could see rolling down her cheeks.

Christ! I could hardly take a damn breath because my chest was so tight. "Nelson Mandela once said that courage isn't the absence of fear, but the triumph over it. You fought your way through it, Taylor."

"But I couldn't fight him," she said in a tearful voice. "And I wanted to so damn badly, Hudson. I didn't want to lay there and submit."

I put a palm on each side of her face. "You did it to save a friend, Taylor. Don't ever fucking blame yourself for that because it's almost impossible to do that when all you want to do is fight. Give yourself credit for what you did for Harlow. Don't hate yourself for doing what you had to do. Most people wouldn't have ever thought about sacrificing themselves to save someone else."

"I don't regret it," she said earnestly. "Sometimes I just wish I could have gotten in a swift kick to his balls, or scratched those lifeless eyes out of his face."

She laid her head on my shoulder again as I answered, "And that makes you human," I told her. "I'd like to kill the bastard myself, but he's locked up, Taylor. He'll pay the price for what he did for the rest of his fucking life."

"I'll be okay, Hudson," she said in a thoughtful voice. "I'll be living my life while he rots in prison. Most of the time I'm all right with that. I guess I just haven't totally resolved *everything* that happened."

"It hasn't even been a month yet," I said gruffly. "You'll get there. I never should have mentioned how I felt earlier, Taylor. I fucked up."

"No," she said in a stronger tone. "Don't ever apologize for being honest, Hudson. Please."

"Bad timing," I said firmly. "Jesus, you aren't even recovered yet, Taylor. And then when you tried to tell me you weren't ready, I didn't listen."

"I never said I wasn't ready," Taylor replied. "You totally misunderstood."

Hadn't she pretty much said she didn't know how to give me what I wanted? Wasn't *that* a good indicator that she'd been completely confused?

"Explain it then," I insisted gently.

I was sick of dancing around a subject that was eating my guts out. She'd listened to me....

"First, I want to tell you what all that stuff you read in my dossier was really like," she said nervously. "You were right when you said all you saw were...just facts."

I nodded. "I'm here to listen."

Apparently, she trusted me enough to tell me anything, and I'd have to be satisfied with that. For now.

Chapter 17

Taylor

I had things I wanted to say to Hudson, and I wasn't going to rest until I did.

He'd cut the evening short once we'd gotten inside earlier, going to his office, and leaving me to my own devices.

I'd watched a movie, and then headed to bed. All I'd done was stare at the ceiling by moonlight in his beautiful guest suite until I'd finally conked out and had the worst nightmare I'd ever experienced in my life.

I was calmer, and it was all because of the man holding me right now.

If Hudson hadn't been so damn determined to get into his office like his ass was on fire earlier, I would have explained exactly why I'd been a little confused.

Burying himself in work was his way of making sure nothing else was said about his whole confession, putting a wall between the two of us until, hopefully, I'd forget about the whole conversation.

That wasn't going to happen.

He'd just have to listen, and figure out that I was speaking *literally* earlier, and it wasn't a hard concept to grasp, but he had to know my history first.

The man had shared enough of his own past for me to realize that he'd never really been a child. We could relate on that part, at least.

I took a deep breath. "I was four when my parents died. Honestly, I don't really remember them much except for really vague flashes of memory. I grew up in Los Angeles, and my dad worked in a factory there. My mom did some part-time work at a fast food place. We lived in an apartment. Both of them were really young when I was born, and they were still trying to make everything work. It wasn't the best area of Los Angeles, but it wasn't the worst, either."

Hudson's arm tightened around me as I continued, "I've never understood why my father snapped one day when he came home from work, shot my mother, and then turned that same gun on himself." I took a deep breath. "I've always wondered why he didn't shoot me, too. I didn't see the incident happen because I was playing in my room, but according to witnesses, I saw it after the fact. Apparently, I was covered in their blood, and begging them both to wake up when I was found and taken by the state."

It wasn't all that hard to talk about the death of my parents because I didn't really remember them, or the homicide-suicide. It was mostly just...facts.

I continued, "My dad's family could barely take care of themselves, much less a kid who hadn't started kindergarten yet, and my mother's family were extremely religious. They wanted nothing to do with me. They cut my mom off completely when she got pregnant before she was eighteen, and worse yet for them, before she was married. So I spent a lot of time during grade school going from foster home to foster home." I smiled slightly. "I was kind of a dorky looking kid, ugly with a face full of freckles, and big glasses that never really fit my face right. And I was angry. God, I was so damn angry at the entire world. I was mad because nobody loved me, but I wasn't exactly a loveable kid, either, and I tended to get in a lot of fights, which would usually end my stay in yet another foster home.

I'd end up slugging another foster kid or one of my foster parents' biological children because they teased me, so off I'd go to start all over again. By the time I was eleven, I was completely convinced that nobody could love me, and that I'd never have a home like most of my friends did."

"What happened?" Hudson finally spoke in a raw voice. "Tell me."

"I'd just gotten booted from my latest home, and I didn't want to go back to foster care again, going from house to house," I explained. "So I ran away. I did what I had to do to eat. I stole food, slept wherever I could, until one morning, I met Mac Tanaka. It was a weird, random thing that changed my entire life. I was sleeping on a bench, and he was just strolling through the park. He sat down and talked to me for hours, and then he took me home with him. Looking back on it, I think we were both lonely. He and his wife had never been able to have their own kids. When Mac's wife died, I don't think he knew what to do with himself. He used to say that I saved him, but he actually saved…me."

"So you stayed with him?" Hudson asked, sounding relieved.

I nodded. "We were probably an odd pair, an eleven-year-old girl, and a guy in his seventies, but I don't think either one of us cared. Eventually, I started to trust him, and he officially made me his foster daughter. He and his wife had fostered before, but he'd stopped once she passed away. Mac started teaching me chess and Tai Chi so I could learn to be at peace with my world, and I cooked and did the laundry because he was really bad at both of those things. I learned to love, and what it was like to be loved by a parent figure. Mac changed my life, and he changed me. When he died seven years ago, I felt like my entire world was falling apart."

"Maybe it was," Hudson said stoically. "It sounds like he was your entire world."

"For a long time, he was," I agreed. "He wanted me to go to Stanford when I was eighteen, but I wanted to stay with him because he'd just been diagnosed with cancer, so I got a full-time job as a cashier in a grocery store. I put my Stanford acceptance on hold because Mac needed me, and I needed to be with him. Treatment was unsuccessful, and he passed away."

"I'm so sorry, Taylor," Hudson said roughly. "The only things I really knew were how your parents had died, and that you were moved around from foster home to foster home. Words on a page. I knew you'd eventually gotten permanent placement, but I had no idea who that foster parent was. Now that I know exactly what happened, I can only imagine how devastated you must have been when Mac died."

"I was. It tore me apart. It took me a year to get back to school, but I knew I'd be doing something Mac really wanted for me, and it was something I wanted, too. He left me everything he had, which wasn't much by the time his life was over, but it helped me get through some of my college years."

"Did he adopt you?" Hudson said curiously.

I smiled. "He wanted to, but that piece of paper didn't matter to me. He was a parent figure to me in every way that really meant something."

"Sounds like an incredible man," Hudson said sincerely.

"He was. He was amazing. And wise. He may not be with me physically anymore, but I'll carry his wisdom with me for the rest of my life," I answered, my voice trembling with emotion.

"You loved him like a father," Hudson stated.

"With all my heart," I said, my voice catching. "Even after seven years, there's rarely a day that I don't miss him. I miss my pendant that he got for me, but I know it was just a talisman to remind me that I was strong enough to make it on my own. Really, I'm always going to carry Mac right here." I laid my hand gently on my chest.

We were silent for several minutes before Hudson asked, "Why don't you wear glasses anymore?"

"Mac introduced me to contact lenses when I was old enough, and he started a special account for me to get laser surgery when I was old enough. I didn't touch that account until three years ago, and I finally got that laser surgery because I knew that was what Mac wanted me to do with that money."

"Not that I'm not incredibly glad you told me," he said lightly. "Or that you trust me enough to share all of this, but why now?"

I swallowed hard, "I was trying to say something downstairs, before you went to your office, but I don't think you were listening. I wanted to explain. I did a lot of things I'm not proud of—"

"For fuck's sake, Taylor, you were a damn kid who never had a single moment of security in her life. Do you really think I give a damn if you stole stuff so you could eat?" he asked in a low, rumbling baritone. "Yeah, I care because you didn't have a single place or person to turn to back then who gave a flying fuck about you until Mac came into your life, but all you were doing was trying to survive."

I smiled because Hudson sounded so disgruntled. I should have realized that he'd understand. "But here's the thing," I said nervously. "I was pretty content spending my time hanging out with Mac, or friends. I had a high school boyfriend that I had a physical relationship with when I turned eighteen, but we were both virgins, and pretty clueless, and we broke it off after a month or two. I was really busy taking care of Mac while he was sick, and before he passed away. At Stanford, I told you there really wasn't anybody, either. And then, there was the kidnapping incident and the rebel leader. Dammit! I'm trying to tell you I have no idea how to seduce someone. That I've never had hot, sweaty, wild sex. I've never felt the way I do when I look at you," I finished in a rush.

"Taylor," he said, and then he stopped like he didn't know what the hell else to say.

I went on, "Hudson, what I meant downstairs earlier is that I want you, too, and I feel the same things you do, but I wouldn't have any idea where to start or what to do if I *could* get you naked."

Chapter 18

Hudson

For the very first time in my life, I was pretty much speechless. It took a few minutes for the truth to sink into my brain.

Taylor hadn't been trying to say she wasn't sure if she wanted *me*.

She'd been trying to convey the fact that she was…inexperienced.

Her first sexual experience had been with a guy who had no clue how to work her body into a frenzy.

Her only other sexual contact had been with an animal who had repeatedly taken her body in hatred against her will.

"Um…maybe I shouldn't have said anything," Taylor said, sounding uncomfortable as she moved to get to her feet.

I snagged her waist and pulled her back to my side.

"Oh no, you don't," I growled. "I'm not letting you drop that bomb on me, and then take off like you never said it."

Since just thinking about her being trapped and helpless made my gut burn, I took one of her legs and pulled it over my lap until she was straddling me.

Much better. Now, I could see her face.

Jesus Christ! She was beautiful. Her hair was loose, all those glorious flame-colored curls were falling down around her shoulders, but I gritted my teeth and tried not to let that get me distracted. "So what you were really trying to say is that even though you're not a virgin, you're sexually inexperienced?" I questioned.

I watched as she swallowed hard, and then nodded before she murmured, "You could probably make that totally ignorant. The will is there, and every time I look at you, I want to crawl up this hot body of yours and beg you to fuck me, but after that, I'm clueless. I know that's kind of crazy for a woman who is twenty-eight years old, but yeah, I don't know a single thing about real passion."

Fuck! I wanted to teach her every damn thing she wanted to know, and then some, but I kept reminding myself that now *wasn't* the time. It was a miracle that she could even *feel* desire after what she'd been through.

We were going to take all this shit slow. *Very slow.*

I nearly groaned when she wiggled her ass a little. My dick was as hard as a rock, and every time she moved...

"What do you want from me, Taylor?" I asked, my voice hoarse with desire.

She wrapped her arms around my neck slowly, her green-eyed gaze locked with mine as she said earnestly, "Everything and nothing. I don't care about your money, Hudson, although if you'd care to let me have your body, you won't hear me complaining. I don't need you take care of me, anymore. I just want...you. I think you're the only one who can show me everything I've been missing all these years."

My pulse was thundering as I looked into Taylor's eyes, and saw the same intense hunger that had been kicking my ass for days. "I don't want to rush this, Taylor. You need to get over the trauma of what happened to you in Lania. When I talked to you outside, I just wanted you to know how I felt, why I act the way I do sometimes, why I'm not always rational when it comes to you, *and* why I *can't* be your goddamn friend."

I reached out and threaded my hands through her hair, letting the silky strands flow between my fingers. It was impossible for me to be this close to her and *not* touch her.

"I'm going to be fine, Hudson. Trust me," she murmured as she stroked her fingers over the nape of my neck. "I have an awesome counselor, and I've always known the difference between those assaults and the way I feel when I'm with you. It's not like I didn't know it would be different someday with somebody I really wanted. I guess I just didn't know I'd start feeling that way when I least expected it."

I searched her face. "I think you're probably the most incredible woman I've ever known, Taylor Delaney. Life has given you nothing but shit, and you still somehow feel like it has some kind of value. How do you find the good when there's been so much bad?"

"It wasn't always bad," she said with a small shake of her head. "Just the early stuff. Losing Mac was hard, but he made me strong enough to get through it."

She smiled, and my whole goddamn world turned upside down.

At that exact moment, I completely understood why guys like Mason and Seth were willing to move mountains to make sure their women were happy.

Because I knew damn well I was never going to be content if Taylor *wasn't* smiling in the future.

She should be getting every bit of joy possible after the whole damn world had let her down as a kid. Only one elderly man had actually seen Taylor's pain, and tried to fix it, but he'd only been able to stay with her for a short period of time.

Well, fuck that! I wasn't going anywhere until she was sick of my surly ass, and in the meantime, I'd make damn sure she got *whatever* she wanted.

"I'm about to ask for one of those favors you so generously offered, sweetheart," I warned her.

Still smiling, she stared into my eyes and said, "Name it."

"Favor number one," I said. "If you don't feel it's ethically or morally wrong, would you fucking kiss me before I lose my damn mind?"

Maybe I wasn't about to maul her like a wild animal, but I needed that damn kiss like I needed to take my next breath right now.

However, I needed *her* to make that first move, so she had control.

Still smiling, she nodded. "I want to touch you, Hudson. Is that okay?"

Oh, fuck, yeah. "My body is all yours, baby," I assured her.

I watched her face as she ran her palms across my shoulders and down my chest, exploring every bare inch of skin she could find. "You feel so good, Hudson. Your body is so beautiful," she said in a suddenly sensual *fuck-me* voice before she finally leaned into me, and placed her lips on mine.

Once she'd made that first move, I lost it.

I fisted my hands in her hair, and really tasted the full, plump lips that I'd only been able to fantasize about.

Until now...

I plundered.

I tasted.

I absorbed.

When she moaned against my lips, it felt like a siren's call for me to give her what she needed, and it gnawed at my entire body because I wasn't willing to push things that far.

Not yet.

Because if there was one thing I wanted more from Taylor than to fuck her, it was her complete and total trust that I was *never* going to hurt her.

I had to let her set the pace. It didn't matter that my dick was always ready to rush to the finish line when it came to Taylor.

She'd come to *me* tonight. Taylor had told me every painful thing that had ever happened to her.

I wasn't about to fuck this whole thing up by allowing my lust to have free rein.

I buried my face in her neck, savoring the softness I found there, and the taste of her soft skin.

She tasted like sin, white-hot pleasure, and smoldering passion, and she smelled like blatant, rampant desire, mixed with a faint hint of citrus and flowers. I knew I'd never be able to get close to her again without the scent of this alluring female driving me fucking insane.

"Oh, God, Hudson," she moaned in a throaty, sultry voice as she speared her hands into my hair, and turned her head so I had better access to let my lips and tongue roam.

Hearing my name on her lips, in that tone of voice, almost broke me.

I could fill in most of the other things I really wanted to hear.

I want you so much, Hudson.

Fuck me, Hudson.

Taste me, Hudson.

Yes, Hudson, yesssss!

I'm coming, Hudson.

"Shit!" I cursed as I lifted my head.

Three little words had left her lips, and my imagination was having a damn field day.

I was panting like I'd just finished a marathon in record time as I looked into her passion-glazed eyes.

I wrapped my arms around her, pulled her body flush with mine, and closed my eyes as I put my lips close to her ear and said in a harsh whisper, "Not yet, sweetheart. Not now. Maybe once you've completely healed and you know exactly what you want."

"I want you, Hudson Montgomery," she said softly as she rested against me. "I already know that."

I held back a groan of sexual frustration.

Yeah, she said that *now*, but how would she feel when my cock was actually inside her, exactly where it wanted to be right now?

I was only going to get one shot at slowly teaching her just how good it could be, giving her memories that were a hell of a lot better than she had right now.

"I want that, too, sweetheart," I assured her. "Don't think for a single second that I don't want to fuck you, but you need to understand exactly what that means when and if I do."

If I got my dick inside her, everything would change.

It would be hot and hard, which wasn't something an inexperienced woman probably needed. But I wanted Taylor so damn much that no matter how much I tried, it couldn't be any other way the first time I sank into her body.

After that, she'd be mine.

I wasn't sure I could *ever* let her go after I'd been inside her gorgeous body.

And right now, Taylor needed choices.

"What would it mean?" she said in a sleepy voice, not sounding the least bit daunted.

"It means it's time for bed. You in your bed, and me in mine," I answered firmly as I stood up, scooped her up, and carried her upstairs.

Chapter 19

Taylor

"S o what did you tell your sister about me?" I asked the following afternoon as Hudson and I were in the kitchen, getting ready to leave his house for Riley's barbeque.

I'd decided to wear my best pair of skinny jeans, a lavender summer top, and white casual sandals. I'd done a fancy, fat braid to tame my unruly hair. It had been a relief to see Hudson dressed just as casually in indigo jeans and a short-sleeve gray Henley that matched his eyes, and hugged every rippling muscle in his torso and powerful arms.

Honestly, it didn't matter what Hudson was wearing, or not wearing, the man took my breath away.

"As close to the truth as possible," he replied. "I told her about the kidnapping, and that you were recovering here with me. Riley won't tell anyone. She doesn't know about Last Hope, or that Jax and I were there for the rescue. In the beginning, when we were gone on a lot of missions, Jax started spinning tales to Riley about us being treasure hunters to explain us being gone and out of contact when we were on a case, and it stuck. She just doesn't know we were hunting human treasure and not lost gold or artifacts."

"If you trust her with secrets, why haven't you told her?" I questioned curiously.

"Riley worried a lot when we were all in Special Forces in the military," he explained. "She was ecstatic when we were all discharged and came back to San Diego to take our places at Montgomery Mining. There wasn't a single one of us who wanted her to know that we were doing more of the same, as civilians this time."

"But now that you aren't traveling as much, couldn't you tell her?"

He shrugged. "She'd be hurt and pissed off that we didn't tell her in the first place, so we're kind of fucked."

I smiled as Hudson slipped his feet into a pair of casual shoes. "Are you more concerned about her being hurt, or being angry?"

He shot me a mischievous grin that made my heart skitter. "She's happy now, and we don't want to screw that up, but Riley can be pretty fierce sometimes. Most of her work as an attorney revolves around wildlife conservation, and I'd rather she continue to rip up large corporations that put profits over conservation than turn that anger toward me."

Okay, so that surprised me. I'd expected Riley to be some kind of business or corporate attorney, not a woman who fought *against* them for animal rights.

I couldn't help but find it a little amusing that her three older brothers, all alpha men who weren't afraid to risk their own lives to save others, were worried about how their little sister would deal with the fact that they'd fabricated stories that weren't true. "She sounds amazing," I said with a sigh. "And she's as beautiful as she is accomplished."

I'd seen pictures of all of Hudson's siblings around the house. Riley was absolutely gorgeous, just like all her brothers.

"She is," Hudson agreed nonchalantly as he prowled closer to me. "Just like another stunning redhead I know."

My breath caught as he placed a hand on both sides of my body, trapping me against the counter I was leaning on.

I shook my head slowly as I met Hudson's intense, heated gaze. "I'm not beautiful. And now I have a couple of scars to go with the ugly freckles that never disappeared when I hit adulthood."

I'd actually used one of the few foundation makeups my skin could tolerate to try to cover the small scars on my face, but it hadn't completely erased the angry red marks.

"You're never going to convince me that you aren't the most gorgeous woman on the planet," Hudson said with hoarse conviction in his voice as he put his hand on my face, and stroked one of the scars gently with his thumb. "So you might as well stop trying, sweetheart. Those little leftover freckles on your adorable face make me want to explore your entire body to see how many more I can find in *other* places. And these tiny scars are always going to get my cock hard because every time I see them, I'm going to be thinking about what a fucking extraordinary woman you are."

My heart was racing as Hudson stroked his thumb over the second small scar on my face. "You're crazy," I said breathlessly as I wrapped my arms around his neck.

I wasn't quite sure how to handle having this big, breathtakingly handsome man looking at me like he was right now.

I knew I wasn't beautiful, yet Hudson made me feel like I was a beauty queen.

Maybe I'd never cared all that much if a guy looked at me with lust in his eyes before, but then, none of those guys had been Hudson Montgomery, either.

Now, I did care, and the way this man looked at me like he wanted to devour me whole was so damn heady that all I could do was drown in his masculine scent and wallow in the heat of his powerful body.

"I'm beyond crazy, sweetheart," he muttered. "You sent me straight to insanity. Worse yet, I don't even give a damn that you did it. Do you want to know what fantasy I used to get myself off after I sent you off to bed last night?"

Oh, God, yes, I wanted to know. "Tell me."

"My head between those beautiful thighs of yours, teasing your gorgeous pussy until you were squirming, panting and screaming my name while you came. You could say we came...together," he finished in a low, sensual tone next to my ear right before he nipped my earlobe.

I closed my eyes as *that* visual flooded into my mind. "I've never—"

"You'd love it," Hudson interrupted. "In my fantasy, you were begging me to make you come."

Slick molten heat flowed between my thighs, and my nipples were so hard that it was almost painful.

Okay. Yes. I masturbated, and I'd been doing a lot of it lately, but my imagination wasn't quite as vivid as Hudson's.

Probably because he knew a lot more about hot and dirty than I did.

My body was on fire, and it was demanding a satisfaction that only Hudson could provide.

His mouth skimmed from my ear to my lips before he took my mouth with an insistent force that completely consumed me.

He kissed me like he needed to brand me, claim me, and there was nothing I wanted more than to be...his.

Hell, yes, I'd beg him to make me come.

I'd scream his name.

I'd be so lost to the pleasure of Hudson touching me that I'd end up completely mindless.

I let out a hungry moan against his lips, and speared my hands into his hair.

Needing more.

Needing...him.

I was panting when he released my mouth, grabbed the braid of hair at the back of my head, and pulled it so my head tilted to give him better access to my sensitive neck.

My entire body started to tremble with need as his tongue stroked over my heated skin.

"Hudson," I said on a long groan. "Please. I need... I need..."

"You need me," he rasped into my ear, one big hand smoothing up my back. "Jesus Christ, Taylor. Don't you *ever* wear a bra?"

I shook my head helplessly. "Don't need it. Too small."

His hands cupped my breasts, each of his thumbs teasing the hard peaks of my nipples. "They're fucking perfect," he said in a harsh voice.

I squeaked as he lightly pinched one nipple, and then stroked it with a soothing, circular motion.

My hands fisted hard in his short hair, my entire body tight with desire as he moved a hand down to the zipper of my jeans.

"Oh, God, Hu—"

My words were completely swallowed when his mouth crashed down on mine, and I lost every thought in my head as his fingers slipped into my panties, and stroked over my throbbing clit.

He tore his mouth from mine before he cursed, "You're so fucking wet."

"Because I want you too damn much," I hissed.

"You could never want me too much," he denied huskily. "Come for me, sweetheart. I'll make that ache go away."

I gasped as he put more pressure on that tiny bundle of nerves, each slick caress of his fingers getting harder and faster.

He was relentless. When he buried his face in my neck again, and started nipping and licking my skin, my head fell back, and I arched hard against him.

My climax happened hard and fast.

"Hudson, yes!" I cried, abandoning all attempts to gain any semblance of control.

My body imploded, and then shuddered as he grasped my ass and pulled me against him until I could feel his very large, steely erection straining against the zipper of his jeans.

I felt utterly overwhelmed as he cradled my body against his muscular form while I tried to get my out-of-control heartrate and breathing back to normal.

I ran my hands down his back, and then up under his shirt, drowning in his masculine scent, and the feel of his hot, bare skin.

He let out a long breath beside my ear. His tone was deliciously wicked as he said hoarsely, "Making you come was probably the best thing I've ever done in a very long time."

"I'd really like to return the favor," I whispered as I tried to get to the front of his body with my hand.

He took both of my wrists and firmly drew my arms around his neck, and I knew he'd done it to get my hands away from his cock.

"You'd be playing with fire, sweetheart," he growled. "Not happening."

I kissed his sensual lips tenderly before I said, "I think I could handle watching you go up in flames."

Not only could I deal with watching Hudson lose control, I'd relish every moment of it.

He kept such a tight leash on himself, trying to control his every emotion, that I'd like to see him completely let go.

"We'll see," he grunted. "Once you're healed."

He took my face between his palms and kissed first one scar on my face, and then the other.

His actions were so tender that they brought tears to my eyes.

Maybe because I knew, deep in my gut, that Hudson really did find me completely irresistible.

He saw some kind of beauty in me that I didn't see when I looked in the mirror at myself.

"Thank you," I murmured as he pulled back and our eyes met.

"For what?" he asked, quirking a brow in question. "For making you come? Baby, I assure you, that pleasure was all mine."

Thank you for wanting me.

Thank you for seeing me.

Thank you for taking care of me.

Thank you for rescuing me.

Thank you for understanding me when I hardly comprehended my own reactions.

Thank you for desiring me.

Thank you for being the hottest damn friend I've ever had.

Thank you for being...you.

One thing Hudson had been wrong about was when he'd declared that he couldn't see me as a friend.

We *were* friends, and he'd never convince me otherwise.

I could tell him almost anything, and *know* he wasn't ever going to see me any differently after those words were spoken.

If it was a painful confession, he'd just hold me and tell me everything was going to be okay.

If I was out of sorts, he'd make me feel comfortable.

If I was sad, he'd try to cheer me up.

That was friendship, and no matter how much we wanted carnal knowledge of each other's bodies, that solid base of comradery and affection would always be there.

It would for me, anyway.

I'd always been able to see beyond the workaholic, the billionaire businessman who ran his empire with a very firm hand, the alpha male with bossy tendencies, and his façade of being a guy who didn't need anything or anyone.

Maybe he fooled most people, but not me. Hudson had his own needs beneath that powerful, cool veneer he showed to most of the world.

The guy carried a lot of guilt. He took on every responsibility people threw at him, and then asked for more. Hudson was a perfectionist when it came to his own actions, but he could easily forgive so many flaws in other people. He was intrinsically kind, however, for some reason, he didn't think he deserved to get some of that thoughtfulness back.

I saw Hudson as a man, because beneath that sometimes cranky, billionaire businessman disguise, he needed somebody to see…him.

I took his head between my palms, and put a light kiss on his sensuous lips before I finally answered, "Thank you for being the most incredible guy I've ever known, Hudson Montgomery."

He grinned. "Sweetheart, if I'd known that making you come was going to get you to kiss me this much, I would have tried it earlier."

I laughed because Hudson's sexually playful side was so damn irresistible. "My turn to touch you next time," I said in a flirty tone I didn't know I possessed. "We better get going or we'll be late for the party."

I fixed the zipper of my jeans while I watched Hudson shove his wallet in his back pocket, and grab his keys as he drawled, "Didn't I already warn you about playing with fire?"

I smiled as I grabbed my purse, not nearly as nervous about meeting Riley and Cooper as I thought I'd be.

"Maybe you've made me into a pyromaniac," I teased.

Our relationship had been so one-sided since the very beginning, and I hated that. Hudson had done all the giving, all the sacrificing. Whether he realized it or not, I was healing, and I was doing well. I was entirely ready to balance the scales.

I wanted to see Hudson smile.

I wanted to lighten the load for him, and see him more relaxed.

Hudson had been born into a world that had expected perfection from him at a very young age.

It was beyond time for him to realize that *he* deserved to be happy, and that he didn't need to be flawless.

Somehow, I was going to be the one to teach him that.

Because, somewhere between his incredible rescue that had saved my life, and this very moment, I suddenly realized that I'd fallen head over heels in love with Hudson Montgomery.

Chapter 20

Hudson

I watched Taylor as she picked up a handful of sand. She carefully let it spill out between her fingers while she talked to Maya Sinclair, her expression lively and animated.

Maya was the young daughter of Aiden Sinclair, Seth's brother, and the little girl looked transfixed as she watched and listened to Taylor. The two females both sat cross-legged on the sandy beach near the back patio of Riley and Seth's home.

From my patio lounger, I couldn't hear a damn thing they were saying, but since both of them were smiling, I didn't give a fuck what they were talking about.

As expected, everyone at the casual barbeque had seemed to adore Taylor, especially Riley and Cooper.

Honestly, I'd been surprised by how easily Taylor had pried Cooper out of his usual, introverted self.

"You look like a guy who could use a beer," Seth joked as he held out a cold bottle, and flopped into the lounge chair next to me, holding a half-empty beer of his own in his other hand.

"Thanks," I said as I took the cold brew from him. "It's hotter than hell today."

"It's summer in Southern California," Seth said nonchalantly. "There isn't much of a breeze today coming off the water, so it just feels hotter." He paused for a moment before he nodded toward Maya and Taylor. "Those two look like they're becoming fast friends. It looks like Taylor is teaching Maya something about the sand or the beach, and Maya is loving every minute of it."

I nodded. Maya had always been scholastically advanced for her age, so she'd probably have no problem following anything Taylor was trying to teach her. "I don't doubt it," I responded. "Taylor is an environmental geologist, and Maya has always loved Earth science."

Seth snorted. "That little smarty pants loves *any* science. Period. She's way too smart for a kid her age. And Taylor is brilliant. I heard her talking geology to Cooper earlier, but that discussion was way over my head. A guy who never got past a high school diploma didn't stand a chance of joining that conversation."

I pulled my eyes away from Taylor long enough to send Seth a quick glance. He looked perfectly happy that he hadn't understood a damn thing that Cooper and Taylor had been discussing. "I'm sure they would have been happy to explain it. Please don't start the I-only-have-a-high-school-diploma bullshit with me. You're one of the smartest guys I know."

While it was true that Seth hadn't gone to college, it hadn't stopped him from building his own commercial real estate and construction empire. He sucked in knowledge faster than anyone I knew, including me, and he'd learned the construction business from the ground up.

At one time, my sister's husband had been a construction worker just trying to get by and help raise his younger siblings. I had a lot of respect for Seth. I just didn't tell him that very often.

"That's high praise coming from you," Seth mused. "You must be in a good mood today. Does it have anything to do with the pretty redhead you haven't taken your eyes off of since the minute you got here?"

"None of your business, and who said I was in a good mood?" I grumbled.

"Oh, come on, Hudson, you've never brought a date to any of Riley's parties, and you've never looked at a woman like you do Taylor. I'm a guy who is, and always will be, madly in love with my wife. I know the signs. Plus, she is staying with you right now. When is the last time you had a woman at your place?"

I took a long slug of beer before I answered. "Never."

"Exactly. Why now?"

"Riley didn't tell you?" I asked skeptically.

Seth shot me a puzzled look. "Tell me what?"

Either Seth deserved an Academy Award, or Riley hadn't even shared the kidnapping incident with her own husband because I'd asked her to keep it a secret.

I looked around. Seth and I were well away from the rest of the partygoers. Everyone else was either in the water, on the beach, or hanging out near the food and bar.

I hadn't meant that Riley couldn't tell *Seth*, so I quickly explained what had happened to Taylor, minus her sexual assault, Last Hope's involvement, and my part in the rescue. "She's a Montgomery Mining intern, so yeah, she's recovering at my place. The woman went through hell. It was the least I could do," I said, finishing the explanation.

"Jesus!" Seth cursed. "I haven't heard a single word about the kidnapping of any of your employees, much less three of them."

"We'd like to keep it that way," I warned. "It would make it a lot harder on Mark's family, Harlow, and Taylor if they were being hounded by the press. The U.S. government isn't eager for it get out, either, so it hasn't been difficult to keep things quiet."

"I'm sure as shit not going to tell anyone, and apparently Riley already knows," Seth commented. "Taylor looks incredible for being not quite a month out from that incident. It must have been hell for her."

"It was," I agreed. "I dealt with Lanian rebels when I was in Special Forces, and they aren't exactly known for their humane treatment of hostages. Taylor is doing incredibly well."

I gave Seth as much information as I could about the kidnapping, how she'd tried to escape, and the state Taylor had been in after she'd been rescued.

"So was she helped by the Lanian government?" Seth asked curiously.

"You could say that," I answered evasively. It wasn't exactly a lie. Prince Nick had brought the doctor and supplies. I knew Seth was talking about her initial recovery, but if he wanted to think some Lanian covert team got Taylor to safety, I was fine with that. "I sent my jet to transport her back to the U.S. and I ended up offering her a place to stay while she recovered."

Not exactly a lie.

"No wonder you're crazy about her," Seth answered. "You'd never even know something like that happened to her. She's so damn friendly and sweet to everybody."

"Who said I'm crazy about her?" I sent him a stare that would intimidate most people.

But not Seth. He stared right back at me, and raised an eyebrow as he said, "Cut the bullshit, Hudson. Like I said, I know the signs. There's nothing wrong with being enamored with a woman like Taylor. She's pretty, resilient, highly intelligent, and she appears to look at you the same way you look at her."

"I like her. Probably have since the moment we met, but I liked her a hell of a lot more once she kicked Jax's ass at chess," I joked.

Seth's eyes widened. "How in the hell did that happen?"

"She was taught by Mac Tanaka, a legendary chess Grand Master, and Jax got way too cocky," I told him.

Seth snorted. "I would have given at least a million bucks to see that. Riley said that Taylor is a Tai Chi master, too. A woman of many talents, which makes her very intriguing."

"She's real, dammit! She isn't impressed by the Montgomery name, or my money, and she's not the least bit intimidated by any of that, or me. When she looks at me, she just sees…me, and she's pretty damn tolerant about every single one of my goddamn faults. If you really want to know how I feel about her, yeah, I'm crazy about her. I didn't mean for that to happen, but I couldn't very well stop it once it started. Are you happy, now?" I sent Seth a disgruntled look.

He swallowed a mouthful of beer before he answered, "The question is...are you happy, Hudson? It really doesn't matter how anyone else feels. But just for the record, yeah, I'm pretty damn thrilled that you met a woman like Taylor. You deserve someone who cares about you, and not your money or the Montgomery name. So what are you going to do about it now?"

I shrugged. "What can I do? Taylor is still recovering. I'm hoping I can talk her into a permanent position at Montgomery Mining, but she's been resistant about that so far because she doesn't feel like she has the experience to be part of the Montgomery lab team. I think she feels like I'm doing her a favor, which I'm not. She'd be an amazing asset to our lab and research center. She's definitely sweet, but the woman is stubborn as hell sometimes."

I watched as Jax strolled over to where Maya and Taylor were sitting, and exchanged a couple of words with the two of them.

Maya got up with an enormous smile, and ran toward the house.

My guess was that Jax had given Maya a fun errand to run so he could chat with Taylor for a few minutes.

"Looks like Jax is making some kind of move," Seth said in a thoughtful voice. "Does he already know..."

"He knows," I assured Seth. "He's going to try to talk her into taking a permanent position with Montgomery, too. He wants her to stay. She's too damn intelligent to let go of without a fight to keep her with us."

"I think you need to fight just as hard to keep her with *you*, Hudson," Seth suggested.

I continued to watch Jax and Taylor. They seemed like they were in an earnest discussion. "Put yourself in my shoes," I told Seth. "The woman was just held hostage, she was beaten and abused, and she's still trying to get her bearings after the entire incident. It doesn't matter how damn badly I want her; she just isn't ready for anything more than friendship right now."

"So be her best friend," Seth answered. "And then convince her that you want a hell of a lot more. Look, I know she probably has lingering issues and fears that nothing but time will fix, but I really don't think she's irrevocably damaged, Hudson. In fact, she seems more together than most people I know. Let *her* decide exactly what she wants, and what she's ready to do. I'm telling you; she looks at you the same way you look at her. I think she wants more, just like you do."

"I told you, Seth, I was her caretaker in the beginning. She's probably just grateful—"

"Oh, hell, no!" Seth interrupted. "Don't even go there, Hudson. This isn't some kind of hero-worship for her. She's eying you like you're some kind of irresistible dessert that she can't wait to sample. Give me a break. I know that damn look, and it's enough to make a guy completely insane. Since I'm married to your little sister, that's all I'm going to say on that particular subject, but please get real. Gratitude and desire are two totally different things."

I crossed my arms over my chest as I confessed, "I hate feeling this way. How in the hell can I want to fuck a woman so damn desperately when she's fresh out of a hostage situation? This entire situation is messed up. Taylor deserves so much better than...me."

"Because sometimes," Seth said solemnly. "When you find the woman you can't live without, you don't care how much shit you have to go through to make her yours. And you know damn well it's not just physical, Hudson. Maybe you don't want to admit it, but how in the hell would you feel if she met someone else she wouldn't mind dating."

"I'd fucking lose it," I admitted hoarsely. "Taylor is mine."

Seth nodded slowly, like he completely got me.

"When I first met Riley," Seth said in a low, serious tone. "I sure as hell didn't want to complicate my life, and the very last thing I thought I needed was to fall in love with the pain-in-the-ass female attorney standing between me and a prime piece of real estate I wanted. But it didn't take me long to realize that it didn't matter if she was my temporary enemy, because I knew damn well we couldn't stay adversaries for long. Hell, yes, we both fought that attraction. Hard. But looking back now, somewhere deep in my gut, underneath all that animosity, I recognized the fact I'd actually been waiting for Riley my entire life. She was it for me. She was the one. Once my brain and my heart caught up with my gut instincts, there was nothing I wouldn't do to make her mine. I had to because there wasn't and never will be another Riley out there for me. It was all or nothing. Luckily, I eventually found out that she felt the same way, and we had to go through a lot of crap to get to our happy ending, but I'd do it all over again and more if it meant that in the end, I'd have Riley. I love her, and if I ever lost her, I'd be one sorry bastard who was just taking up space on the planet. She makes me the man I am today, and I'm not the least bit ashamed to admit it. Before her, I wasn't a big believer in fate, but I do think that Riley and I were always meant to be together. I guess if we'd fucked that up, we would have made our own destinies, but my life would suck without her, which is why I never take a single moment I spend with her for granted. Ever."

I sat there completely stunned for a moment because Seth had never even come close to being this candid with me. We razzed each other a lot, enjoyed each other's company, talked a lot about business and current events, but he hadn't spilled his guts to me since the day he'd promised he'd always love and take care of my little sister when he and Riley got engaged. Even then, he'd never been quite *this* heartfelt about the way he felt about Riley.

Yeah, it was pretty damn obvious that he adored her, and that she returned that affection.

Hell, maybe he'd figured I wouldn't understand, and maybe a few months ago, I wouldn't have comprehended how a man could feel that way.

But now…I did, and I knew it must have been agonizing for Seth when he'd found out that my father had repeatedly molested Riley as a child. "I think that she may have been waiting for you, too," I said in a raw voice. "When she couldn't tell a single soul about what my father did, she was finally able to tell you. I don't know how in the hell you got her through something so painful that she'd had to bury it all those years, but I'm damn glad you did."

Seth shrugged. "All I really did was love her, and tried to make her see that none of it was her fault. Even if she melts down, even when she seems fragile, at her core, Riley is a strong, incredibly intelligent woman. She figures it out. I'm pretty much just there for backup when she needs me." He hesitated before he added, "I have a gut instinct that Taylor is the same way, even though I barely know her. Be there for her, Hudson. Let her cry on your shoulder when she needs it, but have faith that she'll eventually work through it because she's independent and courageous. And for God's sake, don't assume you know how she feels. You don't—unless it comes directly from her mouth. When she tells you something, listen, and take it as the truth instead of overthinking everything."

I wasn't sure how I knew it, but I had absolutely no doubt in my mind that Seth had discerned the fact that Taylor had been a victim of sexual abuse while she was a captive. It was definitely something I never would have shared with him, or anyone for that matter, but it was probably a logical conclusion on his part since he did know that Taylor had been tormented in every other way during her imprisonment in Lania.

I sent him a cautious glance. "It's too soon," I rasped.

He looked back at me with an empathetic expression. "In your mind, maybe. But I think you need to let Taylor make that final decision. Look, you're in one hell of a bad position right now. I get it. But don't let your concern look like a rejection to her if you really want her. No woman on Earth wants to feel undesirable after something like that happens."

I nodded sharply. "We talk. She knows I'm attracted to her, I guess I'm just..."

"Worried that she doesn't feel the same way?" Seth guessed. "Dude, no offense, but I think I can safely say that, judging by the way she looks at you, deep gratitude *isn't* what she's thinking about."

I chugged the last of my beer before I asked, "How in the hell did you ever get through all this? Taylor makes me completely insane, and I used to be a really rational man. I'm not the kind of guy who loses his shit over a woman. Never have, and never thought I would."

Seth grinned. "The right woman will topple some of the toughest guys in the world. Personally, I feel sorry for the poor bastards who think they could never feel that way, and haven't gotten as lucky as me."

"It's hard to feel fortuitous when your balls are turning blue," I grumbled.

Seth chuckled at my misery before he said, "Uh-oh. It looks like Riley can't wait another minute to have a little talk with Taylor alone."

My eyes flew back to the spot where Jax had been having a discussion with Taylor moments ago. Maya and Jax were there eating ice cream—which Jax had probably asked the little girl to get for them so he could get a few minutes alone with Taylor.

I groaned as I saw two redheads strolling down toward the pier. "Do I need to rescue Taylor?" I asked Seth.

Seth shook his head as he rose from the lounger. "Nah. You're safe. Riley seems to like Taylor. If she didn't, you might have to worry. I'm grabbing another beer. I'm not up for volleyball right now. It's too hot."

"Bring me one. I think I need it," I told Seth. "I don't think I want to know what they're talking about right now."

"You already know. This is Riley we're talking about," he called back. "And Taylor is the first woman she's seen you with in a very long time."

Yeah, I knew my little sister, and that's *exactly* what worried me.

Chapter 21

Taylor

I liked Riley Sinclair almost immediately.

Yeah, she was gorgeous, but there didn't appear to be a snobby bone in her body, and she had a beautiful, genuine smile.

She looked at me as we walked down the beach, unable to hide the very real concern in her eyes as she asked, "Are you really okay after everything you've been through? The kidnapping must have been traumatic."

I smiled at her. "It's going to take some time to get back into the physical shape I was in before it happened, and I still have nightmares sometimes, but honestly, I'm doing fine, otherwise. I'm actually just grateful I'm alive most of the time."

"Are you comfortable at Hudson's place?" she questioned hesitantly.

"How could I *not* be," I said with a laugh. "He has a gorgeous home right on the beach, just like you do. It's quiet, he has a lot of privacy, and the man can cook. What else could I ask for? Your brother has been incredibly supportive. I'm not quite sure what I would have done without him."

"Well," Riley said, stretching the word out. "Hudson can be a little…"

"Surly? Grumpy? Bossy? Yeah, I noticed, but he's only that way on the surface. He has a good heart. Hudson is an amazing man. I'm just not sure he sees himself that way."

Riley nodded. "He works too hard, sleeps too little, shoulders way too much responsibility, and you're the first woman he's ever brought over for one of my get-togethers. Ever."

"Really," I asked. "I wonder why."

Riley let out a long breath. "Maybe this will sound a little weird, but it isn't all that easy to be born into money, and have a last name that has a ton of expectations along with it. It makes it really hard to separate the people who really like you from the ones who just really want your money or your name. I think Hudson just gave up on dating after he'd been hurt a few times by women who didn't give a damn about him. All they cared about was his money and his social status."

"I'm not quite sure how *any* woman could fail to see what an amazing man Hudson is underneath all of his wealth and power. He's actually incredibly humble, he's brilliant, he's witty, and genuinely kind. I think those qualities are a lot more important than his bank account," I said a little indignantly.

It really bothered me that not a single female he'd dated had seen *him*.

"I completely agree," Riley said firmly. "But in our world, it's really hard to meet somebody who *doesn't* give a damn about status and money."

"You did," I reminded her.

"Seth is…special," Riley said in a voice that completely revealed how much she loved her husband. "He grew up poor and worked hard to take care of his family. He knew what his priorities were, and what was really important *before* he inherited a fortune. Seth grew up in a house full of love, even though they didn't have much money. We…didn't. Our parents didn't give a damn about any of us. They were abusive, and completely superficial. Because my brothers were all mentally gifted, they were shipped off to a boarding school when they were very young, and were expected to act like adults."

"So none of you really had a childhood," I said sadly.

"No," she answered solemnly. "My father molested me as a child, which made my entire childhood traumatic, and the boys were shipped off to a place that didn't care about anything except academic achievement."

"Oh, God, Riley," I said in a horrified tone. "I'm so sorry about what happened to you."

"Don't be," she requested. "It doesn't matter anymore. My father has been dead for a long time, and my mother might as well be because none of us speak to her after we found out that she knew what my father was doing, but ignored it so it wouldn't sully the Montgomery name. I only told you so you'd understand what a screwed-up family we had."

We walked silently for a few moments before I said, "I can kind of understand. I grew up in foster care after my parents both died in a homicide-suicide incident when I was four. I was shipped from foster home to foster home until I finally found a permanent home when I was eleven. Things got a lot better for me after that, but it does a number on your psyche to grow up feeling unwanted and unloved."

"It absolutely does," Riley agreed. "Why didn't anyone adopt you?"

I laughed. "I was a completely unattractive redheaded wild child, and more likely to slug somebody who was teasing me than to cry about it. I spent most of those earlier years angry, terrified and feeling totally unlovable."

"I don't blame you," Riley replied. "But you're a beautiful woman, Taylor. I have a very hard time believing you weren't a cute kid."

"Believe it," I said flatly. "I had enormous glasses that never fit, a face full of freckles, and crazy red hair. I got to lose the bad glasses after I got into a good home where my foster father bought me contact lenses, and later I had laser surgery to get rid of those, too, but I think the freckles and the crazy hair still fits. Plus, I'll end up with a couple of small scars on my face from taking a beating during my kidnapping."

Riley stopped and gently gripped my upper arm until we were face-to-face. "Those scars will barely be noticeable once they heal, and most of your freckles are gone. If those remaining freckles really still bother you, you can use a number of products or methods to get rid of them."

I rolled my eyes. "Your brother apparently thinks they're adorable. I've tried some of the products, but I have really sensitive skin, and the other stuff has been out of my reach since I've been a struggling student for six years now."

Riley smiled. "I actually think they're adorable, too. But this is about you and what makes you feel beautiful."

I could hardly tell Riley that her brother was the only thing that made me feel absolutely fuckable, but I could hardly mention *that*.

I smirked as I held my arms out away from my sides. "Do I really look like a woman who worries all that much about how I look? This is my general look every single day. Since I'm a geologist, and I'm in the field a lot. Someday, I might need some professional clothing, but until now, that hasn't been necessary."

Riley looked me up and down. "Actually, you do look like a woman who cares about how she looks. That pretty light purple color of your shirt makes your stunning green eyes pop, and you look very well put together for a casual party. You're gorgeous, Taylor, whether you realize that or not. I'd love to be as slim as you are, but I like my food too damn much."

We started walking down toward the pier again before I answered, "I lost weight in Lania, but I've regained most of it. If I continue to eat everything Hudson keeps trying to feed me, I'll blow up like a balloon."

Riley laughed before she asked, "Do you think your relationship with Hudson will continue once you're fully healed? I mean, it's obvious you care about each other, so I guess I was just hoping it might."

"I'm not sure," I answered honestly. "I care about Hudson a lot, but let's get real, I'm a new grad environmental geologist, and Hudson is...well, he's Hudson Montgomery. If it hadn't been for the kidnapping, I doubt we ever would have crossed paths in the first place. Plus, you have to admit that I'm not the kind of woman he'd usually date. So yeah, *I'd* like to see it go further, but I don't know if it will. I'm job hunting for a permanent position, and I might not even end up in California."

"If you two care about each other, you can work that out," Riley replied. "And Hudson rarely hangs out with the ultra-rich crowd unless he's forced to do it because of business obligations, or the charities he supports. None of us do, really. It's a miserable crowd for the most part. Look, I don't want to overstep my boundaries here, but I can tell Hudson's crazy about you by the way he looks at you, and I think you care about him, too."

"I do care. A lot. But I was sexually assaulted repeatedly by the rebel leader while I was being held hostage, and I think Hudson feels like I'm not ready to take this to another level right now." I hadn't meant to tell Riley about that part of my captivity, but it had flown out of my mouth anyway.

It hadn't been difficult to tell her since she'd been so candid with me.

"Oh, God, Taylor. That must have been awful."

I nodded. "It was, but I'm completely capable of understanding that the sexual assault was completely different from a relationship with mutual consent. I'm a Tai Chi master, and I've been highly trained to live in a state of mindfulness since my early-teens. That's means I've learned to always turn my attention to the present moment without judgment, and be open to new experiences and new emotions. Yes, I've had some bad dreams, and right after the kidnapping, I had flashbacks. I'm still working on that stuff with the aid of intensive counseling. My therapist told me that every person deals with trauma and sexual assault differently, and that sometimes, it can take a long time to work through it and have a normal sexual relationship. I completely understand why, and it might take me a while to deal with all of my subconscious issues, but for me, everything I went through during the kidnapping, and the way I feel about Hudson are completely *separate* experiences. I don't associate what happened in Lania with anything that happens *right now* with Hudson. For a while, I thought I was just weird, but my therapist assured me that my brain is perfectly okay, and that it's dealing with my experiences in its own, unique way. However, Hudson *doesn't* get it. I think he's still trying to protect me, even though I don't really need a caretaker anymore. Now that I've been able to go back to some of my Tai Chi practices, I'm actually more focused."

Riley rolled her eyes. "Get used to the protective behavior. Seth's protective instinct *never* went away, and I doubt Hudson's will, either. And I agree with your counselor that you should deal with your trauma and assault issues however they manifest, not like somebody else thinks you should react. Every woman is unique, with vastly different histories and experiences."

"Sometimes, I wish I had the damn sex appeal to just seduce him," I mumbled.

"Oh, you do," Riley said with a smirk. "You just haven't used those skills...yet."

Chapter 22

Taylor

One week later, I was more than ready to dig for any hidden seduction skills I had just to get Hudson to lose control.

I was completely over letting him make me come with all our clothes on. Granted, he was pretty damn creative, but it just didn't feel right to me anymore. I wanted to touch him, but every single time my eager hand reached for his cock, he stopped that action before I could even get started.

I'd made a lot of progress in evening out our lopsided relationship.

Hudson had started going into his office last Monday, so I'd happily taken over the cooking every day. Not that it was exactly a big chore since he had a kitchen that would probably make a chef weep with joy, but I also baked every single day.

Like Hudson, Mac had loved anything sweet, so I'd taught myself how to make just about every dessert on the planet. I still loved trying new recipes, but I hadn't really had the free time to do much baking during my years at Stanford.

Now, I had more free time on my hands than I wanted.

My physical therapist was cutting me loose in two weeks, and we'd scaled back my sessions to once a week since most of our work revolved around my Tai Chi routines, and making sure I could tolerate the faster, harder martial arts movements.

I'd still continue to see my therapist once a week to keep dealing with some of the trauma of the kidnapping, but I hadn't had a single nightmare since the time I'd woken up screaming.

Now that I was back into my Tai Chi every single day, my mind was much calmer, and my body was stronger. I finally felt like myself again.

"I got a job offer today," I told Hudson as we were finishing our dinner at the dining room table.

His head jerked up and he looked at me with a puzzled expression. "Where? I thought Jax talked to you last week about taking the position we have available with our conservation research team."

I sighed. Jax *had* spoken to me about that job. It was a position I coveted, and was so relevant to my specialty area, but I just didn't feel like I had the experience to accept it. "I told him I'd think about it. I already had resumes out, and I did several virtual interviews this week that went pretty well. When I did the one scheduled for today, I was offered the job on the spot."

"What company?"

I told him, and then watched as a disgusted expression formed on his face. "You'd fucking hate it," he said gruffly. "They still do mostly dirty gold mining. You wouldn't be working on remediation, prevention, or new ways to decrease the environmental impact of mining. You'd be too damn busy running from one cyanide or mercury disaster to the next. They don't give a damn about sustainable mining."

"I know. But what if I could help them change that?"

"Taylor, if you spoke up instead of towing the line with that company, they'd squash you like a bug. Don't do it," he warned ominously.

"The salary is decent, and I don't have to stay there forever."

"And where exactly would you be?"

"Their headquarters are in Nevada," I said. "I'll probably have to travel—"

"Taylor," he growled.

I closed my mouth waiting for him to speak.

"I'm about to ask you for favor number two," he rumbled in an ominous voice.

My eyes widened. "If you're going to start harping about the money again, then don't bother. I'm perfectly capable of getting a job."

God, Hudson was so amazingly hot when he started his alpha male bullshit. Not that he intimidated me at all, but watching his face when he turned into a beast made my entire body tingle in response.

He glared at me. "I already told you that I wouldn't bring that up again. But feel free to raise the subject if you're feeling ready to accept it."

"I'm not," I said adamantly. "So if it isn't about the money, let's hear it."

"I really want you to take that job at Montgomery. You know that particular team would be a great fit, and it wouldn't be the first time we've taken an intern into a permanent position. I don't want you to go with another company. Jax and Cooper are both hoping you'll decide to stay, too. This isn't me doing you a favor. I'm asking you to do one for me. You're much too intelligent to be happy in some entry level position at another company that doesn't give a damn about the geological damage they're doing."

Was Hudson asking me to do something I thought was immoral or unethical? No, no he wasn't.

He was being truthful about the fact that Montgomery had pulled outstanding interns into a permanent position, too. Harlow had started with Montgomery as an intern, and she'd advanced up the ladder over time.

I felt almost anxious at the thought of grabbing something I didn't think I'd see for years, until after I'd paid my dues in a junior position at another company.

It wasn't like I *wanted* another company. Montgomery had always been my goal for the future.

But deep inside, I didn't know if I was ready for Montgomery yet. Plus, maybe I still thought that Hudson was offering the job because of this...not-friendship-but-really-not-lovers-either kind of relationship we had going on.

I held his eyes as I answered, "Please don't tell me that you couldn't find someone more qualified than me for that job."

He shrugged. "There's always a benefit in taking on a new grad, especially one like you. It's not always great to end up with a more experienced geologist. If they haven't worked in a company like mine, it's very likely that they could have some bad habits. Plus, you are less expensive since we'd be starting you at a lower level until you get through your initial training, and the probationary period."

"How cheap will I be for you?"

Hudson nonchalantly named a starting average salary, and then told me what I'd get out of training and probation.

I gaped at him. "That's really...high."

"That's the going rate at Montgomery for that position. It's not like I'm making it up. We value your education, and we'll even offer some assistance once you've worked for us for a year to help you get your doctorate if that's what you want."

I swallowed hard.

How could I *not* take the job that was being offered to me? I'd have to be crazy if I turned him down. It was everything I wanted, including tuition assistance to do a doctorate in the future.

The salary was kind of crazy, but Montgomery had always been known as one of the best paying employers out there for geologists. "Is this really what you want? Am I really ready to jump into a team right now?"

Finished with his dinner, Hudson pushed his plate back and rested his arms on the table in front of him. "It's really what I want, Taylor. I don't want you to go somewhere else. And hell, yes, you're ready. It's not like we're going to just toss you onto the team, and expect you to sink or swim. Someone will be assigned to teach you all of our procedures so you'll feel confident once you finish that training."

"I did learn some things during the time I spent with Harlow as an intern," I mused.

"I think you owe it to yourself to give Montgomery a shot," he said roughly. "You'll always have the option to go somewhere else if it ends up not being your thing."

"Not being my thing? It's the opportunity of a lifetime for a new grad, Hudson, and I would have applied with Montgomery at some point in the future. You know that my goal is to assist in the efforts to help mining companies make the least possible impact on the environment."

He smiled. "You'll be working on that with a team of people who have the exact same goals."

My heart was racing as I finally said, "Then I'm agreeing to help you out with favor number two. When do I start?"

I watched as the tension began to disappear from Hudson's gorgeous face. "When your internship comes to an end," he said gruffly. "And there is a part two that comes with this favor."

"Hudson, I don't need another four or five weeks before I can go to work—"

"You do," he interrupted. "Christ! You've worked your ass off without a damn break for years over the last decade. You took care of Mac and held down a job for three years. After that you worked and grieved. For the next six years after that, you went to school full-time and worked. And then, instead of taking the summer off, you uprooted your life in Stanford and came here to do a demanding internship before you went to a permanent position. To top all that shit off, you ended up in a damn hostage situation where you nearly lost your life. Now that you're well and healthy again, you need to take some time to yourself, Taylor. I don't care if you do your pre-employment paperwork over the next five weeks, and you completed the basic orientation before you started as an intern, so it should be a smooth transition. Take this time to enjoy your life before you dive in headfirst into a demanding job." He paused, looking slightly apprehensive before he added, "Also, I want to help you be completely prepared. Let me help you update some of your electronics. You'll need a new laptop, an upgraded phone, etc. etc. etc. I'm not asking you to let me do that as your employer. I want to do that as me, *Hudson*, the guy who cares about you. I'd also really like it if you didn't make any plans to find your own place. Stay, Taylor. Stay with me here. Not because I'm doing you a favor, but because I'd miss you like crazy if you *weren't* here anymore."

Tears blurred my vision, but I didn't care. If there was anybody who needed to completely take some time off, it was the man sitting across the table from me right now. Instead, he was lecturing *me* about taking a vacation. Probably the most touching thing about part two of this favor was it had everything to do with me, and not Montgomery Mining. He wanted this for me because he...cared. Period. Hudson *knew* me. He *saw* me.

I wanted to crawl across this damn table, throw myself into his arms, and never leave.

But I held myself back because I had a few conditions of my own. "Nobody needs a vacation more than you do, Hudson, and I'm not talking about taking time off for family obligations, weddings, get-togethers or parties. I want to spend time with *you*, Hudson, and I want to see you relax. I want at least two weeks. I'll give you an hour in your office every morning, but after that, you're mine."

His eyes grew stormy, like he'd be perfectly happy to put himself into my hands. "Done," he agreed readily. "Hell, I'm already yours anyway."

My heart tripped as I saw the possessive look in those molten gray eyes of his.

Although he should already understand how much I wanted him, how I was already his, too, I wasn't sure he quite understood exactly how I felt.

Maybe I hadn't opened up enough for him to know, but I planned on rectifying that miscommunication as soon as possible.

"Deal," I murmured as I tried to figure out exactly how I was going to get Hudson naked.

Chapter 23

Hudson

L ater that night, I stepped into the shower, my cock aching and swollen, and fucking begging for relief.

Every damn night, I told myself that I could hold off a little while longer before I pushed Taylor for more than hot and heavy make out sessions that always left her coming at the very end.

There was nothing I loved more than watching her when she climaxed, knowing it was *me* who had driven her into that frenzy, but it left me blue-balled and frustrated, too.

I washed my body, and then my hair, Taylor's helpless cries of pleasure still ringing in my ears.

God dammit! The woman was worth waiting for, and I'd fucking wait forever if *that's* what it took to finally make Taylor mine.

When she's ready….

I moved my hand down and wrapped it around my painfully erect cock, just like I'd done every single night since the first time I'd made Taylor come, and had listened to those sweet cries escaping from her lips.

I stroked up and down my shaft to the memory of her *fuck-me* moans of pleasure that had led up to her climax less than thirty minutes ago.

"Fuck!" I rasped, and then closed my eyes as my head fell back against the wall of the shower.

I'd been so damn tempted to let her touch me when her hand had come damn close to stroking over my cock.

But as usual, I'd moved those exploring fingers out of the reach of what would definitely be more than she could handle.

Not ready.

Not ready.

Not ready.

I sped up my pace. I needed to get myself off just to take the edge off...

"Do you have any idea how incredibly hot it is to watch you touch yourself?" a sultry female voice uttered damn close to my ear.

My eyes flew open because I knew I had to be *deep* into some kind of hot fantasy.

I blinked, and then I did it again.

If this was a sexual fantasy, it was pretty goddamn vivid, because I saw Taylor completely naked, so damn close to me that she could reach out and stroke her hand boldly down my body as she said, "It's an incredibly erotic sight, and I'd love to just watch it until you orgasm someday, but right now, I want to participate."

Yep. She was here. No doubt about it.

My eyes traveled hungrily over her body, from her already-damp, unbound hair, down to those perfect, pert breasts of hers, and finally to that mouthwatering pussy. She'd shaved it since I'd seen her fully naked after her rescue, but she still had a landing strip of tight red curls over the mound that I desperately wanted to touch.

I dropped my hand to my side, and simply stared because I couldn't get a single word to come out of my mouth.

I was stunned into silence, mesmerized as I watched Taylor blatantly eating up every inch of my body with her eyes.

She looked at me like she was a starving woman, and I was the only sustenance she wanted or needed.

Moving closer, she didn't even flinch as her body entered one of the sprays of water. Her only focus seemed to be…me.

Every muscle in my body tensed as she explored my nude, slick body with her palms, stroking over my shoulders, my chest and then down my abdomen as she said, "You're so beautiful, Hudson, and I've wanted to touch you for so long. Do not stop me this time, because if you do, I'll just keep trying. I need to touch you."

My head dropped back against the marble enclosure again, knowing damn well I wasn't going to stop her this time.

I'd give this woman whatever the hell she needed.

And, fuck me, I wanted her hands all over me. I'd fantasized about it a million times, but those imaginings had never felt this damn good.

As she moved as close as she could get, her mouth trailed over my chest, and her hand moved to my groin.

I sucked in a breath as she gently fisted my cock.

"You're so big, Hudson," she said softly, close to my ear. "And so hard."

"Your damn fault." I finally managed to get out between my gritted teeth.

She let out a wicked, sexy laugh that I'd never heard come out of Taylor's mouth before. "It turns me on that I can make you this hard."

Holy fuck! When had this woman become a sex kitten? Not that she hadn't always gotten my motor running, but right now, she was completely irresistible. Maybe because she seemed to be having absolutely no hesitation about…exploring her sexuality. With me.

I clenched my fists, my entire body wound tight as she kissed and licked her way down to my abdomen before she dropped to her knees.

Jesus H. Christ! Surely she wasn't going to…

I hissed as her grip tightened on my cock, and I felt her mouth take as much of me as possible before sliding back to let her tongue stroke slowly over the sensitive tip.

My brain screamed at me to put a stop to one of the best damn things I'd ever experienced, but when she moaned, obviously enjoying exactly what she was doing, I shut down that train of thought completely.

I speared my hands into her wet hair, closed my eyes, and allowed myself to feel every single sensation, every emotion, and every damn sound she was making.

"Fuck, baby!" I ground out as I guided her head. "That feels so damn amazing."

I was about to come like a teenage boy getting his first blowjob.

I'd wanted Taylor for what seemed like forever, and her being her, with her mouth happily devouring my cock, was more than I could take.

Honestly, there had never been a woman in my entire life who had ever wanted to go down on me with this much gusto, and I generally didn't let it go very far. I could usually tell that my sex partner wasn't into it.

But Taylor? She was *definitely* into it, and every lusty moan she made was about to send me over the edge.

She paused, but kept her hand stroking my cock as she said in a pleading tone, "Come for me, Hudson. Please. I want that so damn much."

I fisted her hair, realizing that the last thing she wanted was for me to hold anything back. That imploring request had done more than just ramp up my desire. It had set me free from the fear I'd harbored since the day I'd realized that I wanted Taylor.

I urged her faster and faster, raw urgency guiding every movement.

I wasn't going to last much longer.

Not like this.

Not with her.

"Yeah. Fuck! Yeah," I groaned as my balls drew tight. "I'm going to come, baby. Hard."

It was a warning for her to back off.

She didn't.

Taylor moaned and took as much of me as she possibly could.

That set off the most powerful orgasm I'd ever experienced.

"Jesus, Taylor," I bellowed as my entire body shook, and Taylor kept right on greedily swallowing until I was finally spent.

I pulled her up, our eyes locking. I was still breathing hard, and my heart felt like it was going to pound through my chest wall as I saw the arousal in her gaze.

She wasn't scared.

She wasn't traumatized.

Taylor was breathing as hard as I was right now, still lost in erotic bliss as her tongue flicked out and she licked her lips.

I hauled her against my chest and kissed her. She immediately pressed that beautiful body against mine and wrapped her arms around my neck.

Mine! This woman was all mine.

I didn't need to fuck her to claim her. Hell, she'd just sealed her fate by giving herself to me in a way that was so damn intimate that she'd rocked my entire world.

When I finally released her mouth, she said breathlessly, "That was the hottest thing I've ever done."

I slicked her hair back from her face, my chest tight as I looked at the satisfaction mixed with longing in her beautiful green eyes. "My turn now," I grunted as I lifted her body and put her ass on the big shower bench. "You just released the beast. I hope you're ready to deal with him."

Her eyes filled with unbridled lust, and there wasn't a single bit of reluctance in her voice as she murmured, "Bring it on, handsome."

Chapter 24

Taylor

My heart was racing as Hudson went to his knees, spread my thighs, and then moved his powerful body between them. Our eyes stayed locked as he put his hand behind my head and hesitated like he couldn't stand to lose eye contact with me.

Wait for him.

Wait for him.

Wait for him.

Mac's sound advice rolled through my head over and over, because when Hudson looked at me like *this*, I *could* see what I was feeling staring right back at me.

He needed me just like I needed him.

I didn't need to wait anymore.

That reflection of everything I felt was there, in Hudson Montgomery's beautiful gray eyes.

Did he really think that I was going to be terrified to see that kind of passion, that kind of adoration, the fierceness of his desire when it was focused on me?

Oh, hell, no.

I reveled in it because he was the sexiest, hottest beast I'd ever laid eyes on.

He kissed me, and it was a lingering embrace, a tenderness mixed with naked, urgent longing that made my heart ache.

The bench was so large that you could probably throw a party on it, so when he released my mouth, he pushed my body down until I was supine on my back.

We were outside of the water jets, but I could still feel a fine mist that warmed my body.

Hudson didn't waste a moment before his mouth was everywhere.

He took his time exploring my neck, pausing to rasp against my skin, "Don't ever tell me that you aren't beautiful again, baby. You have no idea how stunning you look right now."

"Hudson," I squeaked as his mouth closed over one of my painfully hard nipples, while he pinched the other one with his fingers.

Heat rolled over my body as he licked, nipped and sucked my breasts until I was half out of my mind.

"Please," I cried out, not even certain exactly what I needed. I just had to have...more.

I shivered as his tongue trailed down my belly, and his fingers brushed over the square mass of tight red curls right above the place I needed him to touch the most.

But that sensation was nothing compared to the sharp jolt of pleasure that tore through my body as his tongue stroked through my slick, pink, flesh, not stopping until he laved over my clit.

My body arched, and I whimpered, "Oh, God, yes!"

Hudson buried his head between my thighs with an enthusiasm that rocked my entire body, and the feel of his mouth, nose and tongue working together to make me crazy nearly made me come completely unglued.

I groaned, "Yes, yes, yes. Make me come, Hudson. Please."

My body was completely on fire, and my head was thrashing back and forth because the pleasure was almost too much to handle.

It was nothing like I'd ever experienced before. It was so intense that when his tongue and mouth started really going after that tiny bundle of nerves that was already throbbing, I was breathless.

My climax literally rolled over my body like a freight train. "I'm coming. Oh, God, I'm coming. Hudson!" I cried out as I shattered.

He stretched out the pleasure, his tongue still working, licking at my pussy like he couldn't stop tasting that orgasm.

I just lay there for a moment, completely stunned.

Hudson finally moved, fusing our nude bodies as he kissed me.

Tasting myself on those sensual lips of his made me thread my hands through his hair and keep his mouth on mine to stretch the taste of him out a little bit longer.

When he finally lifted his head, I met his eyes, and said in a lust-infused tone, "Fuck me, Hudson. Now. I want you inside me. I need you."

His nostrils flared, and his eyes flashed with intense heat, but I could see a brief hesitation, too.

Oh, please, don't stop now. Not now.

Every fiber of my heart and soul needed to be as close to Hudson as I could possibly get. I wanted our bodies fused together so badly that I knew I wasn't going to truly find relief from the deep ache inside me until it happened.

I sat up and wrapped my arms around his upper body, and circled my legs around his torso. "Fuck me, Hudson. I know you want the same thing."

He rose, gripping my ass so he took me up with him. When my back was pressed against the very same spot where I'd first seen him stroking himself when I'd entered the shower, he grunted, "There shouldn't be a single doubt in your mind that it's exactly what I want, but it will change everything, Taylor."

I took his head between my hands. "How will it be different?"

His eyes burned into mine, possessive and covetous. "You'll be mine, dammit! I won't share. I can't. It's going to be just you and me, together. No other guys for you, no other women for me. Fuck! Like I'd even *want* to look at another female if you were mine? I'm too goddamn obsessed with *you* to realize any other woman even exists."

I stroked my hand over his wet hair, my heart fluttering. Didn't he realize he'd just said the words almost any woman wanted to hear when she was madly in love with a guy? "I don't want anyone else, either, Hudson. I have absolutely no problem with a monogamous relationship. Now, just fuck me before I lose my mind."

He gave me a quick, hard kiss before he grumbled, "Condom."

"No need," I said fervently. "I have birth control in place, and you've seen every one of my negative tests."

"It's not for me. It's for you," he rasped. "You haven't seen my negative tests."

Hadn't he just said we'd be monogamous? Like I didn't know he'd never do *anything* to hurt me? Ever.

"I. Trust. You." I said the words firmly as I continued to watch his irises change until they were like constantly swirling steel.

"Do you have any idea how long I've wanted to hear you say that?" he asked hoarsely.

"You've had it for a long time," I muttered. "You've just never realized it."

I gasped as Hudson lifted my body, and surged inside me, like he couldn't bear another second of not being exactly where he wanted to be.

"Yes," I hissed, tightening my legs around him.

Hudson was a big man, and the stretching sensation of his enormous, hard cock buried inside me was slightly uncomfortable for a few seconds, but it was totally eclipsed by the pleasure of finally feeling him inside me.

"Jesus! You're so damn tight, baby," he growled.

"I'm fine," I said. "Fuck me hard, Hudson. Don't hold back. I need that as much as you do."

"I doubt that," he answered in a deep, sensuous baritone. "Hold on tight because I don't think this can happen any other way."

He gripped my ass as he pulled back, and surged into me again.

And again.

And again.

I tightened my hold on his back, and fell into the fast and furious rhythm of our bodies as they moved together.

"So, good, Hudson. It's so good," I whimpered as my body reached for his with every powerful thrust.

I buried my face in his neck, my heart soaring, my mind lost to everything except Hudson, and the intense pleasure of having him pounding into me like a madman.

When he shifted so every thrust stimulated my clit, I started to writhe and grind against him.

"Harder," I urged him as I felt my climax building.

"Come for me, Taylor. I'm not going to last much longer. Can't. You feel too damn incredible," he said, his breathing heavy.

My back arched slightly; my body totally lost to anything except the man who was about to make me come apart.

When he gripped my ass harder, and started fucking me at a frenzied pace, I started to implode.

"Yes, just like that, Hudson. Yes! Hudson!" My climax was so intense that my short nails clawed at his back.

This orgasm was different, soul deep and so strong that it rocked me to my core.

My inner muscles clamped around his cock as the pleasure stretched on and on.

He let out a deep, carnal, throaty groan. "Fuck! Taylor!"

I moved back, panting, just to see his face while he found his own release.

His eyes were closed, his head tilted back, his muscles tight, and the look of frantic euphoria on his face made my chest squeeze tight.

I love you, Hudson. I love you so much it hurts.

I had to hold those words back, even though I wanted to scream them out loud.

We stayed just like that for a while, locked together, trying to catch our breath, drowning in post-coital bliss.

Hudson kissed me with so much tenderness, so much reverence, that it nearly made me burst into tears.

I felt adored.

I felt cherished.

I felt wanted.

And I truly did feel like I was the only woman who Hudson really desired.

Feeling like that was intoxicating.

I dropped my head to his shoulder, feeling completely spent, my body finally satisfied. "I think I bit you," I whispered into his ear. "I might have scratched your back up a little, too."

I heard him chuckle. "I noticed. It was pretty damn hot. Feel free to tear me up any damn time you want to do it, sweetheart."

He pulled back a little so he could look at me. "Are you okay? That was a little rough."

I smiled back at him and shook my head. "Not that I have enough experience to know for sure, but maybe I'm a little kinky, and I like it rough," I teased him.

He let me lower my feet to the tile, and then wrapped his arms around my waist. "You won't hear me complaining," he said with a smirk. "I'm more than willing to figure out every one of your perverted fantasies and make them reality."

I laughed softly. "And what about yours?"

He tipped my chin up, and our eyes locked as he said in a genuine tone, "Sweetheart, you just made several of my wet dreams happen in real life."

I was fairly certain I'd *never* been the main attraction in any guy's wet dreams, so I had no idea what to say, but I could certainly get used to being Hudson Montgomery's fantasy.

I pulled his head down and kissed him, and he seemed more than satisfied with that response.

Chapter 25

Taylor

"**O**h, that one is definitely going into the 'yes' pile," Riley Sinclair said with a huge smile as I came out of the dressing room. "It's classy, but it will still make Hudson's eyes pop out of his head."

I shot Riley an exasperated look. "We're supposed to be shopping for work clothes," I reminded her.

I'd spent most of the last two weeks after I'd accepted the position at Montgomery Mining getting my shit together. Meeting with human resources, filling out more paperwork, and squaring everything away so I could start my new job with all my ducks in a row.

Today, Riley had come up from Citrus Beach to San Diego so we could have a fun day shopping at Fashion Valley.

Hudson would be off work for two weeks starting tomorrow, and I'd wanted to get everything I needed for my job completely wrapped up so we could spend that time together.

So far, Riley and I had upgraded my phone to the latest iPhone, and I'd gotten a laptop more suited to a professional than a grad student.

After that she'd dragged me into a spa, where I'd gotten my nails done, and my crazy hair highlighted and cut into a tamer, sleeker style that would actually allow me to wear it down more often without a whole lot of fuss.

I'd also figured out exactly why most makeups gave me hives—because some of the hypoallergenic stuff that had been perfect for my skin had cost a small fortune. It's something I would have never even tried had Riley not hauled me into *that* store, too.

The bags were piling up in the car, and we were *still* checking out clothes.

Riley rolled her eyes at me. "We've picked out some great work clothes, but you really *need* that dress, and some other play clothes. Hudson likes to do a nice restaurant once in a while, so you'll get tired of wearing jeans. And this dress is perfect for any occasion, casual or dressy," she said as she made a motion for me to spin around.

Honestly, I loved the dress, too. The halter started high on my neck, and the silky material fell into a swing dress that ended between my middle and lower thigh. It wasn't exactly a mini dress, but it definitely wouldn't be something I wore to work, either.

"You look gorgeous," Riley said as I faced her again. "And you can get away with going braless, so you wouldn't even have to mess with some kind of adhesive bra."

"Which is a really nice way of saying I have small breasts," I said with a laugh.

Riley was so easy to talk to that it wasn't difficult to say almost anything to her. Over the last two weeks, we'd texted and talked a lot, and I'd learned to appreciate her sense of humor and her honesty.

"Noooo," she said. "It means you can wear a dress like that comfortably, but you're definitely not boob-less."

"Do I even want to look at the price tag?" I asked.

"Absolutely not. You have a very rich boyfriend, and I have his lovely black credit card. You don't need to know. I think he can afford it."

I sighed. "I feel guilty. I know I agreed to let him help me out with upgrading my electronics for this new job, but we bought a ton of stuff, Riley. I want his body, not his money."

Really, Hudson and I probably should be slowing it down by now, but every time he touched me, I wanted him just as much as the first time.

Before he'd left this morning, he'd told me to buy anything I wanted or needed, and not just upgraded electronics, but the amount of stuff we'd bought was getting a little crazy.

Riley laughed. "Believe me, the more you buy, the happier he'll be. Hudson likes taking care of you, obviously, and like it or not, he is an alpha male. If we haul in tons of bags from the stores, he might just start pounding on his chest because he'll feel like a real man."

I wrinkled my nose. "That's so messed up," I said, my lips curving up in a smile.

"You know it's true. Hudson likes to feel…needed. He wants to do things for you, and he wants to get you stuff that makes you feel good. Seth is the same way. He knows I'm filthy rich, too, and we're married for God's sake, but he still wants to be the one who pays when we're together, and he's always buying me gifts, even though I could easily go out and buy anything I wanted."

"So what do you do about that?" I asked curiously.

"Not a damn thing," she answered with a sweet smile. "He's a billionaire. I let him pay with his card, even if I do have one with my name on it in my purse, because it really doesn't matter to me. If he buys me something, I let him know I love it with tons of affection, because it's usually a really thoughtful gift. Don't get me wrong, I'm an independent woman, and if he gets too bossy, I'll put him in his place. But I like to see Seth happy, too, so I don't sweat the small stuff. If letting him do some of those little things that make him feel like he's taking care of me makes him happy, I let him do it."

"But I'm not wealthy, and Hudson and I just started an exclusive relationship two weeks ago," I reminded her. "The last thing I want is for him to think that I want him to buy my affection. He has it, rich or poor."

"He's not trying to buy your affection, Taylor. I think you need to understand that. He wants to make sure you're secure, comfortable, and happy. If you need something, he wants to get it for you because it's an easy thing for him to do. All the stuff we're buying today would be like you picking him up a pack of gum at a grocery store because you know he likes it. My brother is massively wealthy. Let the poor guy buy you a few packs of gum for God's sake. Believe me, he's going to enjoy that particular dress as much as you do." She wiggled her eyebrows.

I grinned at her analogy, knowing she was probably right. "I'm not poor, exactly. I'm just cash strapped after all those years at Stanford. Once I'm working, I'll have a lot more money. My foster father left me everything he had, but not enough for six years at Stanford. The last year was really rough. I nearly passed on the Montgomery internship because I wanted to get into a professional job as soon as possible. Now I'm glad I didn't pass it up. If I had said no, I never would have met Hudson."

I went back into the fitting room and started carefully taking off my dress. I heard Riley's voice through the curtain. "I'm sure you wouldn't have done the same thing if you'd known you were going to be kidnapped and brutalized?"

"Yeah, actually, I would." I replied. "I'd do it all over again. I don't have any regrets, Riley. I'm alive. I'm healthy. I have an amazing future in front of me. And I'm dating the hottest guy on the planet. So yeah, I'd go through it all again if that was the only way I could end up with Hudson."

I finished slipping back into my jeans and top, and when I opened the curtain, I saw Riley leaning against the wall with her arms over her chest. "You are in love with him."

It wasn't a question; it was a statement. Maybe I had deflected that question when we'd been on the beach the day of her party, but she didn't seem like she required an answer this time.

I nodded slowly. "How could I *not* be in love with Hudson? He's the kind of guy every woman dreams of meeting someday. I guess

I never thought it would happen to me. I could never see myself falling madly in love with *any* guy."

She lifted a brow. "Does he know?"

I shook my head. "It's too soon for all that. He wants to take me on dates for the next two weeks. He said he hates that everything happened ass backwards for us, and that I got robbed of the courtship part of the relationship, which in his mind, should have happened first, minus the whole kidnapping thing, too."

"What do *you* think?" she asked.

I shrugged. "I think if you start with the really hard stuff, you know you're relationship is pretty solid. I'm glad we were friends first, although he did say we could never be friends because he was attracted to me. But he's wrong. We are friends. He just doesn't see that. Hudson has been there during some of the toughest days of my life."

"I'm glad you love him, and I personally think he'd be over the moon to hear you say you're in love with him," Riley said softly as she took the dress from me and added it to the growing pile of 'yes' clothes on a nearby chair. "He needs someone like you, Taylor. He needs and deserves some happiness in his life."

"I know. I'm glad he's taking some time off," I replied. "Really, I just want to see him kick back a little. He spends so much time working or taking care of other people, and he put in a lot of hours just watching over me. I want to take care of him for a while."

Riley piled some of the clothing into my arms, and then picked up the rest. As we walked toward the check-out, she said, "According to him, you cook for him every day, handle the household chores, and bake some delicious desserts. He told me he was getting spoiled."

"It's nothing really," I argued. "Not compared to all the things he's done for me, Riley."

We both loaded our clothes onto the counter and the woman at the checkout smiled at us as she started ringing everything up and neatly folding the items.

"It means something to *him*, Taylor," she said in an earnest tone. "Sometimes, what might seem small to you is big to someone else.

He's never had someone do those things for him. He's filthy rich. Women expect expensive restaurants, lavish parties, and very exclusive clubs when they date him. I'm pretty sure not a single one of them could even boil water on their own, and I doubt they'd put any time into something that would make him happy."

I frowned. "That's sad."

She nodded. "That's kind of the way his entire life has gone. People expect a lot from Hudson, but they don't think he needs anything because he's so wealthy and seems so self-contained. That's why I'm glad he's hooking up with somebody who's real, and can see through all his bullshit."

"I do see him," I assured her. "I think I always have."

I could hardly tell her that Hudson and Jax had saved my life, and that Hudson had been there when I needed a shoulder to cry on, or even if I needed to pee.

"I know you see him," she said as she handed Hudson's card to the cashier. "Where to next?"

"I think I saw one of Hudson's favorite candy stores on the way in. I think we should stop there, and *I'm* paying for that pack of gum," I joked. "So keep that black card in your purse until you have a chance to give it back to Hudson."

We both grabbed one of the large bags. "You do know why he gave *me* that card instead of giving it to *you*, right?"

"Because you're his sister?" I guessed.

"Nope. He did it because he knows I have absolutely no problem spending his money for him," she said with a smirk. "He was probably afraid you'd use it much too sparsely."

"I probably would have," I muttered.

"And he knew that. He'll be glad you got everything you need, and you look absolutely gorgeous. Probably the only thing that would delight him even more is if you drove a new car home."

"Absolutely not. My Toyota might be old, but it runs just fine. Mac bought me that vehicle when he thought I was going away to college right after high school. That vehicle and I have been through a lot together. I'll replace it myself when I have to." I'd told Riley almost everything about my childhood, and my history with Mac.

"Okay, we'll skip the car lot," Riley replied jokingly.

"I'd appreciate that," I answered wryly.

"So we'll do the candy place, and then, if you don't mind, I'd really like to grab an iced-coffee," Riley said longingly.

"I'd absolutely be up for that," I said enthusiastically.

Actually, since I wasn't as enthusiastic about shopping as Riley was, it sounded perfect.

Chapter 26

Taylor

I was setting up my new computer when I heard Hudson come through the garage door later that evening.

He'd had to do a late dinner meeting, so I'd ordered takeout for myself instead of cooking.

"Hi, sweetheart," Hudson said in a husky voice as he entered the living room. "You look even more gorgeous than you did yesterday. New haircut?"

I nodded. "Do you like it? They did some highlighting, too. I thought it might be nice to tame it so I could wear it down sometimes. Something a little more professional than the ponytail."

"It's pretty damn sexy, and I love it." He nodded toward the coffee table. "New computer I hope?"

I looked up at him, and my heart tripped, just like it did every time I saw him.

I sighed. He'd worn a custom dark navy suit today, with a silk, wide stripe, blue and gray tie.

Hudson looked incredibly handsome in anything...or nothing at all. But when you put a man like *him* in a custom suit, he was devastatingly hot.

"Yes. Your black card got a workout today," I said remorsefully. "Riley suggested things I never really thought about, so we bought a lot more than I'd planned."

"Good," he said with a happy grin. "What's that?" He nodded toward the side table.

"It's a gift," I told Hudson as I got up, went to him, and gave him a welcome home kiss before I went to the table and picked up the box.

"For you? Who is it from?"

The box was wrapped in gold paper and a bow, so he didn't recognize the company brand until I handed it over.

"From *me* to *you*. And this purchase was not put on *your* card. I saw the candy store and couldn't resist because you told me once that you loved the chocolate turtles there."

Hudson looked taken aback for a moment, and then a little confused. "You bought these for...me, as a gift?"

My heart clenched painfully as I watched his expression, realizing how right Riley had been about Hudson being a giver who never really got anything back in his personal life.

It was so damn obvious, and so damn heartbreaking, that he didn't seem to know how to deal with getting a gift from a lover. At all.

It was an inexpensive present, a casual gesture to let him know I was thinking about him, even when we weren't together.

It wasn't like I'd just presented him with a million-dollar sports car or a high-tech plane.

I moved closer and whispered against his ear playfully, "It's just candy, handsome. It won't bite you."

He sent me a wry smile. "I guess I'm just not used to—"

I grinned back at him. "Get used to it. I *do* think about you, even when we aren't together. And if I see something that reminds me of you, or something I know you'll like; I will get it for you."

"I probably only mentioned that I liked these turtles once, and it must have been a while ago, because I don't even remember telling you about that," he said thoughtfully as he started unwrapping the candy.

"I pay attention," I informed him. "You talked it about it briefly during my horrifying week of eating like I couldn't get enough food, and you said you could probably eat a whole box of these turtles every day, so it was probably a good thing that you didn't have a store close to here or your office."

Oh, sweet Jesus! After *this* reaction, I was going to make damn sure he got used to getting gifts as often as possible from me.

Riley had probably been right about the fact that doing anything for Hudson, even baking him something, was a rarity for him.

Obviously, getting any kind of gift from a girlfriend had just never happened at all.

Operation: Spoil the Boyfriend was definitely on!

"If you ever get that box open, I'd be thrilled if you'd offer me one. I've never tried them," I teased him.

He grinned as he finished unwrapping the box. "Are you trying to say I have something you want?"

I lifted my hand and stroked it along his stubbled jawline as I murmured, "Handsome, you have a lot of things I want, but I'll settle for a piece of candy...for now."

His grin grew broader as he opened the top of the box and held it out to me. "You better get yours before they're gone."

I grabbed a chocolate turtle from the box and watched as he devoured two of them before I'd finished my first.

I had to admit that the gooey caramel and nuts, covered with the best milk chocolate I'd ever had, was decadently delicious.

I shook my head when he held out the box to me again. "I ordered Chinese. I'm still stuffed. I got extra food in case you were hungry. I can heat some up for you."

He put the lid back on the box and set the chocolates on an accent table. "I had dinner, and that chocolate was a perfect dessert. I'm good." He paused before he added, "I have something for you, too."

He shrugged out of his suit jacket, and pulled something from the inside pocket before he draped the garment over a chair.

Hudson held out a small, pink velvet box with an uncertain expression on his face.

I popped the lid immediately, curious as to why he looked so apprehensive.

My heart skipped a beat as I saw what was inside.

"Oh, my God." My hand was shaking as I picked up the pendant necklace.

It was the one Mac had given me, my talisman, but it was also… different.

Hudson said hoarsely, "I asked Prince Nick to try to find it in the rebel camp. Unfortunately, the only thing that turned up was the dragon. No pearl, no chain, and nothing in the eye sockets. I had it restored the best I could. I wished we would have found it intact, but at least the dragon is the original."

I lifted it carefully, temporarily stunned into silence.

The pendant was recognizable as the original, but the additions made it even more beautiful than it had been before.

The eyes that were originally made of green glass had been replaced with small emeralds of excellent quality that shone brightly against the white gold of the pendant.

And oh, sweet Jesus, the pearl encased in the cage tail was stunning.

I moved a little so I was directly underneath one of the recessed lights in the ceiling, and rolled the pearl a little.

Holy shit! The luster was incredible, and it was shaped perfectly round. It was really high quality, and probably somewhere around 16 millimeters.

The pearl was probably the most noticeable difference since the original pearl was manmade. This one…was not.

"Is this a South Seas Pearl?" I asked as I continued to gape at the gorgeous pendant.

"It is," Hudson answered. "It took some time to locate one that large in a high grade. Honestly, I wasn't sure whether you'd be thrilled that the pendant was restored, or heartbroken because it had been so badly damaged."

I fingered the thin but sturdy long chain that was stamped 14 karat, and matched the white gold pendant.

"I wish we could have found the original pearl and the eyes," Hudson continued. "But it just wasn't possible. Nick and his men went through that camp with a fine-toothed comb, Taylor."

The chain was long enough that I could get it over my head, so I slipped it on, and then wrapped my fingers around the pendant.

It felt so damn good to have it back.

Tears sprang to my eyes, and this time, I couldn't stop them from falling.

My heart ached just thinking about the time and energy Hudson had put into finding something that had been precious to me, and then had painstakingly tried to put it back together again.

Just to make *me* happy.

To me, *that* was priceless.

I tried to swallow the enormous lump in my throat, but I couldn't.

There was nothing I wanted more than to tell Hudson exactly how I felt.

How much I loved him.

How much this meant to me.

God, it was killing me *not* to say it, and my frustration was trickling down my face in the form of tears.

"I'm sorry, Taylor. You're crying," he said huskily. "Maybe I should have just let it go."

Anger rose up inside me, a fury born of frustration that he was actually second-guessing his decision.

I punched his shoulder. "I am *not* sad," I said irritably, and then punched his other shoulder. "You gave me back something I never thought I'd see again. And now it's really special because it's part you, and part Mac, the two most important men I've ever had in my life." I started pounding on his chest, tears coursing down my face until I was nearly blinded by them. "Don't you have any idea how much this means to me?"

His powerful arms wrapped around my body, and crushed me against him. "Do you always beat on the men you see as special?" he asked drily.

"No!" I exclaimed. "Just you."

I knew I was out of control, but at least my anger stopped me from telling him the three little words I didn't think he was ready to hear. Hudson hadn't even hinted at those emotions, and he wasn't used to anybody loving him except for family.

If I tell him this too soon, it could destroy our relationship before it has even had time to grow.

Hudson stroked a soothing hand up and down my back. "No offense, sweetheart, but you don't seem very happy."

I huffed against his shoulder. "I am. You're just not seeing it."

I stepped back and swiped at my wet cheeks as I said. "You just did the most incredible thing anyone has ever done for me, Hudson Montgomery."

I reached out and started to unbutton his shirt. If I couldn't *tell* him how I felt, I could show him.

Once the shirt was on the ground, I reached for his belt, and worked on his pants until they went south to his ankles.

"Can I ask what in the hell you're doing now?" Hudson asked hoarsely as he stepped out of the pants.

I pulled my shirt over my head, tossed it, and then shimmied out of my jeans and panties. When I was completely nude, I replied, "Getting us both naked. I need you, Hudson."

I pulled his head down so I could get what I really wanted right now, and started to kiss him.

Chapter 27

Hudson

I kissed the naked, beautiful woman in my arms like a man possessed.

Which I basically…was.

I was hungry for Taylor every damn minute of the day.

I groaned against her lips as her heated, silken skin slid against mine.

Taylor made me completely insane. Having her in my bed every night for the last few weeks hadn't lessened my obsession with her. If anything, it had gotten more intense.

Now, I didn't just want Taylor's body. I wanted every single damn part of her.

Yeah, I even wanted her tears if she *really* needed to cry, although I'd much rather take preventative measures and make sure she was always happy. It nearly killed me to see her cry.

I finally tore my mouth from hers, and held her head to my shoulder, my heart racing so fast that I couldn't catch my damn breath.

Because *that's* what Taylor did to me.

Every damn time she did something sweet for me like she had tonight, like she did every single day, I felt like the luckiest bastard in the world to have her in my life.

My problem? I got more and more desperate to make damn sure she *stayed*.

Dammit! I knew she cared, but I needed...more.

I had to know she was fucking mine, and *always* would be.

Was that completely fucked up?

Yes, it probably was because I *should* just be enjoying every single minute I spent with this woman instead of wanting...something more.

Okay. Yeah. I could admit it. I was terrified I was going to do something that would fuck up the best thing I'd ever had.

So I really, really needed to know what was wrong with her.

"Tell me what just happened, Taylor," I said, trying to keep my voice calm.

I'd given her a repaired pendant, and she'd fallen apart.

I had to know...why.

Why she'd gotten angry.

Why she'd cried.

If she really loved the restored pendant, none of it made any sense.

Taylor wasn't the type of female who was mercurial. Her moods didn't swing like that. She didn't go from happy to angry, and then burst into tears all within a ten-minute timeframe.

Something was eating her up, and I wanted to know *exactly* what it was so I could get rid of whatever was making her unhappy.

Correction: I wanted to get rid of it as long as it wasn't...me.

This last few weeks of having her in my bed every night, seeing her beautiful, smiling face every evening when I got home, her touching me whenever she damn well wanted to do it, and me doing the same, had made me happier than I'd ever been in my entire life.

I'd been dead wrong when I'd said that Taylor wasn't my friend. What I guess I should have said back then was that I couldn't be *just* her friend.

Dammit! I had every damn thing I'd ever wanted with Taylor, and I wasn't going to lose her. *Ever.*

I finally truly understood what Seth had been trying to say at the picnic.

I'd be a sorry bastard, too, if I didn't have Taylor in my life.

I *needed* her, and I wasn't ashamed to admit that to myself.

"Just fuck me, Hudson. Please. I need you," she said in a sultry, sexy voice.

Holy fuck! I wanted to give her anything she needed, and I wanted that, too, but I couldn't just sweep what had just happened under the rug.

I *had* to fix it.

I picked her up, and sat down on the leather couch with Taylor on my lap. "Something is wrong, sweetheart. I can sense it. Talk to me."

She scrambled off my lap, stood up, and started gathering up her clothing. "If you don't want to fuck me, you should have just said so," she said indignantly. "I'm not going to keep throwing myself at you. I feel kind of ridiculous."

I watched as she marched her beautiful naked ass toward the stairway and disappeared.

Okay, what the fuck had just happened?

I got up and followed her. I got to the stairway just in time to see her turning the corner upstairs.

Oh, hell no.

I wasn't going to just let her run away from this.

I sprinted up the stairs, and to my bedroom.

Taylor wasn't there, but the bathroom door was closed, and the light was on, so I sat down on the bed, determined to wait for her to come out of there, even if I had to wait all damn night.

I pulled off my socks, getting ready to be comfortable while I waited, when the bathroom door flew open, and there was Taylor, looking a lot more composed than she had earlier.

She'd pulled on a pair of the thin shorts and a tank top she usually slept in while she was in the bathroom.

I watched her as she crossed the room and sat down on the bed next to me, but not close enough for me to touch her. I was okay with that if she needed her space, as long as she talked.

"I'm sorry," she said in a remorseful tone. "I had absolutely no reason to be angry with you, and you didn't deserve the way I acted, either. You just got home from work. Maybe you weren't in the mood to get naked with me, and that should be perfectly okay if you weren't. I guess my gut reaction was that maybe you're tired of us fucking like bunnies all the time, or maybe you're getting bored... with me."

My gut twisted when she wouldn't meet my gaze. "Seriously, Taylor? There is *never* going to be a day that I don't want us to get naked and sweaty, but there's more to all of this. I know it. Something is bothering you. A lot." I paused before I continued, trying to figure out what to say. In the end, I just decided to be honest like we always were with each other. "You know, I was wrong when I said we could never be friends. We're best friends, and even though that's just one part of our relationship, it's important. I can't just fuck you and pretend that I don't know something is bothering you. That just doesn't work for me. Tell me what's going on in your head. I want to help you fix it."

She shook her head. "You can't fix this, Hudson. It's my issue, not yours. It isn't you, it's me."

"That's bullshit, and you know it. Your issues are my issues, too, Taylor," I cajoled. "Tell me that if you knew something was bothering me, that you wouldn't pry whatever problem I had out of me somehow."

"I probably would try," she admitted with a ghost of a smile on her face.

"You'd succeed, just like I plan on doing. I'll be following you around until you get sick of hearing me ask you what's wrong, and you just fucking tell me. I don't get it. You've never had a problem telling me any of the really hard stuff before. As soon as you trusted me enough to talk about it, you told me. How much more time do you need to trust me enough with whatever is bothering you now?"

Son of a bitch! I knew I was losing it, but it hurt to know that no matter what I said, she just didn't trust me enough to share something that was obviously eating her alive.

She shook her head as she said in a frustrated tone. "This isn't about trust. It's about me. It's about *my* fear."

"Jesus! I'd happily give my life to protect you, Taylor. Don't you know that?"

"It's not *that* kind of fear, Hudson. Oh, screw it. All we're doing is arguing, and that's the last thing I want. Do you really want to know what's wrong?" She finally met my eyes.

She sat up straighter, and I could see her determination as she stiffened her spine.

I gazed into her beautiful green eyes, and the vulnerability I saw there tore my damn heart out. "Only if you really want to tell me, sweetheart," I said, backing down a little because she looked so damn...open and defenseless.

Maybe I'd pushed her too damn hard.

"Fine," she said in a short, tense voice, her eyes still locked with mine. "I have one very big problem. I love you, Hudson. I'm madly, completely, totally in love with you. I know it's way too soon, and you probably think I'm crazy, but I can't stop it. And when you do ridiculously thoughtful things for me like you did with the pendant, I want to throw myself in your arms and tell you just how much I love you. I want you to know that I've never, ever felt this way before, and I know in my heart that I'll never feel this way again, so I didn't want to lose you by jumping the gun. But I just cannot contain it any longer. You don't just have my body and my mind. You have my heart and my soul, too."

I could see it. Jesus! I could see it in her eyes.

I was so stunned that I couldn't speak. I couldn't react.

Taylor fidgeted as she broke the silence, "So, yeah, that's it. I love you. I wanted to be able to tell you, but I didn't want you to freak about it. That's all."

She stood up, and I could tell she was feeling awkward as she started to move away from the bed.

Oh, hell no!

I snagged her around the waist, and pulled Taylor onto the bed. She landed on her back, and I pinned her wrists beside her head. "Have I ever, in any way, given you the impression that I wouldn't want to hear that?" I snarled.

Her eyes widened. "You never seemed to be leaning that direction," she said hesitantly. "I didn't know how you'd take it, but I had to say it, Hudson. You had to know I was crazy about you. For me, I'd come too far not to be honest, but I was trying to wait. I know you want me really bad, and I know you care—"

I slammed my mouth down on hers so she couldn't say another damn word.

I kissed her like I wanted to inhale every ounce of love she wanted to give me, and I groaned when she tangled her tongue with mine, pushing back, entwining us together.

I was breathing hard by the time I came up for air, but that wasn't going to keep me talking. "Don't say anything, Taylor. Not right now. Just listen," I said in a voice that sounded like I'd just run five miles at a sprinting pace.

Obviously, I'd given her some mixed signals. Somehow, she'd missed the obvious, and that was ending right now.

I took a couple of deep breaths. "I probably started to fall in love with you from the day I rescued you. You were so damn brave, so smart, and so incredibly resilient that I was drawn to you almost immediately. By the time I got you back to the States, I was fucking obsessed with getting you better, and making sure nobody would ever hurt you like that again. Did I feel guilty? Yes. Was that my chief motivation? No. You are and always will be the most fascinating woman I've ever known. I didn't want anybody to touch you except me when you were vulnerable, and I wanted you to trust me so damn badly that I was obsessed about that, too. By the time you started getting my dick hard, I knew I was screwed. I was already madly in love with you. I love you, Taylor. I have almost since the beginning. I have never, and will never feel this way again, either, and I was probably way more scared of losing you than you were about losing me. Jesus! I thought it was pretty damn obvious how I felt. Had I known that you would have been okay with me saying those words out loud, I would have. A long time ago. So, hell no, it's not too damn soon. I've just been waiting for *you* to catch up with *me* in the obsessive love department." I searched her eyes, trying to gauge her reaction, but she just seemed to be laser-focused on what I was saying. "Maybe I'm a greedy bastard, but I want it all, Taylor. Your heart. Your soul. Your body. Your mind. I want you to be mine, and I want to be yours. And I want that forever. Tell me that's what you want, too."

Tears started to trickled down her temples as she nodded. "I do. So damn much."

I let out an enormous breath that I hadn't even realized I'd been holding. "Thank fuck! I guarantee that I'm going to screw up in the future, and the way I feel about you is pretty extreme, but I'll always do anything in my power to make you happy, Taylor."

She yanked to get her wrists free, and I let her go.

When she wrapped her arms around my neck, and gave me a blistering kiss, anything that had been wrong before was now absolutely perfect.

Chapter 28

Taylor

I finally let go of the death grip I had going on with my arms around Hudson's neck, and ended the frenzied kiss.

For several heartbeats, our eyes locked before I said, "Mac once told me that when I found the right guy, I'd feel it with my entire soul, and I'd see the way I was feeling reflected back to me in his eyes."

His gray gaze turned intense. "And do you see it?"

I nodded. "Yes. I saw it that night in the shower with you, too. I should have had more faith—"

He put a finger to my lips. "Don't, Taylor," he said harshly. "I've screwed up, too. This is new for both of us. There's going to be a learning curve. We just need to keep talking to each other."

I wrapped my legs around his waist. "There's something else I'd rather be doing right now. I need you, Hudson."

Now that I knew that he loved me, I wanted him so badly that my entire body ached for him.

The heat that flashed in his eyes was white-hot and hungry.

He sat me up, and yanked the tank over my head. "I'm not sure why you bothered to get dressed. It's always going to end this way for us," he rumbled. "No matter what disagreement we had earlier."

I hadn't bothered with panties so I lifted my hips and let Hudson slide the thin shorts down my legs.

Honestly, we didn't argue very often, but when we did in the future, I hoped it *always* ended like this.

He shucked his boxer briefs, and I opened my legs wider, hoping he'd come down on top of me.

I wanted his body flush with mine, his weight on top of me.

I sighed when he lowered himself over me.

I savored the feel of his soft skin over hard muscles, smoothing my hands over his back and his shoulders. "You feel so good," I murmured, getting lost in his masculine scent. "Fuck me, Hudson. I can't wait any longer."

He moved to roll me over on top of him. "No!" I insisted, holding onto him. "Just like this. Please."

For some reason, he never wanted to be on top of me. I had a feeling he thought it might make me uncomfortable because I'd been assaulted, but right now, I needed him to take me just like this.

He stared down at me. "Are you sure?"

I nodded. "I'm not afraid of your strength, Hudson. I wallow in it because I know damn well you'd never hurt me."

"I love you, Taylor," he said with a groan as he buried his face in my neck.

I tilted my head, giving him access to whatever he wanted as he licked and nipped at my skin.

I squirmed, wrapped my legs around his waist, and ground up against him. "I love you, too, Hudson. Now fuck me before I lose my mind."

He slipped one of his hands between our bodies, and grasped his cock. He teased my clit with the head. "Is this what you want?" he asked in a wicked, low tone.

"No teasing," I whimpered. "I want you inside me now."

"Fuck! You're so wet, sweetheart," he hissed.

I threaded my hands into his hair, relishing the feel of the coarse strands between my fingers. "Because you make me that way," I whispered in his ear, and then nipped his earlobe.

"Dammit! I can't wait any longer, either," he rasped, and then surged into me with one powerful movement of his hips.

"Oh, God, yes!" I gasped.

He pulled back and thrust in again. "Mine. You're fucking mine, Taylor. Say it," he demanded coarsely.

"I'm yours, Hudson. I always will be."

I was never going to hesitate to tell him that. I knew he needed to hear those words whenever he needed reassurance, and I'd happily give that to him.

Any way he needed it.

I met every furious forward movement of his hips, wanting him as deep as he could get.

The intensity, the way we were straining to get as close as we could get, gave me so much pleasure that I could already feel my climax starting to build.

I tightened my legs around Hudson's waist. "Harder, Hudson. Fuck me harder," I pleaded.

He buried his hands in my hair, tilted my head, and fused our lips together, his tongue working my mouth in the same crazy, rapid tempo as his cock.

I moaned against his lips, surrendering to the madness I always felt every time Hudson was inside me, around me, surrounding me.

My hands fisted his hair as my body got lost in the seductive rhythm.

When he finally lifted his head, I panted, trying to catch my breath.

"I love you, Hudson. I love you so much," I told him breathlessly.

My heart soared, and my body pulsated.

I could tell Hudson exactly what I was feeling, so I felt so damn...free.

He shifted slightly, and I moaned when he put his hand under me and gripped my ass, pulling me hard against him with every stroke of his cock.

"Yes-oh-my-God-that-feels-amazing," I babbled.

"Come for me, baby," he said gutturally.

I was already close.

So close.

"Hudson!" I keened his name as I shattered, my body splintering as my orgasm took control.

My back arched, and when I looked up, I could see Hudson's gaze locked on my face, and *knowing* he was watching me fall apart made my climax even more intense.

"Fuck!" he cursed. "Can't wait."

"Then don't," I pleaded. I didn't want him to wait.

I wanted him to ride his orgasm with me.

I needed him to feel as unrestrained as I did right now.

My eyes were drawn to Hudson's face when he found his own release, and I was transfixed by the myriad of emotions that I could see in his expressive eyes.

Intense pleasure.

Desperate need.

Hot desire.

Adoration.

Pure happiness.

And infinite…love.

He dropped his forehead to my shoulder when he was finally spent. "I love you, Taylor. I hope you never doubt that for a single moment again."

I could feel his breath coming hot and heavy against my neck until we both started to catch our breath.

His voice was rough and graveled when he finally spoke. "Stay with me and love me forever, Taylor. If you do, I'd be the happiest asshole on the planet."

My heart squeezed tight inside my chest. "I'm not planning on going anywhere, Hudson. Why would I when you're everything and all that I need."

Sometimes it was really hard to believe that a guy like Hudson would even contemplate the possibility of any female walking away from him.

But he did.

Like every other person in the world, Hudson had his insecurities.

And as baffling as it was to me, many of them seemed to revolve around...me.

I wasn't sure if I was awed or absolutely terrified that I seemed to be Hudson's Achilles' heel.

Honestly, *he* was *my* greatest vulnerability, too.

I guess as long as I *knew* I was his weakness, I could do everything in my power to become his greatest strength, too.

He rolled onto his back, and drew my body into his like he couldn't stand to have any distance between us. "You'll probably be the death of me someday, baby, but at least I'll go with a smile on my face."

"That's never going to happen," I assured him. "I'm always going to have your six, handsome," I told him, using the slang military term for having his back.

He chuckled. "And you know I'm always going to have yours. Watching your gorgeous backside is one of my favorite activities."

I smacked his arm playfully. "Pervert."

"Only with you, sweetheart," he retorted. "Do you have any complaints about that?"

"Just one," I mused.

"And what's your objection?" he said with humor in his voice.

"If you're watching my ass, it's virtually impossible for me to be watching yours. Just for the record, I'm pretty sure I was drooling over yours long before you even started looking at mine."

"Doubtful," he said skeptically.

I sighed. "Why do you think I always wanted to be sitting at the breakfast bar when you were cooking? I had a perfect view."

"Please don't try to tell me you were lusting after me when you couldn't even walk," he said dubiously.

I moved so I was on my side, and wrapped my arm around his waist. "Okay, I won't tell you that, but I was. I can't really explain it, but I was drawn to you even before that, from the moment you got me out of that hellhole in Lania. I trusted you, even when I was out of my head, and I probably shouldn't have put my faith in anyone back then."

He stroked a gentle hand over my hair. "No offense, baby, but I was pretty much all you had."

I shook my head. "It wasn't that," I assured him. "It wasn't just because you rescued me."

"Hell, maybe I get that," he rumbled. "I think I knew you were trouble from the time I saw your damn picture. I barely slept before Jax and I got to Lania. All I could think about was whether or not you could just hold on a little bit longer. It probably wasn't logical to think we'd even find you alive, and I have no fucking idea how you managed to hang onto life, but I wasn't giving up hope, either."

I stroked a hand down his chest and his stomach. "Maybe I was waiting for you to rescue me, handsome."

"Fuck! I definitely took my sweet time getting there. If Jax and I had known as soon as it happened, we would have had a team there within twenty-four hours. We wouldn't have counted on Harlow's release, either. Maybe nothing we could have done would have saved Mark, but could have made it a hell of lot less traumatic for you, and for Harlow."

"Hey," I said as I threaded my hand into his hair, and turned his head toward me so I could look into his eyes. "It's over, Hudson. You came for me, and I was alive. I'm here, and I'm healthy again. Do you know what a miracle that is to me?"

He searched my face. "I'm always going to come for you, Taylor. Count on that. If you're ever in trouble, or you need me, there isn't a damn thing I won't do to get to you."

I put a gentle kiss on his lips before I replied, "I know that. I hope that someday you'll realize that I'll always find a way to get to you, too."

"I think I already know that," he said huskily. "And it scares the shit out of me. You're way too ballsy, woman. Don't you dare ever put that beautiful ass of yours on the line to save mine."

I smiled as I straddled him. "Oh, so it's okay for you to do that, but it's not okay for me to do the same thing."

"Exactly," he said in a clipped voice. "If something were to happen to you now, Taylor, I'd never survive it. I've seen you as close to death as a person can get. I can't handle seeing you like that again."

There wasn't an ounce of playfulness in his voice. He was dead serious.

I stopped giving him a hard time the second I saw the tension on his face. I could tell he was still haunted about the way my kidnapping could have ended.

"Nothing is going to happen to me, Hudson. I'm here. I love you. And we're going to have an amazing life together," I murmured as I stretched out on top of him.

He suddenly rolled, and trapped me under him. "And you're finally mine, Taylor," he growled as he loomed over me. "Fuck knows you've had me by the balls almost from the beginning. I've been yours pretty much from day one."

I wrapped my arms around him. "Then I'm claiming what's mine right now," I purred, my entire body tight with anticipation.

"We're going slow this time," he grunted. "We have all damn night."

With Hudson, there was no slow and easy, and I knew it.

We were frenzied about claiming each other's bodies in less than a minute.

The same thing happened the next time he tried the whole 'taking his time' thing.

And the next.

But I certainly had no complaints if he wanted to keep attempting the impossible, because hard, hot and fast just got better and better every single time.

Chapter 29

Taylor

"**S**weetheart, did you really think you could put *that* dress on and *not* make us really late for our dinner reservations tonight?"

I glanced at Hudson, noting the predatory look on his face as he stood in the kitchen watching my every move.

"Not this time," I told him sternly.

Granted, Hudson looked good enough to devour whole right now in a pair of khaki dress pants, and a deep burgundy polo shirt, but this time, I refused to be diverted.

He'd been the most relaxed I'd ever seen him over the last ten days of his coerced vacation.

Most of those days, he hadn't even bothered going into his home office. At all. His brothers had promised to let him know if they needed something, and Hudson didn't bother checking in with them every single day.

We hadn't gone out every single night. We'd spent a few days just enjoying the beach, swimming, and playing around outside.

However, as promised, Hudson had done his best to woo me on his date nights, and he'd been successful every single time.

Probably my favorite date had been a romantic dinner harbor cruise. It had been a nice warm evening on the water, which had made the entire night seem...magical.

I'd been beyond grateful that I'd let Riley talk me into so many outfits when we'd gone shopping.

So far, I hadn't worn this comfortable, black swing dress, but I'd slipped it on tonight, and put my hair up in a sexy style that left some loose curls around my face.

I'd gone all out tonight, even doing a very careful makeup job, and adding a pair of strappy black sandals that had been an impulse buy to match the dress.

"Taylor, you take my breath away," Hudson said in a raw, hoarse voice. "Just when I think you can't possibly get more beautiful than you already are, somehow, you do."

I sighed as I stopped right in front of him. "When you say things like that, I realize exactly why I love you so damn much," I muttered as I carefully kissed his lips, trying not to smudge my lipstick.

There would always be a big part of me that wasn't a dress up, fussy type of woman, but I had to admit that I enjoyed Hudson's reactions when I was in the mood to explore the ultra-feminine side of myself. Honestly, before Hudson, I hadn't even known that part of me even existed.

He kissed my bare shoulders, and my neck, his hands exploring the silky material. "Jesus, Taylor, you aren't wearing a bra. I think you could fall out of this thing at any time. Normally, I'd be the last one to complain about that, but one wrong move and every damn guy in the restaurant will be gawking."

I laughed. God, sometimes I really adored his alpha possessiveness. I stroked his jawline. "Number one, I won't fall out of it because my boobs are too small for that to happen."

Okay, maybe if I got really crazy in this dress, the drape might fall forward enough for somebody really close to me to see the tiny curve of my breasts, but it wasn't going to happen when I was sitting at a table eating dinner.

"Second," I added. "You're the only guy who's really going to be looking."

"I highly doubt that," he grumbled as he wrapped his arms around my waist. "I notice every single guy who looks at you just a little too long. Shit, Taylor. Don't you ever see how men look at you? And tonight, they'll definitely be looking."

Personally, I thought Hudson was delusional, but if he wanted to believe that I was irresistible to every man on the planet, I doubted I was ever going to convince him otherwise. I wound my arms around his neck. "Does it ever occur to you that I really don't give a damn about any man in the room except you? That maybe the only eyes I see looking at me are yours?"

He only looked partially placated as he said huskily, "Oh, mine are always going to be all over you. Count on it."

I shivered at the predatory note in his voice.

Sometimes it was still difficult to believe that this drop-dead gorgeous, thoughtful, intense, brilliant guy was madly in love with me.

Not that I could ever truly doubt it, because he showed me just how much he loved me every single day.

Still, for a woman who had never been loved with this much devotion, this much passion, this much adoration, it was going to be a while before it wasn't just a little bit overwhelming sometimes—in a good way.

I smiled up at him. "Just when I think I can't love you more than I already do, I realize that I love you more every single day, Hudson Montgomery," I told him lightly. "What's going to happen when I simply love you too much."

His intense gray eyes stared gravely into mine. "You could never love me too much, sweetheart. Not in my opinion."

Yeah, he could never love me too much, either. The more he showed me how much he did, the more I wallowed in it.

Unable to resist feeling his mouth on mine, I pulled his head down for a real kiss.

To hell with the lipstick.

I had more in the tube in my purse.

I could fix it.

Hudson took control of the embrace almost immediately, putting his hand behind my head, and ravishing my mouth until I was breathless, and my heart was racing.

When he finally lifted his head, he rasped into my ear, "Do you have any idea how much I want to bend you over and fuck you until you have a mind-blowing orgasm right now?"

Okay, so my resolve was cracking just a little. "Reservations," I reminded him.

He pulled back a little and shot me a cocky grin. "Baby, your man is Hudson Montgomery. Do you really think anybody will say a word about us being late when I've always been a very good customer?"

Nope. I already knew there wasn't a single person who would ever butt heads with a man like Hudson.

Any business would be crazy if they didn't cater to him.

I swiped a smear of lipstick from his face as I asked, "So you always get exactly what you want, Mr. Montgomery?"

He nodded arrogantly. "From just about everybody except you."

"I hate to break it to you, handsome, but you're not getting exactly what you want from me right now, either. I'm starving, and you promised me some amazing seafood. It's a nice place, and I don't want to get there with my makeup a disaster, and a body that's hot and sweaty," I insisted as I stepped back from him.

Honestly, the whole alpha male I-get-what-I-want-whenever-I-want-it façade was hotter than hell, but we'd already been late for two reservations.

Maybe he didn't mind being late.

But I found it a little bit unnerving.

"Shit! I'm sorry, Taylor. If you're hungry, let's hit it," he said remorsefully.

I beamed at him.

It was amazing how Hudson could be demanding one moment, and then apologetic the next.

If I wanted or needed something, by God, he'd make sure I got it, even if that meant putting his own desires on hold.

Honestly, I knew damn well that's why I loved him so much.

Yeah, he had a cocky, arrogant, demanding side.

But inside beat the heart of the sweetest guy in the world.

And honestly, I was okay with the fact that I was one of the few people who knew that sweet, thoughtful side of him, because I'd always make sure it was appreciated.

I paused as we made our way toward the garage door as I said, "I'm not taking the whole being bent over the table and satisfied off the table. I won't give a damn if I get hot and sweaty once we get home."

He lifted a brow. "I hope you plan on eating quickly."

"I thought you were working toward slow and easy," I teased.

"I think you and I both know that's never going to happen, but I won't rush dinner," he said in a wicked tone. "But I might explain to you exactly what I have in mind for later while we're eating."

My heart tripped as he opened the garage door.

I ended up eating a little faster than I would have liked.

We took our dessert to go, but once we got home, we didn't get around to eating it until the following day.

We were entirely too busy later that night getting exactly what we *both* wanted.

Chapter 30

Jax

"Do not slam this door in my face, Harlow. I think we need to talk." I tried to keep my tone somewhere between don't-even-try-it and please-give-me-a-few-minutes, but I had no idea where I'd landed on that scale.

Hopefully, I hadn't come off as a complete prick, because Harlow looked like she could use a friend.

After many attempts to contact Harlow on the phone and via text, I'd given up and come to her apartment now that she'd returned from her mother's home in Carlsbad.

I saw her hesitate, and for a moment, I thought she *was* going to tell me to fuck off and close the door.

"I won't keep you," I persuaded. "Come on, Harlow, you've hung up on me and my legal department at least a dozen times now."

"I don't get it," she said in a frustrated voice. "I've already said no to *everything*. What in the hell do you guys want from me, Mr. Montgomery?"

"If you don't want the money, that's fine," I told her calmly.

"As my employer, Montgomery Mining paid a small fortune for my ransom so I could be released from a hostage situation. That was more than enough. I don't need some kind of settlement, *and* for some unknown reason, I'm still getting paid by your company, and that needs to stop. I resigned, Mr. Montgomery."

I grinned. "Yes, and we refused to accept your resignation, so you're technically on a paid leave. You have way too many important research projects in the lab to just…leave."

"I gave my resignation to the lab director weeks ago. I don't want to go back to Montgomery Mining," she retorted sharply.

"Look, I know you've been through hell, but you might feel differently in a few months. What's the harm of staying on the payroll right now," I said as persuasively as possible.

Honestly, Harlow didn't look like she was in a position to decide much of anything, and that bothered me worse than it probably should.

I barely knew Dr. Harlow Lewis, but I'd seen her in action in our lab enough times to recognize that she definitely wasn't herself right now.

Okay, maybe I *had* asked her to have dinner with me two years ago, and she'd laughed in my face and turned me down flat, but it wasn't like I'd held a grudge.

Not really.

Well, okay, maybe a little.

Truth was, she was the first and only woman who had *ever* turned me down.

I was Jaxton Montgomery, billionaire co-CEO of Montgomery Mining, the largest mining company in the world. So yeah, I didn't get many women who laughed in my face and blew me off.

Actually, there had just been *one*.

Her.

Harlow intrigued me from the moment I'd met her a couple of years ago. She was a gorgeous blonde bombshell who also happened to be a brilliant scientist in our laboratory.

I had to admit she'd had a point when she laughed and told me that the last thing she wanted was to be my one-nighter, and then end up being hounded by the press for the next several weeks after a single date.

No, thanks.

Have a nice day.

Goodbye, Mr. Montgomery.

It wasn't like I could have assured her that she *wouldn't* be a one-night woman, because I was, after all, the king of one-and-done.

I was the master of never dating a woman more than once.

Unfortunately, the price I paid for that habit was being hounded by reporters every time I had a new woman on my arm.

She finally answered, "The problem is, you're paying me for a job that I can't come back to...ever. My bad decision-making led to the death of a colleague and someone I cared about, and the hostage situation nearly killed my own intern."

"Harlow, that wasn't your—"

"Don't say it!" she warned. "Do you really think I don't know what happened to Taylor, Mr. Montgomery? How am I supposed to live with that?"

Taylor Delaney, Harlow's intern and friend, was now the love of my eldest brother Hudson's life. "Have you actually asked Taylor what happened? She's doing fine, Harlow. You've talked to her. She's healthy, she's moved on, and she and Hudson are almost nauseatingly happy."

"She won't discuss it with me, or admit that she was sexually assaulted every night, but I'm not an idiot. Maybe I wasn't in my right mind at the time, but how am I supposed to live with that, or Mark's death."

Harlow looked haunted. She still looked beautiful, but she had dark circles under her eyes, and the woman was always immaculately groomed. Maybe she looked different because I'd never seen her dressed so casually. She was in cut-off denim shorts and a T-shirt, but I didn't think it was her attire. It was more about the defeat that seemed to be hanging over her head like a dark cloud. Physically, she'd healed, but emotionally, she was obviously still struggling.

"Last Hope sent you a counselor," I reminded her.

"They didn't rescue *me*. You paid my ransom and I was released, remember?" she said drily. "But I'm seeing someone on my own. And yes, I know I can never tell anyone about Last Hope. Marshall and I had *the talk*." Her hands made air quotes.

"No, we only had to rescue Taylor, but once you knew about Last Hope, you were under our protection until you're physically and emotionally ready to tackle the world on your own. That's one of the reasons I'm here, Harlow. Marshall made me your assigned advisor. I want to make sure that you're okay, and I'd like to check in with you once a week, more often if you need it." I wasn't about to reveal that I'd actually volunteered to do follow-up with Harlow. Maybe because I didn't really understand why I'd offered in the first place.

Harlow let out a laugh that was completely devoid of humor. "Seriously, Mr. Montgomery? *My advisor* is the guy who never dates a woman more than once? Ever? No offense, but I can hardly see *you* as my go-to guy. I'm sure you're much too busy lining up your dates. Finding a new woman every night has to be exhausting and extremely time-consuming. No worries. Tell Marshall I'll be just fine without an advisor."

"If you needed me, I'd be there," I said, feeling offended. "I'm dependable."

Harlow rolled her eyes. "Yes, I'm sure you'd be rock solid, but I'm all good. I think this conversation is over."

"No, Harlow," I said in a cautionary voice as I put my hand on the door to keep her from slamming it in my face.

The woman had to have someone checking up on her, and she definitely needed to talk. I had no idea who she was using for a counselor, but it was obvious she was getting nowhere with her guilt issues. And honestly, none of the whole kidnapping situation had been her fault. She'd been a victim. Period.

"I'm done here," Harlow said in an obstinate tone.

"I'm not," I said flatly. "I propose we make a deal."

She crossed her arms over her chest. "What?" she said impatiently.

"Let me be your advisor. Check in with me once a week. I want at least two hours a week, and if you ever need me, all you have to do is call." I dug my hand into my suit pocket. "This is my contact info. All of it. Including my cell and my home address. Maybe it's a little too late, but you'll have a Montgomery on speed dial now. If you agree, I won't have a single date or see any female for as long as I'm your advisor. I'll be available at *all times*," I finished in an adamant tone.

She shook her head with a wry smile. "No offense, but you won't be able to keep that promise for a week, much less a month or two, Mr. Montgomery. Your latest conquests are in the gossip rags on a weekly basis."

I shot her my most charming smile. "Then I guess the reporters will have to find someone else to follow. Because I'll be dateless for a while."

She lifted a brow. "I'm almost tempted to agree because it would be easier. You'll fall off the wagon."

"I won't. But you'll also have to agree to staying on the payroll on a paid leave of absence, and re-evaluating your decision to leave Montgomery at a later time if I do follow through," I said smoothly. "So if you're so sure I'll fail, the easiest way to get off our payroll and get everyone to leave you alone is to agree, and wait for me to be photographed with a female—other than you, of course."

Harlow immediately snatched my contact info from my hand. "Deal," she said. "But we schedule an appointment for two weeks from now. If you aren't photographed squiring some woman around, I'll make that meeting. I guarantee this is goodbye, Mr. Montgomery."

I smirked. "I'll expect your check-in two weeks from today. I'll also expect you to call me Jax, not Mr. Montgomery. I'll be functioning as a Last Hope advisor, not your employer."

"Yep. I'll agree to call you anything you want since it won't be necessary to call you at all. Have fun on your dates," she said, like she couldn't wait to close the damn door.

I scanned her face one more time before I removed my hand from her door as I said, "We'll be talking soon, Harlow."

The door banged closed the minute I started to walk away. I smiled as I just kept on walking toward the parking lot.

Harlow Lewis had no damn idea how dangerous it was to challenge me.

I generally *wasn't* a good loser.

So I always made damn sure I was in a good position to win.

Harlow hadn't seen the last of me, and she wouldn't for a very long time.

Epilogue

Taylor

Three Weeks Later...

"**Y**ou don't have to wear it right now," I said as Hudson affixed the new watch I'd given him onto his wrist. "You have a couple of watches that are a lot more expensive than most people's vehicles."

Operation: Spoil the Boyfriend had gone so well that I could now give Hudson a gift *without* the awkward moments.

Most days, it was something small, like a new pen, candy, or just something totally ridiculous.

Since I'd gotten my first full check for my new job, including a sign-on bonus that had been offered by human resources for that position, I'd bought Hudson a dive watch.

A week or two ago, he'd said something about losing his dive watch, and that he should get a new one since he'd offered to take me out and teach me to scuba dive.

Okay, it wasn't a Rolex or something outrageous, but it had been affordable with all the features Hudson would need.

"I want to wear it," he insisted. "It's really nice, Taylor. I love it. And thanks for handling dinner."

I'd made lasagna since I'd had plenty of time to do it before Hudson got home.

I shrugged. "You were working late. I didn't mind."

Although he usually got home at a decent hour these days, he'd had a special meeting that had kept him at the headquarters longer than usual today.

"You work all day, too, sweetheart," he said as he closed the dishwasher, and turned it on.

"I cooked, you cleaned," I teased him, knowing he was very aware of the fact that I'd been watching him from my seat at the breakfast bar.

In a more serious voice I added, "I love my job so much. I got placed on such an amazing team, and I don't feel like an idiot. I think I have a lot to contribute. I'm so glad you encouraged me to take this position."

"You seem really happy, so I'm glad you accepted," he said with a grin as he came toward me and held out his hand. "Should we take a walk and check out the sunset?"

Hudson had changed into jeans and a T-shirt when he'd gotten home, and I'd put on a pair of shorts and a casual top.

"Sure." I took his hand, happy we could sneak in some outdoor time.

Really, I was happy doing anything with Hudson.

It seemed like every single day, I found one more thing to love about him.

Honestly, my life seemed almost scarily perfect.

The only thing I was still worried about was Harlow. We talked every day, and now that she was back in her own apartment, we had plans to meet up. But she still didn't sound like herself right now.

Hudson and I strolled down the beach, watching as the sun started to set.

"Okay, so, I'm about to ask you for favor number three," he said, sounding a little bit nervous.

I stopped. "Is something wrong?"

He shook his head as he dug into his front pocket. "No, baby, everything is very right, but I want a favor."

I let out a relieved breath. "Ask me. Whatever you want."

He lifted a brow as he pulled out a little black box from his pocket. "This one is kind of a big one," he warned.

I beamed at him. "Lay it on me. I'm sure I can handle it."

"This is more about whether or not you can handle me," he said huskily as he flipped the box open. "For a lifetime."

I let out an audible gasp as I saw exactly what he was holding.

"Marry me, Taylor. Put me out of my misery. Favor number three—please say yes."

The ring was absolutely gorgeous, and it was all diamonds, so it flashed brightly in its bed of black velvet. There was one large center stone, surrounded by a smaller circle of gems. It was set in either platinum or white gold. "Oh, my, God, Hudson. That ring is beautiful. I think you already know that my answer is yes. Yes, yes, yes!"

He grinned, looking relieved as he pulled the ring out, and slipped it onto my finger. "I love you, Taylor."

I threw my arms around him the moment the ring was on my finger. "I love you, too, Hudson." I pulled back to kiss him.

The embrace was long, and filled with emotion and tenderness.

I was breathless when it was over.

"Can we get things ready soon?" he asked.

"How soon?" I asked, my voice filled with excitement.

"Next month?" he said hopefully.

"Only if you want to run off to Vegas," I joked.

"I'll let you decide on a date." He kissed the top of my head. "Really, I'm just damn glad you said yes."

"Like there was ever any question that I would," I said as I smiled at him.

Hudson turned me around, his arms circling me from behind, so we could watch the last of the sunset together.

I leaned back against him with a happy, thoroughly contented sigh.

As usual, Mac had given me sound advice.

The *right guy* had definitely been worth the wait.

~The End~

Please visit me at:
http://www.authorjsscott.com
http://www.facebook.com/authorjsscott

You can write to me at
jsscott_author@hotmail.com

You can also tweet
@AuthorJSScott

Please sign up for my Newsletter for updates,
new releases and exclusive excerpts.

―――――――――――――――――――――

Books by J. S. Scott:

Billionaire Obsession Series

The Billionaire's Obsession~Simon
Heart of the Billionaire
The Billionaire's Salvation
The Billionaire's Game
Billionaire Undone~Travis
Billionaire Unmasked~Jason
Mine for Christmas (Simon and Kara Short Novella)
Billionaire Untamed~Tate
Billionaire Unbound~Chloe
Billionaire Undaunted~Zane
Billionaire Unknown~Blake
Billionaire Unveiled~Marcus
Billionaire Unloved~Jett
Billionaire Unchallenged~Carter

Billionaire Unattainable~Mason
Billionaire Undercover~Hudson
Billionaire Unexpected~Jax

Sinclair Series

The Billionaire's Christmas
No Ordinary Billionaire
The Forbidden Billionaire
The Billionaire's Touch
The Billionaire's Voice
The Billionaire Takes All
The Billionaire's Secret
Only A Millionaire

Accidental Billionaires

Ensnared
Entangled
Enamored
Enchanted
Endeared

Walker Brothers Series

Release
Player
Damaged

The Sentinel Demons

The Sentinel Demons: The Complete Collection
A Dangerous Bargain
A Dangerous Hunger

A Dangerous Fury
A Dangerous Demon King

The Vampire Coalition Series

The Vampire Coalition: The Complete Collection
The Rough Mating of a Vampire (Prelude)
Ethan's Mate
Rory's Mate
Nathan's Mate
Liam's Mate
Daric's Mate

Changeling Encounters Series

Changeling Encounters: The Complete Collection
Mate Of The Werewolf
The Dangers Of Adopting A Werewolf
All I Want For Christmas Is A Werewolf

The Pleasures of His Punishment

The Pleasures of His Punishment: The Complete Collection
The Billionaire Next Door
The Millionaire and the Librarian
Riding with the Cop
Secret Desires of the Counselor
In Trouble with the Boss
Rough Ride with a Cowboy
Rough Day for the Teacher
A Forfeit for a Cowboy
Just what the Doctor Ordered
Wicked Romance of a Vampire

The Curve Collection: Big Girls and Bad Boys Series

The Curve Collection: The Complete Collection
The Curve Ball
The Beast Loves Curves
Curves by Design

Writing as Lane Parker

Dearest Stalker: Part 1
Dearest Stalker: A Complete Collection
A Christmas Dream
A Valentine's Dream
Lost: A Mountain Man Rescue Romance

A Dark Horse Novel w/ Cali MacKay

Bound
Hacked

Taken By A Trillionaire Series

Virgin for the Trillionaire by Ruth Cardello
Virgin for the Prince by J.S. Scott
Virgin to Conquer by Melody Anne
Prince Bryan: Taken By A Trillionaire

Left at the Altar Series

Temporary Groom (Book 1)

Other Titles

Well Played w/Ruth Cardello

Made in United States
North Haven, CT
28 October 2021

10671133R00142